P9-CAR-391

POPULAR TITLES PLAN BOOK

81

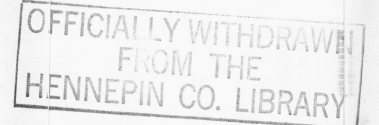

OFFICIALLY WITHDRAWN
FROM THE
HENNEPIN CO. LIBRARY

Hennepin County Library

The borrower is responsible for all
books drawn on his card and for fines
on his overdue books. Marking and mu-
tilation of books are prohibited and are
punishable by law.

SDP AUG 2 1978

A DIFFERENT KIND OF RAIN

By DeWitt S. Copp

Novels

RADIUS OF ACTION
THE PURSUIT OF M
THE MAN THEY CALLED MISTAL
THE NOTEBOOKS
THE MAN WHO WASN'T HIMSELF
DEAD MAN RUNNING
THE FAR SIDE
A DIFFERENT KIND OF RAIN

Non-Fiction

BETRAYAL AT THE U.N. (WITH MARSHALL H. PECK)
THE ODD DAY (WITH MARSHALL H. PECK)
INCIDENT AT BORIS GLEB
OVERVIEW (WITH BRIG. GEN. G. W. GODDARD, U.S.A.F., RET.)
FAMOUS SOVIET SPIES

A DIFFERENT KIND OF RAIN

by

DeWitt S. Copp

W · W · NORTON & COMPANY · INC ·
New York

HENNEPIN COUNTY
LIBRARY

JUL 3 1 1978

Copyright © 1978 by W. W. Norton & Company, Inc.
Published simultaneously in Canada by George J. McLeod Limited,
Toronto. Printed in the United States of America

All Rights Reserved

First Edition

Library of Congress Cataloging in Publication Data

Copp, DeWitt S.
A different kind of rain.

I. Title.
PZ4.C784Di [PS3553.O637]   813'.5'4   78-3748
ISBN 0-393-08818-9

1 2 3 4 5 6 7 8 9 0

For George and Frank

Although all the characters in this book are fictional, with no intent to portray persons living or dead, certain Weather Modification operations described in Quebec, Iran, Cyprus, Alaska, and Vietnam are based on fact—as are references to Congressional hearings, and international conferences and governmental reports.

JULY 1975

TWO martinis for lunch is one too many, and I came back to my office in the National Press Building, grumbling my way along humidity-sodden 14th Street, disturbed by my inability to count, particularly on an afternoon requiring work. I tacked past Annie, my secretary, saying, "No calls, no nuthin', unless the President requests my company in the Rose Garden."

"Oh, boy," was Annie's all-encompassing response.

I went into my office, closing the door with one hand, blotting sweat with the other, and plunked myself down on the couch, there to chew the cud of the article I had been unable to complete that morning.

Subject: Coming global food shortages.

Reasons: Population growth, climatological changes.

Sources: The World Food Congress; CIA report on rapidly changing climate; top secret long-range projection by Ashton Lee's Scientific Research Group on crop failures in the USSR and the PRC.

Possible conclusion: Global conflict.

One problem in the writing was not being able to quote Ashton's SRG predictions—at least until some Administration eagle saw fit to leak the word to CBS-or whomever.

"The hell with it," I muttered, and between visions of mass starvation and nuclear holocaust, I drifted away on the droning hum of the air conditioner.

Somewhere between here and there, I began to dream, and no wonder, either, that the dream, despite the hour, became a variation on a well-worn nightmare.

This time we were pulling out of the dive, coming in on the ridge very fast. Coming in on the bright-carpeted green of jungle and the white limestone cliffs near Mu Gui Pass.

"The G factor is very strong here," I said, fighting against the leaden pressure which was trying to force me through the bottom of the cockpit as I struggled to bring the Blad 500 to bear.

"He's doing it on purpose," I said to her. "He doesn't want me to take these pictures, any more than the Colonel wanted to okay the flight. Any more than you wanted me to be here."

"John," she said, and it was her voice. I heard it distinctly and started to call out when Major Glenn's voice richocheted around inside my helmet. "We're hit! Punch out! Eject! Eject!"

My fingers sought the eject button, but it had been sealed over by the Colonel, who was in his office. He turned from the sectional map that covered the well behind his desk. "It's too late now," he said. "A Telex just came in from DaNang."

The pilot was dangling in his chute, drifting down toward green velvet, shouting, "Punch out! Punch out!"

The ridge was hurtling up and the news would be there, but it didn't matter whether the jungle was defoliated or not, because Nan was calling my name.

My body convulsed, and I awoke. I could feel my heart pounding —could hear it—could feel sweat coating neck and face, the numb ache in spine, and within I could feel the agonizing gut-wrenching sense of loss, of unfillable emptiness—all perched on the *buzz-buzz* of the intercom like some goddamned, shafted gargoyle on the point of a spear.

The distance between couch and desk was no more than a giant step, but at the moment I wasn't a giant, and it took some getting there as I sought to disconnect mind and body from a wretched incubus.

The garbled sound I made in silencing the intercom brought Annie's worried query: "Boss, are you all right?"

"No. I fell in my soup. Been asleep." It came out like my mouth was full of popovers.

"Well, it's a good afternoon for that, and it's not the President who's calling, but it is long distance—a Mr. Picard. I didn't get the first name. He's calling from someplace in Quebec. Sounded like Sceptered Isles or something."

"Sept Iles," I corrected, but it didn't read any better in the translation. "He's the pilot I had during the wildlife series. Tell him to hold on." While she told him I went to my corner sink and put my head under some tepid water, hoping the fluid would help to wash the whole man back into shape as I used my hands to douse face and neck. It helped. But the thought of René Picard on the phone—bush pilot *extraordinaire*—*courier de bois* with wings—helped more than the water to chase the gloom of my gin-inspired wanderings.

"René! Comment ça va, mon ami!" I gave it the best of my limited French, still a bit hoarse.

"Ahh, John! That is you! Oui? This is René here in Sept Iles. You remember?" It was as though he had practised his greeting so long that he hadn't heard mine. His heavy accent was in place, but the connection or some other factor had smoothed the sandpaper out of his voice and pitched it into an unfamiliar register.

"John, I need you here at once. I cannot say for why on the telephone, but you must come now," the words came spewing out.

If I had been asked to give a one line description of René Picard's emotional balance, I would have said nothing ever fazed him. At the moment I would have been dead wrong. He sounded fazed to hell and gone.

"Écoutez, John," he managed to slow down, "You come to Montreal—to Dorval, and I will meet you at the Butler hangar, like before, and we will fly here. Oui! I will—"

"Wait a minute! Wait a minute, René! What's it all about? I just can't drop everything so you can show me your newest fishing hole."

"Non, non, non, non! It is not for sport! It is very serious! John, please, you tell me when you arrive in Dorval!"

"I can't, René. At least, not until you tell me why you want me to come up,

There was a long pause, and I waited trying to assimilate his totally unexpected and somewhat incoherent demand.

"Listen, John," and now he sounded more like the bush pilot I recalled, his voice assuming its familiar rasp, the pace slower, the words coming in English. "I am not so good on this telephone. . . . This is something of great importance—very great, or I would not bother you. Comprenez? You understand? I am sorry for this call that I cannot explain. But please, please can you come? I will pay for your ticket to Montreal. When I have brought you here you will see."

"You can't tell me more, René?"

"On this telephone, non!"

I knew that a man like René would instinctively shy away from discussing anything confidential on a telephone, not because he was up on the latest bugging scandal but because automatically he would suspect his words were overheard by some faceless minion of the state.

"How long will this take?"

"If you come this afternoon, I will be at Dorval at five. We will come back here and tomorrow I will take you flying for about four hours altogether. After that—"

"Hold on a minute." While he got his breath, I asked Annie to check on airline connections. "Okay, and after you take me flying, what then?"

"You will see! You will know, John!"

"I wish to hell you'd tell me what I'd know, René."

"I . . . I cannot say. I do not know. But before God, I tell you, you must come!"

And so, of course, I went.

*

I went partly because his cry of urgency was so out of character and his plea was a hook in the gullet of my curiosity. I went also partly because I knew whatever had him up the pole dealt with my own work, or he never would have called me. But beyond that, beyond finding a legitimate excuse to put off writing the article that faced me, and getting clear, however briefly, of polluted, over-heated Washington in mid-summer, I went because I saw the move as a chance to escape. As though to flee physically would help me to flee mentally from the trap of an oncoming siege of depression.

René and I had first met in January, where I was on my way to meet him now—the Butler Aviation hangar at Dorval Airport.

He had brought his high-wing De Havilland Beaver gargling down out of a snow-filled sky, surprising me a bit because I'd figured with a blizzard forecast he'd have delayed his flight from Sept Iles and left me to explore the mid-winter festivities of Montreal for a day or two.

There was something about the first sight of him, moving away from his snub-nosed yellow-and-blue aircraft, that suddenly cheered me, shooting a needed squirt of enthusiasm into my bones for the assignment that lay ahead. His head was domed by a brightly hued woolen cap with a bright-tasseled red knob on the peak. Black beard and mustache were trimmed and snugly mortised, giving his face a slightly wolfish aspect. His eyes were concealed behind Polaroids. But it was not his features that attracted me first; it was the way he moved. Parka open against the fist of the cold, he came striding toward the hangar office, a big man moving lightly. Measured against the pale presence so many exude, he stood out not so much in bulk as in motion.

He came into the office riding an icicle, his voice a frosty rasp. "Bonjour, McCloud. Bonjour, mes amis. Is no one flying today?"

He'd taken his glasses off and I saw black Indian eyes—magnetic, glittering—French beak, dark weathered skin.

"Only you are flying today, Picard," McCloud said from behind the operations counter. "The rest know better."

"Ah, you are wrong, McCloud. M'sieur Erikson et moi, we are flying. You are M'sieur Erikson?" He turned toward me, grinning, his hand out-thrust.

And we had flown that day, first to Quebec City and then on to Sept Iles. For me it became the damnedest, wildest flight on record. Before it was done, I had cursed myself ragged for ever having accepted the nature magazine's assignment to do a feature on wildlife in the winter wilderness of Quebec. I was sure the turbulence was going to tear the wings off or unhinge my head. Either form of extinction might be precluded by freezing to death. I'm sure it was only the huge jug of McElroy's fine Scotch whiskey, which had formerly been anchored to the co-pilot's seat, that prevented the latter method of departure and made contemplation of the former possibility more an act of anger than one of fear.

We flew into snow-clotted limbo. In fact, it was snowing so hard when we landed at Quebec City I didn't know we were on the ground until René told me. Certainly he hadn't bothered to throttle back at any time.

I remembered while the Beaver was being gassed and rubbed down, or whatever they do to an aircraft that has four feet of ice and drifted snow all over it, I drank a great deal of very hot coffee in the airport cafe. I could have said to him that far enough was far enough, but whether it was the McElroy, or advancing rigor mortis, or just dumb stubbornness, I was damned if I was going to insist that we stay on the ground. I wasn't going to start out by losing face with this wild bastard, who at that point I was sure was putting me through the wringer to see how much I could take. He was going to have to fly me around for two months, and if the dumb son of a bitch wanted to start by creaming himself, I reasoned with stoneheaded clarity, I wasn't going to stop him. My initial enthusiasm for René Picard had been frozen into the ice pack.

The only difference in the remainder of the flight was that the grey without turned to black, and we polished off the McElroy, while he hummed merrily out of tune with the protesting racket of the engine. Occasionally he would turn and grin at me, and in the pale luminosity of the instrument panel, the teeth framed in the matting around his mouth made him look fiercely carnivorous.

God knows how hard the wind was blowing when we landed at Sept Iles, or how he ever found the place. At full throttle he somehow taxied the Beaver up to a hangar door that was swung open and we went blatting out of the white inferno, into the concave sanctuary.

"Voilà!" he said, leaning the mixture, flipping off the magnetos with a flourish. "Bienvenue à Sept Iles!"

"You can kiss my ass," I sighed wearily.

He checked in surprise, and then roared with laughter. "Bon! Bon! You are okay!" he said, clapping me on the back.

*

He was there at Dorval ahead of me. As the taxi made the turn toward the hanger, I saw his Beaver parked on the line, and when I entered the office, there was McCloud behind his counter as I'd last seen him, checking his forms, a pale man with a sour stomach and a leaden voice.

"He's been expecting you," he said, peering at me as though the six months between our last brief meeting were non-existent. He indicated with a turn of his head that René was outside.

"Nice to see you again," I said, moving toward the door to the hangar.

It was not the season for bright-tasseled caps, and from the rear René's head had the look of a beaver pelt. At least his shirt was a flaming red above faded corduroys and boots. He was on his knees by the landing gear, examining the pontoons which had replaced the skis. They extended only a few inches above the wheels, and it could be in landing that he scraped their bottoms.

"What's the matter? Did you think the runway was water?"

He came up and around, plucking cigarette from mouth. "Ahh, John!" He bore down on me, grabbed my arms and then wrapped me in a bear hug. "Oh, bon! Bon! Merci! Merci!"

I got loose and we had a mutual look. "You didn't shave this morning."

"No." He smiled. Something in his eyes seemed to have filmed over the glitter, shadows reflecting substance. "I would have met you, but they said your plane was late." He plucked the bag from my hand. "Allons-y! We get out of here."

"We get out of here when you tell me what we're getting out of here for, René." I said it good humoredly, but I meant it. I wanted some answers right now.

"When we are in the plane, John." He opened the cabin door.

"Once we take off I won't be able to hear a damn thing."

"Before we take off." He gestured for me to climb aboard. He wasn't smiling, and I had the impression that he was holding himself in check, like a man who wanted to run but was forcing himself to walk.

Aside from his own equipment, the cabin was empty of cargo and felt roomier than I'd recalled. I got myself into the right hand seat and he slid into his own behind the yoke. He'd thrown away his cigarette and now he produced the pack, offering it to me. I shook my head. He shoved the window open on his side, and I did likewise on mine while he lit up. It was eventide, the light going soft and yellow, the heat fading before a cool breeze. The cockpit—the faint raw smell of gasoline, of engine fumes, the instrument panel with its dials of flight. Somehow it was all very familiar. Only the season was different.

"Tell me why I'm here, friend."

He rested his hands on the rim of the half wheel, the wood worn smooth with use. The gesture was more a movement of resolve than one signifying flight. At some point he would take the cigarette from his mouth. Now he looked straight ahead, and had I been a painter I would like to have caught him in profile—a pilot in repose, contemplating survival.

*

We followed the long eastward reach of the St. Lawrence, angling gently through the fading twilight into on-coming night. Externally, we were moving away from a point of departure. We were winging through still air, the high-timbered river bank below losing detail, becoming rounded bulk—then losing that, blending into the irrevocable sweep of darkness. Lights filtering the land, winking on the water, offer reassurance and tranquil illusion.

My physical immobility, my stillness was not altogether the result of what he had told me. Internally the weasel of irony was enjoying my liver. I had flown a thousand miles to trap myself—a kind of third-rate appointment in Samarra. It wasn't from death in the market place that I was fleeing, but from memory that would not die. Instead of helping to stifle it, René Picard's bizarre tale had set fire to its cage. I couldn't put out the fire. I could only stand back and try to examine its cause, not sure that the cause was real, only sure of what it had done to my own thought process. It was a process blessed with the curse of having total recall. And so, as we flew, I played and replayed René's words, his voice within my mind broadcast harshly on the monotone of the slipstream.

"Seven days ago I am coming back to Sept Iles by way of Mushalagon from Great Whale. It is mostly clear with some scattered nuage —cumulus, the puff balls, n'est-ce pas? I am at three thousand, and these clouds, they are moving above my line of flight. Comprenez? Well, all at once there is something different."

A shake of the bushy head, hand raising to pluck cigarette away, smoke exhaled, a pause before continuing.

"One of the clouds at about eleven o'clock from where I am sitting suddenly begins to change. It begins to grow, gonfler, escalader—to climb, as though within the winds are very great.

His hands mold the air.

"And yet, this is not that kind of cloud, not a nimbus, not a storm cell. I think what I am seeing is most unusual. Extraordinaire. And more because the other clouds do not change at all."

His choice of words, the intonation, the accent, painted the impression of what he had observed.

"I change my course, beginning to climb toward this strange thing. The top must be nearing twenty thousand with a round cap full of ice, and then I can see as I am flying closer all the cloud is like that, like it is growing a fur, and at the same time its color is changing, not white, not black, but a pale green. I know I am seeing something that I do not understand, and I am asking myself what in the hell have I been drinking. Comprenez?

"Then, all at once there is more. La pluie—the rain is falling. Not from any other cloud but only from this one, and John, before God, this rain is the same color of the cloud, it is—green!

"Green rain, son of a bitch!" Palms slap down on the wheel yoke. "I tell myself I am crazy! I am dreaming! There can be no such thing, but there before me is such a thing!

"I do not fly any closer to that cloud. I am spooked like I have seen a Wendigo. I circle wide. I fly at a secure distance, watching to see what else can happen. Shortly, in perhaps fifteen minutes, the rain is finie and the cloud begins to lose its high top, its bad color, and in a little while more, it is looking like the others.

"Alors! When I land at Sept Iles, I say nothing to anyone. I wait to see if there are any reports. Anyhow what can I say without everyone thinking I should change my whiskey?"

And now a long pause, as cigarette is stubbed out, smoke expended, air taken in.

"Yesterday, I am coming back over the same course. For three days there has been a low with rain and fog, but now it is clear. There are no *nuages* at all. But there is something else. I see that everything on the ground in a certain place has turned grey, as though a fire had made a burn long ago, but not like a burn because I can see the needles, the leaves all in place. When I had seen that damned raincloud I had marked it over a certain *lac* that I call Lac Poitrine because it is shaped like a woman's breast, and Lac Poitrine was in the center of all that was grey, and so I knew the cloud with its rain had passed over that land. Comprenez?

"I had this bad feeling. I fly low, and there is nothing to see but the color of winter in summer, and it was a strange thing to see. So I knew what I have to do. I have to land on Poitrine, and I am nearly not here to tell you. Never did I make a landing like that! Never!

"John, the *lac* was full of dead fish, and the smell came in, and it was not just the dead fish, but of dead everything! Elk! Bear! Caribou! Birds! Birds! All dead! *Tout mort! Tout mort!*" His voice reached for his raised hands. It caught like a saw hitting a nail.

"How do you know that?"

"I saw! I saw!" His arms thrown wide. "They were all around the lac. Peut-être they had come for water. Something had driven them. Some were floating in the water with the fish. But everything in that goddamned place where I saw the rain falling, was dead!"

And now the anguished voice chops off, caught in mid-cry. It is a matter of regaining control. Beads of sweat on the forehead and the breathing deep. And then finally, "I could not tell you this on the telephone, John. You can see that, but I knew you must come because you would know what to do."

"Have you ever heard of Angus MacMurry?"

"MacMurry? Non. Who is he?"

"One of your countrymen, a scientist. How come you didn't report all this to your own people?"

"What people?"

"Well, fish and game, forestry—for starters."

"Merde! So what would they do, arrest me for poaching!" His eyes full of murderous disdain.

"They'd investigate, René."

"Écoutez, John, I know them. I know you!"

And I knew the inherent built-in rejection of dealing with *official-dom by* a hard-headed Canuck.

"You are the only one—"

You are the only one! Oh yes, I'd heard that line somewhere before and had stupidly believed it.

Now, locked in flight, a gentle darkness soiled by the engine's bleat, we had come full circle. Well—not entirely, but from last night's lack of sleep to this point of no return, the lines were close enough so that all I had been fighting to hold back—other faces—other times— other circumstances with similar connotations—swept in. Then it had been herbicides and defoliants, and *only I* could investigate and write about them.

"I knew you would see how bad this thing is." I had heard his voice from afar. His unintentional irony helped close the distance. "We will fly to Poitrine demain. You will bring your camera, and—"

"A camera won't mean much, René. We'll need an ice chest, the kind you carry fish in. We'll have to collect specimens and get them to a laboratory to tell what did the killing."

"Oui, oui."

"It's possible that whatever caused the thing is contagious."

"I thought about that, but nothing has happened to me."

"Sure you feel all right?"

"Oui, sure." An examination of hands, palms and backs, proved it to his own satisfaction.

"Tell me, did you see any other planes in the area at the time?"

"I have thought of that, and I am not sure because when I am looking at the top, the casquette, I think for the blink of an eye I see the sun flash on something, but then it is gone, and I see nothing else but what the cloud is doing. Pourquoi?"

Why, indeed?

*

Sept Iles is named for seven islands that front its great circular bay. Until 1950 the place was just another fishing village on the Côte Nord with nothing much to commend it but its stone bluffs overlooking a vast expanse of river surrounded by a no-nonsense wilderness, reaching out forever. Then the Canadians ran a rail line north into Labrador and began hauling out iron ore, and today Sept Iles—its bay over-stocked with ships from everywhere—is Canada's third largest port with a population of about twenty thousand.

I had come to know the place and René Picard in the white-wolf season of winter. But seeing it now at the peak of its brief summer added a new dimension to its character. Winter had given it a locked inside, careful feeling. Now it was wide open, full of vigor, thriving, alive. The sun threw gold on the water of the harbor, concealing its dirty face. An ore ship, riding high with a rusted stern, eased in toward a berth. A dust-coated Land Rover went past to the sound of raucous laughter, a voice calling back, "Hey René! Comment ça va?"

And, as we walked in the early morning brightness from the log-fronted inn to rue Napoleon, with its tourist shops and banks and easy-moving traffic, on our way to pick up a bag of ice and an ice chest, it was "Bonjour, René!" "Ça va, René?" Ho, René."

And I was thinking, Thank God I slept last night. I went out like a light at whatever time it was. I can hack it today. Just take it slow.

The air, even with the faint stink of the harbor—dead fish and diesel fuel—had a full-throated purity that made for breathing deeply.

This is the first day of all the days that are left. I said it every day, but this one starts well, and all that matters now is this moment. The past is nothing. It cannot help you. Working on it can only kill the present. So leave it! Leave it! Let sleeping ghosts lie. Never mind circles, full or otherwise. Never mind connections, made or not. That ship moving in, that's real. Nothing is real but what you can see, and the future does not exist until it is now. And now is just fine with a belly full of bacon and eggs and good strong coffee. Yeah, and then the spoiling thought—and a lake full of dead fish, waiting.

"Holá, René."

"Ça va, mon ami."

We flew over what seemed an unending carpet of green that had been white when I saw it last. We had crossed the Sainte Marguerite, the rail line running to Little Manicouagan, and ahead and all around the green carpeting was knifed and torn with rivers and lakes bearing French and Indian names.

The sameness went on, with all its variations in contour, in coloration of the carpeting, in size and configuration of watersheds. And we noisely traversing it, proving some celestial formula of time and motion. Further north the trees would begin to lose height, thin out, and finally disappear. But here, above the high plateau, the green appeared limitless.

"You remember that?" René's voice rose over the engine's bark as he jerked his head toward my side.

The lake off the wing was long and narrow, with a bulge at one end.

"No."

"We landed there after the big storm. You got some good photographs."

I stared down and saw nothing familiar. We had landed so many places before, during and after big storms.

"Oh, yes! . . . where and how much farther to Poitrine?"

"Tout droit!" He sliced with his hand. "Ten minutes."

His mood changed. He was more like the René of past flights, but unlike my change, I didn't think his mood shift had anything to do with a good night's sleep and fresh air. It was because he felt whatever the problem was, my knowing it would not only ease the burden of proof that he'd actually seen what he had described, but also that I would know what to do about it.

The momentary lift felt in Sept Iles had faded; put out of reach by time and distance, like that indefinable platter's rim of the horizon, devoid of substance. Felt, passed over, passed by, past. Maybe I could conjugate it.

My thoughts were circling our destination. I knew René had expected me to ask more questions, but there was nothing more to ask. I was not about to tell him that I had observed the type of rapid cloud growth and glaciation he had described; that I too had seen rain fall as a result. But then the precipitation had been colorless—the cloud hue normal and the object had been to preserve life, not to destroy it. Nor was I about to tell him there was a way in which green foliage would turn a gun-metal grey very swiftly, and the overall effect within the stricken area could be sudden extinction. But it required an erupting volcano to produce the condition and somehow what he had seen and what I knew did not gibe. Beyond that, from having long drunk at the trough of ecology, I had learned not to waste time questioning environmental claims, but to go to the source and find my own answers.

"John! There!" He thrust his hand out.

Our goal was ahead, slightly off to my right. He skidded the plane left, then lowered the nose to give me a better view while reducing power.

The grey swath was roughly tear-drop in shape, with an irregular boundary and a ragged point, indicating the precip had dwindled out in a normal fashion, leaving an exact mark of the cloud's passage during the rain fall. As we descended I judged the affected area to be about five miles in length and around three at the widest point.

"Level off and circle from this distance," I said. I had brought my camera and began to get some shots. "I'll tell you when to go lower."

From a thousand feet the discoloration could have been taken as evidence of an old fire or perhaps a swamp. But at tree-top level, the shots I took would show clearly enough that neither was the cause. As René had said, the thick woodland and the brush around the lake retained their normal foliage. The effect through a telescopic lense added weight to the centrifugal force I was feeling in the tightness of René's turns; nor did having the window open by my head have anything to do with the coldness I began to feel. Pale grey leaves, pale grey hemlock and birch, pale grey earth, jarred me like the sound of someone running fingernails down a window screen.

"All right, stop trying to twist my head off!" I shouted, as he swung into another turn. "Let's get down!"

Before we did that, René flew his Beaver the length of the lake a few feet off the surface. The water was not grey. It was a normal black velvet. I saw no dead fish until we reached the south end where Poitrine's out flow emptied into a stream. We pulled up and circled and I could look down and see the outflow was choked and bloated with a sargasso of white bellies that extended out into the lake and along its lip.

René came out of his turn and landed the Beaver heading away from the carrion. As soon as we touched, speed and sound fell away swiftly. With the engine throttled back to idling, the water slapping on the pantoons, I felt a quality of silence about us that went with being surrounded by a grey wilderness in mid-summer. The blue of sky didn't seem right either.

"You want to anchor there?" René had turned the plane and nodded toward the lake's end.

"No. Go in there by that ledge."

"The stink will be formidable. I have a bottle of balsam spray. Soak your handkerchief, tie it over your nose." His voice sounded hoarse, as though he felt he had to whisper.

"At least we won't have to worry about mosquitos and black flies." My joke was hollow. I had already caught a whiff of what he was talking about, and as he taxied in toward the shore, the odor came out to meet us—an overpowering stench that passed through the nostrils into the lungs and rooted itself in the gut.

I pulled my handkerchief out fast, grabbed the bottle of spray from his outstretched hand, trying not to gag.

He gave a bark of laughter, a cross between a howl and a giggle. "When you landed here before, did you go ashore?"

"No. I saw all this, and I said, *vite!* Get out of here! John, I do not wish to get in too close now. Maybe snag a log or a rock."

"You anchor where you think best."

"Oui."

He moved in with the propeller ticking over delicately, and I was thinking, I've got to get out on the pontoon and drop the anchor, and when I do, my feet are going to get wet. I really hadn't been listening to what he'd said, or if I had I hadn't been able to translate his words into the enormity of what they had described. The water, normal appearing as it was, could still be contaminated.

"Do you have waders aboard?"

"No need to wade. We use the rubber dinghy. I think we are close enough."

He reached down beside his seat and pulled a lever. Over the engine, I heard a splash. He cut the switch and the Beaver eased around, nose to the wind.

The stench was more concentrated, and I gagged as I got up and away from the seat, going back to where we'd tied down the ice chest. He followed me.

"Maybe you'd better stay with the plane," I said. "I'm going to make this fast."

"We make it faster together. I take care of the dinghy." He unfastened the pack from the cabin ceiling, opened the cabin door, shook out the rubber and pulled the CO_2 cylinder.

"René, make damn sure you don't get wet!"

He looked at me, and I wondered if my eyes reflected the same sense of impact. He'd seen what was here once, so he had to be prepared. With me, the shock had been cumulative—sight, smell, hearing. Absolutes. There was absolutely no other sound than that of the water gently spanking the pontoons.

In the wilderness anywhere, the lack of man-made sound is a kind of blessing, but always there is the muted pianissimo of life which offers reaffirmation. Man, the noisiest and most obstrepherous of creatures, has become, through his technology, an alien breaking down the laws of nature. Now beyond the plane's reach there was a total silence—no bird song, no whir of duck wing, no splash of fish rising, no movement, no faint crackle of life in the underbrush. Nothing but a forest stained an unnatural grey with an ugliness that wrenched at the eyeballs, and issuing from the still greyness a monstrous charnel house stench that was all pervading.

René paddled the dinghy with great care to the rock ledge, and with equal care I made contact against the sloping granite face and eased myself on to it.

"No point in your getting out," I said. "See what you can get in your fish net. I only need one."

He grunted and hefted the ice chest to me. I forced myself to concentrate on what I had to do. I was wearing gloves he'd given me, and I had his hunting knife. I went after the flora first. Moss on the rocks, lichen growth, marsh grass, a flower, birch bark, spruce bow, alder leaves. Each went into a separate plastic bag. Then it was fauna. I didn't have to go far, for as René had said, whatever hell had come down from the cloud, it had caused a stampede for the lake, and I could make my choice from the rotting remains of every species in the area. Chipmunk, blue jay, fox, weasel, bittern. Strewn about in profusion, they lay on the ledge and in the nearby underbrush, small creatures amidst the larger species.

I fought against throwing up, as I selected and collected. I was soaked with sweat and the sun wasn't that hot. I looked up and saw René, bringing the bright yellow dinghy. He seemed to be creeping over the water, and I wanted to shout, *"Hurry up! Hurry up!"*

Wordlessly, he came in and extended the net with two fish in it. I reached for it and nearly lost my footing.

"Watch out!" His shout was a massive sound.

I got the fish into the bags and into the chest and the chest shut. When I hefted it, I knew René was going to have to make two trips. I knelt down and eased the chest down the rock incline so he could get a hand on it. There was no need for conversation, no desire for it. He slid the chest over the rubber gunnel and into the dingy. I watched him start paddling back to the plane, and then I began to heave and vomit, and I felt as though my innards were coming up with everything else. I knew it was more than the stench and the enormity that had me. I had a fierce desire for water. I went down on all fours. Hurry, dammit, or I was going into the lake and drink it up!

"John!" Suddenly he was there with a hand outstretched. I went into the raft on my belly, and felt his grasp steady me.

"Water!" I said. "Got to have!"

Something plopped on the rubber beside me. It was a pint bottle of McElroy, and I went after it like a camel reaching a water-hole after two weeks lost in the desert. The sun lathered the cold sweat on my body. The Scotch saved my life.

When we reached the plane René suddenly remembered I'd left the net.

"Leave it! Leave the dinghy, too."

I was jack-knifed over the cabin entrance, and was hauling myself inward when I became aware of an alien noise. I couldn't immediately identify it. A hard knot of sound growing in volume, then the knot being torn apart, shredded furiously, and then all the parts collected into a frenzied roar, ripping at the eardrums.

Over it, I heard René's shout, and as I came to my feet and swung around, I had identification. A diving jet! I saw it just as the sound engulfed us, a white arrow, targeting upward, turning, the sun striking fire on its knife-like wing, then coming back down toward us, looking as though it was going to make us the bull's-eye.

I was still standing slack-jawed and deafened when René brushed by me. He had the prop turning, the anchor up, and the Beaver at full throttle before I'd secured the chest and climbed back into my seat.

"Watch for him!" he ordered, his head swiveling as he eased the yoke back and we lifted off.

Neither of us saw the other plane until its pilot tried to kill us. He waited until we were several hundred feet up. Then he came from behind and under us and pulled up in our faces at full throttle. The sudden violent turbulence created by the jet's turbines nearly had us on our backs. It happened so quickly and René's reaction was so immediate that there was no time for fear, only the startled sensation of being flipped almost upside down. René got control with one wing brushing a tree.

"The son of a bitch!" It was an enraged bellow.

"Who the hell was it?"

"I don't know, but when I find the bastard I'll kill him!"

We made the return flight to Sept Iles at tree-top level, "hedge-hopping" they used to call it. Every so often René would rack the Beaver up into a 360-degree turn in order to check our back trail and the sky above. We saw no sign of the white jet or any other aircraft.

As for my own condition, the demanding need for water and the awful sense of sickness passed swiftly. Perhaps we had found a new claim for McElroy. Between the two of us, we nearly finished the pint in short order; and yet, I felt cold sober, more cold than sober. The godawful stench seemed to have come with us. It clung to me like a net, and when René brought forth his cigarettes I extended my hand.

"But you don't smoke!"

"I just kicked a bad habit. I'll have one, thanks."

I don't smoke, but I thought exhaling the stuff through my nose might help. It did, proving that in spite of all the medical research and statistics that there is something beneficial in tobacco and booze. Withal, my mind began to fumble around.

"René, did you recognize the other plane?"

His expression showed he was still primed for murder. "Non! A Lear jet. He was not familiar to me."

"Wouldn't they have some record of him at Sept Iles or at Air Traffic Control?"

"We will learn that. There was no registration number on his wings, no markings."

"It was so fast, I couldn't tell."

"But I could tell!" He was gripping the yoke like he might break it off the control column.

"He was out to make us crash?"

He glared at me angrily, annoyed that I would have to ask. "You think maybe he was playing some kind of joke?"

"I don't know, René. Do they play jokes like that around here?"

"Not more than once, not with René Picard."

"Before we get back we have to agree on something."

Again the angry, glance. His fuse was really lit.

"And we can't do that till you simmer down."

He stubbed out his cigarette in the overloaded ash tray he had attached to the instrument panel. "Okay, I'm listening."

"Suppose we fly what we have in the chest to Montreal. I'll contact a friend in Washington. He'll recommend a laboratory we can take the specimens to, and—"

"Non! Non! Non! Non! Non!" He jammed the throttle forward, building up more sound than speed. "Those idiots would throw us in jail!"

"Now cut the crap!" My shout topped the engine's bleat. "Nobody's going to throw anybody in jail for bringing in some dead wildlife. I'm not a toxologist. I don't know a damn thing about forensic medicine, but I damn well know that stuff has got to be checked out right now. I don't know what it means, and you don't either, but. . . ."

"And, mon ami, we won't know if you try to get those sots in Montreal to tell you! He shook his fist not at me, but at the sots in his mind.

"René, you're the greatest bush pilot in the world, but you don't know your ass from your propeller in this league. Whatever this is all about, it's happened in your country. For starters, just how do you think I'd get past Fish and Game with that box?"

"No problem at all. We put more ice in, good trout on top, and you take it as your catch. I give you the paper to show tu es un bon pecheur. Voilà!"

"No, not voilà. We're not playing games. We may be contaminated ourselves. We're going to have to be checked over, too."

"You think maybe we get malades and die?" The thought didn't trouble him. In fact, he was calming down. He put the plane into another turn, this one gentle.

"It's a possibility. When you first described what you saw and what you found, I ruled out nuclear radiation because it's not supposed to kill that quickly. If I'd had any brains I'd have asked you to bring your Geiger counter along, because now I'm not sure."

He showed me most of his teeth and gave a snort of oneupsmanship. "My propeller and my ass go pretty good together, non?" He reached under his seat and brought up by its strap a Geiger counter.

I had known that once upon a time the counter was standard equipment with every bush pilot, hoping to hit the big one. But I hadn't seen René's on board and I figured he'd given up carrying it. What interested me most was its silence as he dangled it between us.

"Thank God for that!" I sighed. "But we're still going to have to be checked over and get this collection to Montreal."

He completed his turn of the empty sky and flew us into a narrow pass between pine-covered hills. "We will talk about it on the ground," he finally said, and that was all right with me because it would be easier on the throat, and he'd be able to concentrate on what I was saying instead of distracting me with the possibility that I could reach out and pluck pine needles out of the passing slipstream.

For the remainder of the flight I fixed my thoughts on *what.* What had caused the slaughter—the sudden extinction of all life from a passing cloud? My own inner conflict had been splintered on the rock ledge where I had done my collecting. The rock was literal, but its figurative meaning was devastating. It left no room for somber ironies or doom-laden analogies from the past which I had perceived earlier, during our flight from Montreal. The realization of what we had been amidst was overwhelming, and I could now clearly understand René's initial reaction. He had been both the observer and the discoverer of the results. Agonizing thoughts of yesteryear had no place in this. Although, of course, at the time I was not aware of their departure.

My knowledge of poisons did not deal with pathology. I dealt with more leisurely forms of extinction: pollution of the sea and air, herbicides and defoliants, 2-4-5-T and dioxin, nuclear waste. Man's technological excretions. I sought them out, exposed them, wrote about them, attacked their causes, because I knew their effects could be corrected—that it was possible to stop before it was too late, just as it was possible to stop killing whales or bald eagles.

Besides, American germ warfare research had been halted at Fort Detrick two years ago. I could do no more than put what we had gathered into the right hands and let them figure out the killing agent that made no allowance for life, whether it was warm- or cold-blooded, plant or animal. Ashton Lee would know the direction to go. I would get him to come up and meet us in Montreal. The need for haste was goosed not only by the obvious, but also because in my own field of investigation I believed I had knowledge that would answer another question almost as large as *what.* And that question was *how.*

I suppose if I'd been a detective, my thought process would have worked by who, how, and what. Instead, because I had been in the environmental pond for so long, I swam in the opposite direction. How? Certainly not an act of the Lord God Almighty, testing out his wrath in a remote wilderness. Unless the actions of the jet had been somebody's idea of fun, it had, if nothing else, eliminated any thought of an inexplicable phenomenon brought about by an equally inexplicable act of nature. Brought down to earth, I knew at least one method which could have been used to produce the killing rain. And if I was right, it could be used again and again and again!

As for *who?* I hadn't a clue, only an idea of someone to whom I might talk.

The blue of the day had been bled grey by the time we landed. The sky was solidly overcast, the ceiling lowering, the wind beginning to whip. The first drops of rain pecked at the windscreen as René swung the Beaver around on the flight line and cut the switch.

We sat silently for a moment, in the ears ringing aftermath of the engine sound. As some of the tension drained, I felt the heavy weariness of reaction set in.

René shoved his seat back, and I said, "Wait a minute. Let's have one for the road before you go hunting." I held out the nearly empty bottle.

"When I come back," he said.

"All right, but before we go I want to get something straight. If there's a regular flight to Montreal I'll get on it with the chest. If there's not, I want you to take me there. I'll pay for the gas."

"Listen, John." He used a heavy finger to tap my arm. "First, we see what we see here. There is no flight to Montreal until the morning."

"Then we should go as soon as we can get out of here."

He stood up. "I can fly you to Presque Isle, even to Washington."

"No. Montreal or I'll have a word with the RCMP about our catch."

He swore at me in French, and there was no bonhomie in his look. Nor was there in mine.

He had parked his plane in front of the Alouette Airways hangar, actually a timbered shed, and by the time we had walked the distance to the blocky, single-story terminal building, the rain was beginning to pelt. The flight line had that pungent odor of wetness on heated asphalt. The smell matched our simmering moods. We had not spoken since he had locked up the Beaver and as we strode along I rehearsed a conversation with Ash Lee, letting my annoyance at René's stubbornness ease down to a stubborn resolve.

He held the door open for me, and I grinned at him and said, "Merci bien, mon capitain."

He grunted, still sulking.

"Let's have a cup of coffee and talk this over," I said. "There's no point in our disagreeing."

"We talk with operations and Air Traffic Control first," he said.

He talked *en français* with M'sieur Maurin, headman in the three-man operations office, although all present were fluent in English. But I gathered there was no record of a Lear jet of any coloring or degree on any flight plan in northeastern Quebec. Maurin checked with the tower and then with several air traffic control centers and came up with *rien*.

On a wall map René indicated the general area of the encounter which was festooned with small lakes, and while the information he gave was duly recorded, I got the definite impression that Maurin and his boys weren't taking it all that seriously. We were fishing and someone had done a buzz job on us. Not exactly in the rule book, but not exactly unusual in a place like this, where pilots still flew with a certain élan. The pull up in front of us—*eh bien*, it wasn't a totally unfamiliar maneuver, either.

The one thing that did concern them was an unknown high-speed jet flying loose in the region. Air Traffic Control at Goose Bay, Bagotville, Monkton, Quebec, Presque Isle, and Montreal were alerted to be on the lookout for it.

Maurin, rather diminutive with pencil mustache and red bow-tie, had a self-important air. He had made a few notes of the high points of the incident, but he wanted both of us to write a complete report on it right now.

René said we would do that later. M'sieur Maurin said, toute de suite. René replied with a look that summed up his attitude and held open the door for me. I did not look back, but I felt the chill of official displeasure in the silence that marked our departure. There was much I hadn't understood, but I was left with the impression that what the jet had nearly done to us was not important, but where it might be now was. Trying to kill a couple of fishermen didn't stack up against a possible mid-air with Air Canada.

"You see what I mean?" René said.

"I don't speak French very well." I purposely sounded miffed, although I wasn't.

He was contrite. "I'm sorry. I speak better French to those rond de cuirs than English—but comprenez?"

"I think I got the message. Now where's a telephone?"

"We have coffee first."

He was wrong. A familiar voice called after us, "Picard! Un moment!"

It was Maurin, and for a moment I thought we were in for a clash of wills. He came down the short corridor toward us, cloaking his size in the authority of his position. I could feel René starting to bridle.

"Picard, une crise à Lac Chacun." I got that much, but the rest of it and the exchange that continued was too fast for me. I followed them back into the operations office where René shouted questions to someone via a radio telephone. By the time he hung up I had the gist of that message, too. For my benefit René now spoke to Maurin in English. The concerned look on his face had shifted from one of annoyance to doubt. "There's no one else who can fly in there? Fortin? Coutour? McRae?"

Maurin shrugged. "They are all out. Don't worry, the company will pay you for it. More than for a fishing party, I should think." His eyes slid over me.

"It will be dark before I can get in there," René said as a matter of observation, chewing on his own thoughts.

"So? Are you afraid of the dark, Picard? And a little pluie?" Maurin was being cute, and his two assistants took the opportunity to smile and gaze at the deteriorating weather outside.

René ignored them. "You understand this?" He said to me.

"Someone is hurt at Lac Chacun."

"Oui," Hè moved to the wall map. "Ici," he indicated the lake. "It's about trois-cent kilos northeast. They want me to come right now."

"Maybe we'd better go talk it over."

"M'sieur, what is there to talk over?" Maurin got into the act. "A man has been crushed by a falling tree. There is no doctor in a logging camp."

"No one else can fly in, hey?" I spoke to René. He shook his head. "How long will it take?"

"Two and-a-half, maybe three, hours, with luck."

"What will you do? Fly a doctor in with you?"

"If he can find one," he nodded at Maurin who had gone into his cubicle to make the call.

"Well, René, we'll just have to hold tight till you get back. Meantime, I'll call my friend in Washington, and we'll see who he can recommend."

"John!" The stubbornness was mixed with the desire to inform. "Demain—tomorrow—is a holiday for Quebec! As is the rest of the week—which means that by tomorrow Canada could be attacked from outer space and no one would do a thing about it until Monday. Now when I am back we will depart for Presque Isle. Believe me, I know this will be quicker and better than anything here."

His glance indicated that the operations room was a good example of what he was trying to convey. At the moment there was no time to argue the relative merits of our individual bureaucracies.

"Il n'y a pas un docteur accessible, Picard." Maurin was back.

"I'll call you when I'm ready to leave Chacun. You have an ambulance waiting here."

Maurin's thin nose rose against René's tone of command. "You will file a flight plan, oui!"

We had gotten fairly damp, making the run back to the plane. Now I sat listening to the rain thrumming on the wings, watching the rivulets streak the windshield as René talked to the tower. When he signed off I got down to cases. "I think it would be a good idea to leave the cargo with me."

"Oui, that's why I got you wet. I will taxi you to the terminal, and you can take it into town. Get some fish, some ice. Fill it up and meet me back here at eight o'clock. Then we'll go."

"Won't you be très fatigué?"

"One can always sleep later, John. I know what we have is more important than any single man who is hurt, but if I said non, I would never be able to fly out of here again. You understand?"

"Of course. What about my coming with you?"

He shook his head. "No reason. Better you rest." He looked at me, and in the somber light his expression was cautious, bear-like. "Do you have an idea what may have done this thing?"

"Right now I'd only be guessing."

"By that jet, maybe."

"I don't know."

"We have got to find that bastard." His hands moved to start the engine.

From the window in the terminal I watched René take off and saw the Beaver disappear into the murk. Then I carried the ice chest to the entrance and caught a cab back to the inn. It seemed a very long time since breakfast and a bright summer morning.

The manager was eager to have me store my catch in his freezer, but I held him off, saying I'd be checking out shortly, after a shower and a change of clothes. My first move was to put in a call to Washington.

Muriel Morgan, Ashton Lee's protective earth mother of a secretary, had a voice that was cool and in command.

"I'm sorry, Mr. Erikson, but Mr. Lee is not here."

"Where can I reach him, Miss Morgan?"

"Well, I'm afraid that's not possible."

"Why? Has he died, or gone to Mars?"

She did not approve of my humor. "He's simply out of reach until Monday."

"Miss Morgan, I'm not calling all this distance just to tell him the fishing is good. This is an emergency. I'm sure he left a number with you."

"Mr. Erikson, Mr. Lee gave me my instructions, and I am following them."

I could see her neck, rather thick and made for choking. "I need the number, Miss Morgan. This is a matter of extreme urgency." So far I had kept my voice flat and in control.

"Mr. Lee should be calling in, I can give him a message."

"When do you expect him to call?"

"When he's free."

"Look, Miss Morgan," and now I was fighting against shouting, "I don't have much time, and right now I have even less patience. I want his number. If you fail to give it to me you could be responsible for a major catastrophe. I've got to speak to him right now!"

She didn't reply for a moment, struggling I realized to keep her own temper and to make a decision. We both knew that when Ashton was out of reach like this, he was engaged in secret government R&D, and it wasn't something that could be explained or discussed on the phone. I was hoping the urgency of my need would get past the barrier of standard-operating-procedure and her overzealous nature.

"If you will leave your number, Mr. Erikson, I—"

"Let me speak to Mr. Zeller."

"He's with Mr. Lee. Mr. Cartright is here if you'd like to. . . ."

I blew. "Miss Morgan if it's the last thing I do I'm going to get you canned. You're being just damned ridiculous and we both know it! If—!"

"Mr. Erikson!" Her voice went off key. "No matter what number I might give you, you could not reach Mr. Lee at this time! I don't know how soon he will be reachable, but when he is he will call me. At that time I will give him your message!"

It could be so, but I didn't believe it. Ashton, whether airborne or in a submarine, could be contacted if necessary. I gave her my number and said I would be available from five to seven-thirty, but if I didn't hear from Mr. Lee, I'd hold her accountable.

I hung up before she could goad me further. It had been a long day, and it wasn't getting any better with age and my disposition.

Within the next hour I managed to buy a ten-pound bag of ice and a half dozen freshly-caught walleye. They supplied a normal enough top-cover to the chest and the specimens below. There were a few

35

tricks René would miss, and I couldn't see the thing arousing a Fish and Game official's suspicion or interest.

When I finished the job, I bundled my clothes into a pillow case and packed it in my bag. They, too, would bear examination. Then I thought I'd lie down and think things over. It was a mistake. The effect of the day slugged me, and the next thing I knew I was being dragged unwillingly back to wakefulness by the unmusical summons of the telephone.

"Ash." I mumbled, my hand fumbling for the receiver, my mind as dim as the lighting in the room.

"Ash?" I repeated, sitting up.

No response. Emptiness.

"Hello. . . . Ashton!" A faint humming. "Hello. operator?" I held the receiver, tightly. My watch said a quarter to seven. "Hello!" Nothing. And then a faint metallic click put a period to the one-sided inquiry. I hung up. I waited a couple of minutes for the phone to ring again, thinking that long distance can sometimes get tangled in its own long lines. When I decided such had not been the case, I left the room and went looking for the inn's switchboard operator. She was blonde, petite et très jolie.

"Non, M'sieur. I have received no long distance call for you."

"Would all calls come through your switchboard?"

"Oui, M'sieur." She had nice teeth.

"My phone rang a few minutes ago, but there was no one on the other end, so I—"

"Alors, M'Sieur, there was a local call. I am sorry, I did not understand."

I looked at her stupidly. "Who? Was it M'sieur Picard perhaps?" The laugh said a lot for René's popularity with the ladies.

"No, it was not René. I did not recognize the person."

"Did he ask for me by name or by room number?"

"By name, M'sieur. He said Erikson."

I went back to my room, taking a chill with me. So far as I knew there was no one locally who knew where I was staying. If René had called Maurin from Lac Chacun and asked him to give me a message, Maurin would have done so in a normal manner.

Before I headed back to the airport I had one more try at Ashton but got nothing. Muriel Morgan had gone home to her unlisted number. There was little to be gained by dwelling on uncharitable thoughts, and besides I was far more concerned, at the moment, as to the identity of the unknown caller. I didn't have an inkling, but certainly the writhing strands of my imagination had no trouble in fastening on to a pretty fair reason as to why. Someone knew my name. Someone knew where I was. And someone must know where I'd been and what I'd brought back. But no one appeared at all interested in my return to the airport, ice chest in hand.

I found M'sieur Maurin crisp and faintly aloof. "No, M'sieur, there has been no word from Picard, and we have no knowledge of his ETA."

"He said he'd call you before he took off, and he told me he expected to be here by eight. How long a flight is it from Chacun?"

"A bit more than an hour and-a-half perhaps, depending on the weather."

"Then he obviously isn't going to be here by eight."

Maurin shrugged. "We do not consider him very dependable, M'sieur."

"I gathered that. What about the jet, any report on it?"

"*Comment?*" His eyebrows rose, needle-nose questing, and then he remembered. "No, no. Nothing. Probably one of Picard's bush flying friends having some fun." Very poor fun as seen through the eyes of the operations chief.

"I wonder if anyone has been trying to contact me? My name's Erikson."

"Oui, I know your name, M'sieur, but we have had no messages for you here. Perhaps Air Canada."

"I'll check back in an hour, and see if you've had any word."

"As you wish, M'sieur Erikson."

The airport cafeteria didn't have much going for it. Rustic with slab wood walls and exposed ceiling beams, it was cluttered with tables and the heavy smell of too much fried food and cigarette smoke.

I settled for black coffee and a piece of gluey-looking apple pie. The lighting was dim, which was all right by me. I tucked myself off in a corner with a wall to my back and took in my fellow diners. They numbered a half dozen, and from what I could see of them they were not the follow Erikson type. Ahh . . . but what type was that?

The pair of woodsmen sitting nearest me were on their eighth beer, arguing good-naturedly about the next flight out to St. Pierre, using a beer-soaked airline schedule to make their points.

In the far corner were a couple, he with his back to me, the overhead light revealing that he was going bald. I was unable to get a clear look at his female companion, but it seemed that she was a well-shaped blonde.

The other couple were youngsters, apparently soon to be torn asunder. She was clinging to his arm, eyes puffed from crying, he, needing a shave, staring straight ahead, chain smoking.

The assembled group just didn't fit anyone's idea of lurking menace.

I drank the coffee and ate the pie, aware that both were wretched. Rather than quiet what little appetite I had built up, they killed it. The ice chest sat beside me, my travel pack on its top. "René," I muttered, "You'd better get your ass back here soon."

The couple across the room rose, and as he turned, I saw his face. He didn't notice me staring at him, which gave me a chance to double-check my recognition of him. Six years lay between us. Aside from the grey hair and general physical wear and tear, he hadn't changed that much. He still loomed large, with slightly bent shoulders and a melon-shaped head. His features, heavy in repose, cigarette in mouth, conveyed a faint air of disdain. Captain Liam Ganin didn't look out at the world; he looked down on it, in or out of his cockpit.

The fact that he was here now gave me a powerful jolt. The distance in time and space between the Elburz Mountains in Iran and the forested wilderness of northern Quebec was suddenly collapsed by his presence.

"Ganin!" I hadn't meant to shout.

The woman spun around, her startled expression making a mash of her handsome features. He came around more slowly, unhurried but with fluid ease, the watchful look in his eyes betraying nothing.

"Liam Ganin," I said, going across the room toward him, smiling broadly. His handshake was limp. His face had taken on a puffiness, particularly beneath the flat, pale eyes. The nob of his chin was spangled with tiny red veins, but there were few lines indenting his forehead or his features.

"I think I know you," he said, his voice a light rasp, the trace of a smile, a fixture, not a fact.

"John Erikson," I filled him in, "Tehran, 1969."

38

"That's really ancient history, chum. You were with the Embassy?"

"No, I was a visiting newsman. Your boss, Angus MacMurry, invited me to fly with you on a couple of those missions over the Sefid Rud."

"Well, what d'yuh know." The smirk became a bit more pronounced. "You must have a good memory. That was quite a deal old Mac had with the Shah."

"Are you still working for him? MacMurry, I mean?"

"Hell, no. He went bust way back when. Last I heard he was in the happy farm." Ganin took his companion's arm. "Nice to see you again, chum."

They moved off-stage, and I was left with the remaining audience of four and a cleanup waitress, to judge my performance. I ended the scene by buying another cup of coffee and retreating to my lair in the corner.

The long arm of coincidence—cliché that it is—had me by the short hairs. Dr. Angus MacMurry, Canadian meteorologist and cloud physicist, had been weaving through my thoughts since René had described the cause of his own cry for help. Running into Liam Ganin brought MacMurry into sharp focus. But as I focused, it was with the realization that in Canada there are not that many pilots and even fewer weather modification wizards, and that Ganin's, presence, since he had flown for MacMurry on a long-gone, cloud-seeding operation, and his being in Sept Iles at the present moment, were facts well within the reach of logical explanation. Or so I sought to convince myself, and did a fairly good job of it while disposing of the coffee, which was hotter this time around and therefore more drinkable. On reaching the dregs, I had two remaining questions: What, and for whom, was Ganin now flying? Why was ebullient, tough Dr. Angus MacMurry in a mental hospital? He had hardly seemed the type to me, which on reflection was a stupid observation. What did I know about his type, or anyone's type, behind the mask we all wear? I could take my own face for starters. What was the old Irish saying? —"He left his fiddle at the door." Well, MacMurry was no Irishman, and whatever he left at the door I still wanted to know why he was on cloud nine, instead of being busy out seeding it.

As for Ganin, and his not exactly warm greeting—he hadn't even bothered to introduce me to his lady fair. He was, as I recalled, not exactly the friendly corner grocer by habit or by nature. Now, if I'd been a fellow pilot—Ahh, well . . . Maurin could tell me who Ganin was flying for, and if he didn't know, René would.

I looked at my watch, wondering how soon René would be reporting his time of arrival.

By ten o'clock I had worked myself into a pretty fair lather. René had not only failed to contact Maurin, it also appeared no one had heard from him since his take-off. Neither of these points seemed in anyway to disturb the operations chief and his lieutenants. Their blasé attitude did not help to control my blood pressure.

The picture was clear enough to them. René Picard was a free spirit who had survived a thousand northern whiteouts and le bon Dieu knew how many other aerial phenomenons. As a fixed base charter operator, flying the bush, he observed only those regulations that were mandatory to prevent his license from being revoked. In this part of the world, once you were out of sight of the settlement, it was just you and the wilderness. You made damn sure your engine was in good shape, your radio was working, and you had survival gear. As for the rules, you flew from point A to point B, and as long as you were not traveling an airway, you were free to file or not file. I suppose not filing could enlarge your freedom of action. You could go where you pleased, as we had done earlier and with no Maurin looking over your shoulder. On the other hand, if you didn't show up as expected, they wouldn't drop everything and start looking for you, at least not until you were missing long enough. If it was necessary for officialdom to launch a search, and they found you, they'd never let you forget it. I gathered it was a kind of running battle that René and some of his fellow bush pilots fought with the administration. The disdain was obviously mutual. As for Maurin, his manner indicated that René's failure to contact him was normal.

A couple of things I did learn in the course of my long wait. Captain Liam Ganin was chief survey pilot for Northern Quebec, a division of the Hydro Quebec Power Company. He lived in Sept Iles and the plane he flew was a Grumman Goose—no jet by a long shot. I rechecked with the switchboard at the Inn and found there had been no follow-up by the unknown caller.

At eleven o'clock Maurin informed me he was closing shop. It had been a busy day. Operations would open again at five. The Air

Canada flight from Goose Bay was due in at six. The tower would handle all traffic and communications during the interim.

"Is it possible for you to call the camp where Picard has gone?" I tried to keep the stridency out of my voice.

"There is a radio telephone at the headquarters, M'sieur, and since Picard has not bothered to call us, I do not think anyone will be there at this time."

"Would you please check it out? If there's any charge I'll pay for it." I was losing on the stridency.

"M'sieur. . . ." I could see the resistance in his mouth and eyes.

"He told me he would be back here by eight!"

"So I understand, but—"

"I want to know if he's left!" He must have seen something in my own mouth and eyes. He turned away from me, a man trained to reject suggestions from the outside, a "no" man. He spoke to his number one in French, but in any language he was obviously irritated.

Number One cranked up the equipment and began calling. It was a two-way radio. You called the station, identified yourself, and asked the other party to come in. But he came in over a phone. So when Number One made contact and began speaking, I gave a knowing nod at Maurin and felt some of the tightness ease off. The respite was brief.

I didn't get what Number One was saying, only that he had a puzzled look on his face when he summoned his boss. Maurin took over the phone and the wrongness of something came through without need of translation. It was all there in the quick burst of his words, the rising inflection of his voice.

"What's the problem?" I said to his back as he put the receiver down.

He came around, but he wasn't seeing me. He spoke to his assistants, explaining, and the three of them went at it. Maurin's expression was aroused and wary, a man who wanted to be sure of his own position before he worried about anyone else's.

"Goddammit! What's going on! Where's René!" My bark stopped them in mid-exchange.

"M'sieur," Maurin was in command, "Lac Chacun has no report on Picard. Further, there has been no accident there. No need for him to fly there. They did not call us here."

My departure from Sept Iles on the early morning flight for Mont-real was not auspicious. Fear, anger, and frustration snapped and yowled within me, spinning on the ragged pinwheel of my mind. René's disappearance, his failure to make contact, had been viewed by Maurin and his attendant clowns as some kind of mid-summer joke, a hoax played by fellow bush pilots. All fun and games. The silly bastards were smart enough not to come out and openly say what they thought, but the implication was clear. It was all in keeping with buzz jobs by jets and other flights of fancy. Maurin did alert Air Traffic Control and informed the local RCMP office that Picard was long over due on a flight to Lac Chacun. Then he announced again it was time to close up shop for the day.

I hit the fan. "What the hell do you mean you're closing down! Don't you consider this an emergency?"

"If it is, M'sieur, there is nothing we can do here until daylight."

"Planes don't fly at night! You can't start a search!"

"Not in this weather."

"He said he'd contact you. Suppose he tries?"

Maurin began putting forms in a drawer. "The tower operator will be listening and so, of course, will ATC."

"And then what!"

"*Comment?* Why, in any case, when it is light and the ceiling has lifted, we will go look for him, a search will be made. Believe me, M'sieur, this is not an unusual occurrence."

"It's a damn sight more unusual than you think, bub." And I was forced to leave it at that.

Before I returned to the inn for the second time that day, I had paid a call on the tower operator, a friendly young man with little traffic during the small hours to interrupt his studies. He agreed to call me should there be any word on René.

At the inn my old room had been waiting and, "Oui, M'sieur," they would be happy to wake me at 5:30 and see to a cab, and would M'sieur like to put his catch in the kitchen freezer?

There was no need to wake me. I thrashed away the hours. There were no phone calls from persons known or unknown. For added protection I had tilted a chair against the door, its edge under the knob. Around dawn I sank into some kind of coma in which I managed to half way convince myself that old René and his Beaver were down safe somewhere. But the thing was I knew I couldn't wait around to find that out.

It was a miserable morning of rain and fog, but the operations chief was a different man, far more pleasant and outgoing. He assured me that as soon as the ceiling lifted to minimums, at least three planes would be out hunting for René. He, too, was full of reassurance. René Picard was indestructible!

The Air Canada flight was a half hour late, coming in with its twin landing lights blurred orbs, gleaming in the murk. Somehow they reflected my state of mind, for before the landing I had fought a battle and lost.

"No, M'sieur, I'm sorry, the coffre du poisson cannot be carried on board. It will not fit under the seat and—"

"I can stow it in the area where coats are hung."

"No, M'sieur, that is not permitted."

"But there are baggage racks. I put my travel pack there often."

"A small travel pack as you have, M'sieur, is permitted, but not the chest. It is not a carry-on. It is too large. Your fish will be taken good care of, in the proper compartment for the baggage."

"Look, dammit—!"

I retreated with a green claim ticket and a full head of steam under the curious stares of my fellow voyagers. I could blame my behavior on knowing that I had only two choices: either to go, losing sight of the chest, or to stay—and do what? Charter a private plane. I went. The Air Canada clerk was happy to see the last of the ridiculous American who couldn't bear to part with his fish!

Flesh and bone can stand only so much. I sat, fastened my seat belt, and all my worries disappeared into a black hole, pulling me down with them. In spite of all, I slept.

On the ground at Dorval, the stewardess shook me free from the nether lip of nowhere and announced our safe arrival. Groggily, foggily, I gathered the tattered remains of self together and managed to debark without falling down the landing ramp.

I noted the weather had improved, a steady northwest wind was at work, sweeping away the overcast. If the same wind was doing its duty at Sept Iles, the search for René should be in full swing. At the moment I had two courses of action to follow: claim my box of fish and then get on to the first flight south. It was just after eight, too early to try to call Muriel Morgan but not too early to try to contact the tower at Sept Iles.

The baggage claim area was a long room, badly lit with a half-dozen rotating bins to handle the inflow fed from conveyor belts. At its far end there was a bank of pay phones. I latched on to one, and the call went through swiftly. I learned the search had just begun. There was no additional news.

Even though the call did nothing to melt the lead in my gut, the action had been swift. The same could not be said for the baggage return. Nor was I the only one to become impatient. After fifteen minutes of watching the sterile merry-go-round of empty drums, one of my fellow travelers began to protest to a uniformed attendant. There was, of course, a logical answer to the delay. Due to being required to work on the holiday, the cargo handlers were working to rule. What could be more natural? The assembled gave muttered voice. Finally, at the end of some interminable debate, the insults gave way to a ragged cheer as the parade of assorted duffle began.

I kept my eye on the tunnel opening where the bags made their entrance. I waited. In time the parade was over. The conveyor belt was empty. The white styrofoam chest had not arrived. The awful reality of its absence was made more final by the mechanized remoteness of the baggage operation; an inhuman malevolence at work. I was alone in the room.

The attendant was on his way down the corridor when I gave voice. "Hey, wait a minute! My bag! My fish chest didn't arrive!"

"Pardon." From his reaction I knew he'd heard the complaint often. "Quel avion, M'sieur?" Ours had been the only flight at the moment. He, too, was working to rule, and from his detached manner, I suspected he always had worked to rule.

"From Sept Iles. Has all the luggage come in?"

"You have le billet—the ticket, M'sieur?" He had turned and we walked back to the baggage area as a much larger group of passengers began filing into the room.

I showed him the detached claim check. "Has all the luggage come off the flight?" I repeated, knowing the question was asinine.

"You should have left this cart attached to le billet," he lectured me.

"Don't give me any crap! Just find my chest!" Reaction was beginning to ride the shock wave.

44

Unruffled, he led me into a cluttered cubicle and handed me a form. "If you will fill out the spaces." He picked up the phone.

The result of his call hung me higher than a plucked goose. Flight 602 had been completely emptied.

"Can you call Sept Iles and see if my chest was put on?"

"Possibly it was taken off by error at Quebec."

"Well, all right, call Quebec and find that out!" I was aware of the shrillness in my voice.

He was reluctant to comply. He was a very thin, bald individual with a greyish complexion and faded features, but observant enough to realize that the passenger was likely to wring his scrawny neck if he didn't do as demanded.

The cargo office in Quebec did not have the chest. The cargo office in Sept Iles did not answer the phone. "They will only be there when there is a flight," was the explanation.

"Working to rule, of course. When is the next flight?"

"I do not know, M'sieur. If you will inquire at the ticket counter."

At the airline counter the young lady was as helpful as it was possible for her to be. "I'm sure your chest will come in on the next flight. When it does we can call you, and. . . ."

"When is the next flight due in?"

"Three-thirty this afternoon."

"What about calling your office there, now?"

"We'll send them a Telex right away." She had a nice smile. "Where can we contact you?"

"I haven't decided yet. I need a cup of coffee first."

"Well, I'm sure your fish will keep, whatever you decide." She was comfortingly efficient.

Whatever I decide. Sweet Jesus! I sat huddled over my coffee in the airport's airy dining room, the sun streaming in amidst the gentle flow of arrival and departure.

Question: Was the missing evidence lost, strayed or stolen?

Question: Did I wait to find out, or get the hell back to Washington with some undeveloped film and a story to tell?

Question: René missing, evidence missing. Will you be missing next?

Paranoia? Not in this time, not in this world! Out of nowhere Pete Scott came into my mental view. Five years ago, standing outside the Hotel Calais on the Rue des Capucines, the bulb of his nose blotched in the raw February chill. "Believe me, John, there are things that do go bump in the night and bang in the day." His raucous laugh made a puff of vapor in the cold air. "There's only one rule in the game. You have to make a plan; doesn't matter if you change it later, but make it to begin."

He was showing off, of course. As a political correspondent he liked to imply that he was involved in all manner of secret things, that possibly he was working for Somebody's Intelligence. He enjoyed trying to impress me because he knew my journalistic efforts concerned only the elements in nature, while his concerned the elements of man's political nature. But it wasn't all show-off, and whatever his plan had been, it couldn't have been that good, because two weeks later the Sûreté fished his body out of the Seine with a bullet in his head.

All right, make a plan and see how many bullets you can get in your head. They can toss you in the St. Lawrence.

It's very simple. You're going to have to sweat it out until they get a Telex back from Sept Iles or the afternoon flight arrives. If it doesn't show up then, you know it's been stolen, and you might be a sitting duck.

I looked around to see if any of my fellow breakfasters were waiting for me to quack. Not a one of them had the look of a hunter.

Could someone have stolen the thing to get some fresh fish? It didn't seem likely, not in Sept Iles certainly. But it could be, and if it was, how much danger was the thief in from the specimens? I went round and round on it. I saw myself trying to explain to the pretty airline clerk, saw her smile freeze, her body stiffen, and her foot reach for an alarm button, saw guards rush in and the potential airplane bomber being hauled away. Exaggeration? I saw myself confronting an officer and trying to explain. I saw myself stepping outside the terminal, and then I was either run down or gunned down from a racing black car, in the standard television style.

I was in a spider's web, suspended in time by René's disappearance, by the loss of the chest, by Ashton Lee's unavailability, by the Quebec holiday—caught between the horror of yesterday's find and the need to be in Washington today. Since time was the only factor that could resolve any of it, my plan must be to get a hotel room, to try to reach Ashton, and barring all else, to attempt to get some more sleep.

The first part worked, thanks to the pretty airline attendant, who got me the last available single at the Dorval Arms. The Telex inquiry had brought no response. I would check the three-thirty flight. She would contact me, should word come down between now and then. "Merci, à bientôt."

I found the Dorval Arms to be low-slung and unpretentious, with a somewhat lodge-like appearance. Its lobby boasted a large fireplace, exposed beams and assorted metal artifacts that for some reason appeared more Mexican than Canadian. Or maybe it was the hour and my condition. In the short ride from the terminal, I had been overly aware of all other vehicles in relation to the one I was in, and then in the lobby I was particularly observant of who and what was around me.

Once I had checked in to a room on the ground floor, the bellhop tipped, door bolted with 'Ne déranger pas' card on the outside knob, I calmed down a bit.

I pulled the drapes and lay down on the bed and had a go at reaching Ms Morgan. I would remain calm, I told myself. I would be pleasant. But I didn't get the chance to prove it. There was no answer. Maybe, she too, was working to rule, although it was still a bit early. I fell asleep framing an impressive conversation with her.

I must have been dreaming about him, because four hours later when I came awake, it was with the realization that at some point in times past Dr. Angus MacMurry had told me his office was in Dorval, not far from the airport. I moved from the dream world to the real world, a part of me in both places. Not until I turned on the bed lamp and began going through the phone directory was I fully awake. I stopped long enough to decide that what I was doing made sense.

There was no listing for MacMurry's company, Weather Operations, Ltd., in Dorval or in Montreal, but there was a phone number for its president. I wrote down both the number and the street address and sat looking at my scribblings, feeling glazed over and limp.

My watch said noon. I went in to the bathroom. I needed a shower and shave. Before I accomplished both, I made three calls. Nothing on the chest. Nothing on locating René. Nothing on Ash Lee because his charming secretary had reported in sick. Strike out! Oh, you're good at that Erikson, you're good at that! My only success was making contact with room service and ordering an *omelette jambon* and coffee.

While in the shower I made a decision on phase two of my plan. Maybe MacMurry was in a mental institution as Ganin had said, but then again, maybe he wasn't. Instead of calling to find out, I'd take a cab to his house. If he was there, if he was okay, he'd see me. And I'd have someone I could talk to who would know what in hell I was talking about, and he'd have some ideas on how to move next. If he was not there, I could pay my respects and get rid of some time before going to meet the three-thirty flight.

On the ride to MacMurry's home, I sat back and thought about him, thought about both our first meeting and our last.

*

The International Water For Peace Conference back in 1967 was a piece of Lyndon Johnson hoopla. I had written that the idea for it had undoubtedly spurted from the brow of the President's hustling Secretary of the Interior, Stewart Udall.

There was the war in Vietnam, and even though there was plenty of butter to go with the guns, much of the rest of the world was beginning to notice it was running out of fresh water. What a grand idea for the State Department to send a "you-all come" to the thirsty of the earth. They would be invited to attend a flock of prestigious environmental seminars at the Sheraton Park where the learned experts could bore each other with information already known to them all. In tandem with the talks and slide shows, countries as well as corporations in the water-producing business were invited, for a sizable fee, to exhibit their latest technological developments in extracting fresh water from the ground—by pumping, from the sea by de-salting, and from the sky by cloud-seeding.

From the point of view of publicity, Stu Udall was hot on this last. A few months previous to the conference he had made a whirlwind tour of the Middle East and Subcontinent, declaiming as he went, "We are going to tap the rivers of the sky!" This I had considered utter bullshit and had so written, but in more scientific terms.

I believed that what had inspired the Secretary's hyperbole were the hearings in both House and Senate that had recently been held in an unsuccessful attempt to produce legislation on the badly tangled subject of Weather Modification. This couldn't be done because neither the Department of the Interior nor the Department of Commerce were going to surrender their vested water prerogatives to the other. Interior had control of the water needs of the 17 Western States and under Commerce came weather forecasting and all that it entailed.

Consequently, while reams of testimony given by the Ph.D.'s, the professors, the experts, the academicians, the statisticians and the rainmakers, filled hundreds of pages of Congressional testimony, representing both departments, only one cogent fact emerged. It was not laid down by a witness, but by the Hon. Peter H. Dominick, the junior Senator from Colorado. He told the assembled that for ten years they had done absolutely nothing to advance the science of cloud-seeding and that they had no more knowledge or understanding of how to make the technology productive than when the task to do so had been handed over to the National Academy of Sciences a decade ago.

Udall must have failed to take note of the Senator's point—that, or he figured the sales pitch of being able to make rain was a dandy way to win friends in the Arab World.

At the Conference the success of his pitch was apparent. Of the 105 nations and companies that attended the four day water parley, only two of the exhibitors suggested cloud seeding as a method to add to the water supply. Somehow the U.S. exhibit, which was naturally the largest of all the displays, made no reference to weather modification at all!

I got a chuckle out of it as I drifted through the exhibits on opening day. Then I came to the Israeli display and, lo and behold, there were photographs of seeding aircraft with pyrotechnic flares on their wings looking like miniature rockets. According to the man on the spot, Dr. Hyman Goldsmidt, the flares, containing silver iodide, were being used to good advantage over the Negev Desert during the rainy season. The doctor was careful to explain that the operation was experimental and that rain was not being conjured from the cloudland, but was being increased between 10 and 15 percent from already precipitating weather systems. This, of course, was substantial but nothing all that new or newsworthy.

The only other tapper of the sky among the exhibitors was Dr. Angus MacMurry of Montreal, Canada, President, clan chief and cloud milker, of Weather Operations, Ltd. I had never heard of him or of his company. But as I came around the corner of a row of displays, the sound of his voice came to me from a booth looking a little like a Punch and Judy show. It was tucked off to one side, as though it didn't quite belong. Along the top of the booth's proscenium arch was emblazoned the company's name and beneath it in red a slogan for the thirsty: More Water Where It's Needed! On each side support were a series of aerial photographs, but what drew me, of course, was MacMurry's clarion call.

He stood center stage, selling his wares to a small but growing group of visitors, attracted like myself, by his vibrato. It didn't boom, as the saying goes, but it carried, and its scornful tone brought automatic interest.

Red thatched, big hawkish face with Scottish ancestry all over it, the man was holding forth and obviously having a good time at it. "It's bloody damn rubbish!" The trap of his mouth showed a flash of wicked molars. "How much does it cost to pump a thousand gallons of water out of your deep well? About fifty cents a gallon, give or take the depth of the damn thing! How much does it cost our Arab friends in Kuwait to de-salt a thousand gallons out of the Persian Gulf? About a dollar and a half! And how much does it cost Weather Operations, using my new Weathermaker?" He held up a red cylinder about a foot and a half long. "I'll tell you how much, one bloody cent! That's thirty cents an acre foot!"

He paused for the effect staring down at his audience. He got some, an undercurrent of derision and a couple of laughs thrown in.

He laughed back, his heavily tufted eyes, gleaming with a light of merriment.

"Oh yes, it's a bloody laugh, all right! For educated men to be such damn fools that they'll throw their money into the ground or into the sea when they could toss it in the air and make it pay! But if there's no water left in the ground, for we all agree the water levels are sinking everywhere, and you live five hundred miles from the sea— then how are you going to get the water you need, no matter how much you're willing to pay?"

"Are you trying to say," a voice spoke up, "that, that, that—"

"Weathermaker." MacMurry helped him out.

"That that Weathermaker can actually *make* rain?"

50

"Now there's a man who listens. You're a fine lad." He picked up some laughter.

"Now look here," he looked at his creation, "This little bit of scientific development, into which have gone nearly twenty years of my life, can revolutionize the whole need for more water right now! Yes, it can make rain, or snow, or whatever precipitation you have in mind, and it can save billions in the doing of it. It can help to bring an end to drought! It can wet down forests to prevent fires. It can fill catchment basins, and extend the growing seasons! It can. . . ."

"What can it make without clouds?" The questioner's tone was full of ridicule.

MacMurry, caught in full stride, played it neatly. His mouth closed slowly. He stared down at his interrogator, blinked his cagey sky-blue eyes, shook his head, and said with a great sigh, "Nothing, laddie, absolutely nothing! But!" Up came his arm with the cylinder, holding it like a torch, "as every enlightened meteorologist worth his radiosonde will tell you, most places on this globe have weather systems that pass through during certain seasons of the year. And they are highly seedable!

"Look! I'm not saying to put an end to your well digging or close down the de-salting plants. What I'm saying is, here is a new technology that man can use for his great good benefit, and at damned little expense!"

"If they're that cheap, I'll take a dozen," a listener proclaimed and the gathering ate it up.

MacMurry waited for order, rubbing his chin thoughtfully. When he had quiet, he said, "Well, I'll tell you what, laddie, if you've got a bit of land, say a hundred square miles or so, in need of watering, I'll fly over, and I'll show you what I can do for you with just one Weathermaker."

He turned and said to someone I couldn't see, "All right, Paul, we'll show the philistines."

A screen was lowered, a projector activated, booth lights turned off, and I moved closer to see the show. What I saw was an 8 mm. color film sequence: MacMurry and some helpers putting a box of red cylinders on board an old Lockeed Lodestar bearing the company name; the plane in flight coming up on a line of altocumulus clouds.

"If any of you are Met people you know these are fair weather cu, tops about seventeen thousand. They don't precipitate. This was taken up over the Laurentians near Charlevoix. Now watch."

We saw the plane fly over the middle cloud, caught sight of the red cylinder tumbling from the ship, disappearing into the cloud top.

"The Weathermaker is an explosive device." MacMurry said. "It goes boom in the heart of the cloud."

Next we saw the cloud from a greater distance, in line with its confrères.

We saw that it was changing shape, an anvil formation flaring from its top.

"This is twenty minutes after drop," our host explained. "What you're seeing is the effect of dynamic seeding. The latent heat of fusion has been created in the cloud, its temperature has been changed, its top has become super-cooled, and now it's glaciating. Do you know what that means, laddies? I'll show you."

The shot was at a different angle now, much lower, and we could see that it was raining like hell out of the cloud. The same could not be said for the other clouds. The film ended. There was a moment of silence as the lights went on and then the questions began with an excited rush.

Although I didn't know who MacMurry was, I knew I'd gotten myself a good story out of what I had decided was an obvious exercise in State Department blah mixed in with some Interior Department glug, all cooked up for the benefit of some big-name water merchants. I had planned to write accordingly, but now here was a drummer with a different beat, a red-headed water magician with the eye, beak, and voice of a zealot. He fielded questions with angry joy.

"Sir, Doctor Bork, Chief Cloud Physicist for the South Dakota School of Mines, spoke this afternoon," said a round, coffee-colored man with the clipped British accent of a Pakistani.

"Did he now?"

"Yes, he did, sir. And he said quite distinctly and unequivocally that precipitation cannot be induced in any appreciable form unless the rain is already falling, or is about to do so, sir."

"Well, now, isn't that a wondrous piece of information! Doctor Bork, hey!" He gave the name heavy emphasis. "In my unlearned opinion, your Doctor Bork wouldn't know a raindrop from a gumdrop. But what about you!" He glared balefully at his questioner, "Don't you believe your eyes? Did you not see what everyone else here has seen?" He waved his arm at the screen. "Go get your Doctor Bork and all his friends, and we'll see what they have to say! You know what they'll say?"

"I cannot speak for them, sir," said the round man.

"No, but I can. They'll say they're too busy to come!" His grin was triumphant. "They don't want to see! They don't want to know! They don't want to believe, and do you know why?" He waited a moment. "Because they would have to admit they are wrong and have been for the past twenty years!"

He went on, scooping up questions, flinging sarcastic curves at the meteorological profession in general and at some of its better known lights specifically. He was a rainmaker come down out of the north, ready to up-end the profession not only with the red weapon he held in hand but also with the working of his own jawbone. I had to wait a good twenty minutes before the last of his audience drifted away, bearing the supportive package of brochure and articles.

I had the feeling that although everyone had enjoyed the performance, he had not made many converts. He had come on too strong, like a man in a bar room who is entertaining, but has had one too many. Still, with the film he'd given them all something to think about, even if they weren't quite sure what to think. Neither was I. In 1967, it was "Go ask Stu Udall," and I considered that a waste of time.

As I approached, MacMurry was talking quietly to the dark-haired young man, who I assumed was Paul, his assistant. He was busy rewinding the film in the projector while the boss was attending to the screen.

The boss turned, and, closer to, I saw there was a gauntness about his face, the cheek bones knobby, the flesh dished in below. His reddish mane was shot through with tufts of straw. The eyes were deep set and within their blueness I caught a glint of something explosive.

"How did it strike you?" he asked with a wolfish grin.

"I beg your pardon."

"Well, you stood over there long enough, watching like a young laddie outside a brothel, so it must have struck you."

I laughed. "My name is John Erikson. I'm a writer."

"Erikson . . . Erikson." He tried the name out like he was sampling a taste of Scotch. "Oh aye, I've seen your column in the press. You did that piece for *Science Magazine* on grain shortages."

Momentarily, my liking for him soared. "Why yes! That's so."

"I didn't like it." We both laughed. "You had everything right but the cure."

"I should have consulted you."

"Pity you didn't. But you can start now, if you'd like. What can I tell you?"

"Let's start at the beginning. Who are you?" From the expression on his face I could see that I'd gotten even.

But we had started at the beginning, and I learned that Dr. Angus Colin MacMurry had quite a background within Canadian academic and meteorological circles, or so his publicity sheet attested. He was an Arctic explorer, had been a research-fellow at McGill in microwave communication, and during World War II had worked with Dr. Henry Tizzard on radar development.

As an example of his expertise, he showed me the finer points of his weather-satellite tracking-console, constructed to receive printouts from the weather satellite Nimbus 2. He claimed it was the only privately-owned satellite tracking station to be found anywhere; each printout covered 4 million square miles of earth surface and the weather systems over it. He declared the equipment was an invaluable tool for cloud-seeding operations.

"Let's go to that," I said.

"Let's go get a drink first, laddie. From all the talk, I'm dry as a sand spit, and I don't mean let's get a drink in this carpeted mausoleum. Here the bastards rob you and don't even smile. Do you know a decent bar?"

I did, and before we departed and went to it, he introduced me to his young assistant Paul Dufore, a dark-visaged, intense-looking French-Canadian meteorologist.

"Back in an hour," he said to Dufore.

We sat in a dimly-lit corner of Louie's, he with a double Scotch and me with a beer.

"To your doubts and disbelief." He raised his glass, one eyebrow lowered.

"To your ability to dispel them."

"Before I try, what do you know about the state of the art?"

"Langmuir, Vonnegut, Shaefer," I recited. "G.E. scientists, two of them started the rain falling by seeding a cloud with dry ice or silver iodide over Mount Greylock in Massachusetts back in 1945, and it's been raining ever since."

"What you mean is, there hasn't been any progress ever since."

"Well, that's about what Senator Dominick said a while ago, but I'm also familiar with the general meteorological attitude of the Doctor Borks of the world. It's tough enough to try and predict the weather without having someone come along and screw it up, producing unknown results."

"Unknown results, blah!" He set his glass down hard enough to slop some of its contents on his wrist, which he licked off as he continued to talk. "It's because the pack of them are bloody fools who would rather waste good time arguing about their methods of statistical proof in order to prove the technology doesn't work, than to put their minds to making it work!"

"So much for the meteorological profession, and I am aware of their hostility, or caution, or whatever. What about you? Where's your proof, aside from an 8-millimeter film? Fill me in."

And so, for an hour, he filled me in, while he filled himself with Scotch, downing it like water and going on with a contained yet furious enthusiasm. Some years ago he had asked himself why cloud water could not be engineered and utilized the same as ground water. The technique of static seeding had been well established by a few hardy souls such as Irving Krick. Using ground-based generators, and, where possible, aircraft, they sowed frontal systems from which rain was already falling—or about to—with particles of silver iodide, and they reaped, if lucky, small increases in the total downfall. Or so they said, and ran headlong into the counter-arguments of the meteorological community who proclaimed that proof was no proof, and even if it did work, the seeders were milking one man's clouds to dry up another's, etc., etc.

MacMurry claimed he wanted no part of either the existing technique, which at best was primitive and selective, or the meteorological bureaucracy out to block it and any other cloud-seeding technique.

The Weathermaker was the product of years of research and experimentation in the laboratory and in the clouds. He had made a revolutionary breakthrough; he had changed the whole concept of seeding. Fair weather clouds, with super-cooled tops, which ordinarily would give no precipitation, could be made to produce billions of gallons of water. The precipitation in existing systems could be increased anywhere from eighty to three hundred percent.

"My God, man! Think of what that means! The arid areas of the earth can be made to bloom! You wrote about coming food shortages, and you touched the tip of it, mark my words, you only touched the tip of it. Our climate is changing, drought areas are spreading, water tables are sinking, and the population of places like China, Africa, Russia are going up and up. With proper planning, the right engineering, the construction of catchment basins, the arid areas of this old earth can be made to produce! Granted, it's a new science—but Jesus, man," he grabbed my hand, "Think, think of the potential!"

"In a world where the accent is so much on the negative, you make it sound very positive, but I have to get back to basics, where's your proof?" I retrieved my hand.

He had been caught up in the bagpipes of his own enthusiasm and I had halted him in full skirl.

He glared at me and then simmered down. "When we go back I'll give you a paper from last month's Meteorological Journal. It's on the results of tests made at NCAR on fair weather cu, using the Weathermaker. You know NCAR?"

"Sure, the National Center for Atmospheric Research at Boulder. Have you used your Weathermaker any place else?"

"On some forest fires in Labrador. They were burning out of control, no way of stopping them. I offered to put them out. There were desperate and said go to it. We went in in the Lodestar and had them out in three days. We worked on a weak system that offered showers along the frontal line outside the fire area. We made it come down on the fire like it would never stop. Hah!" He banged his glass again, only this time it was empty.

"Did it get reported?"

"Not bloody likely! Hushed the whole thing up." I waited for him to tell me why, while he caught the eye of the waiter and gave a wave.

"Couple of years ago Western Quebec had a bad drought. Word got out that there was some seeding being done in the East. The farmers in the West claimed the cause for no water in their territory was the seeding. The East had robbed them of their water. Two-headed calves were being born and the world was coming to an end unless the provincial government paid them for their crop losses. The government, in its magnanimity and facing an election, bowed to the weight of scientific evidence and its own gutlessness and paid up twenty million. I might add, the Administration lost the election, but before it went out of office it managed to pass a law forbidding any more seeding in Quebec."

"Doesn't speak very well for the future of the technology, does it?"

"Ahh, not here laddie, not in your country or mine, but where men know the need, where men have not become buried in the ruts of their own conformity."

"And that's why you came here, to—"

"Water for Peace! I thought, what better place to unveil it?"

"And are you going to give a presentation, a paper at one of the seminars?"

He looked at me disgustedly. "Now laddie, you wouldn't be pulling my leg! Give a paper—waste my time and energy on a mountain of jelly! I'm here to do business, not wrestle with the bloody boobs!"

"Have you found any customers?" I was tempted to tell him his form of presentation wasn't exactly geared to immediate success.

He offered me his grin. "I'll be having a meeting with some real thirsty customers from a dry place in the Middle East, and then we'll see."

"Can you tell me the country?"

"I'll tell you laddie, when they tell me, yes. And then if you like, you can come and see the Weathermaker at work."

He let me pay for the drinks, and I left him on Connecticut Avenue and watched him go striding away in the early evening darkness, a man in a hurry, sure of where he was headed, no matter how many windmills he had to knock down to get there.

Several weeks later, after I had done a lot more looking into the subject of rainmaking and deciding in spite of MacMurry's full-blown assurances, the technology was in a very embryonic state—I had a note from him in Montreal, announcing that he had signed a three-year contract with the Iranian Government. Anytime I wanted a look-see, I was welcome to do so. I used the information to conclude my article. But it took me nearly two years to catch up with him so that I could accept his invitation.

*

Tehran's Mehrabad Airport lies in the wind-scoured flat lands west of the city, backed by the long, high reach of the Elburz chain. The mountains are compelling, their massive stone frontings like the paws of some many footed behemoth, towering up in jagged nonconformity to snow-furred peaks.

Without the mountains as a backdrop, the ugliness of Tehran would be more manifest, and as though in recognition of the fact, the city's growth has been out and upward, the Shah's technocrats swarming to take possession of the bare foothills. Coming in from Beirut on the gentle light of a March eventide, I was not concerned with the sprawling city's lack of architectural beauty, nor even the affairs of the long-gone Canadian rainmaker, for as we made our approach I was absorbed in the drama of the mountains.

Mountains have always drawn me. Perhaps I see in them a subconscious form of protection, a sense of security that I find totally lacking in the sea or in the lowlands. Or perhaps it's an anterior memory from the days in the Dordogne when we did finger-painting in the caves of Lascaux. Whatever it is, the connection is there, and as the plane descended, flying parallel to the range I observed a great jumbled layer of pillared clouds, making contact with a line of peaks. The rays of the sun sliced down, and through the rents in the clouds fans of opaque light bathed the snow flanks, creating a wonderous blending of shadow and color.

Shadow and color, I thought, the quicksilver of life, and I wished Nan were there to paint it. . . . But just as I was beginning to absorb the scene, the plane turned again and the sun and mountains were gone. I glimpsed the ant-like pile of tightly-compacted flat-roofed dwellings, grey and whites, the thumb of a minaret and the upthrust fingers of modern construction, then the yellowish, arid earth. We came down to it, and my mind returned to the questions that had been riding with me since take-off. Would I extract whatever time was necessary to seek out the Canadian, MacMurry? Or would I go on to Karachi, where my presence was anticipated by some Rockefeller Foundation types who had invited me to come and see the results of their green revolution using a strain of wheat perfected in Mexico? I had not given them a firm date of arrival, so a day or two in the Shahianshah's capital was not going to leave anyone waiting at the airport in Pakistan. There was the bother of the thing—customs delay, hotel, and taxi driver: they don't use headlights in order to conserve the battery; the accelerator is inoperative unless flat on the floorboard.

But mostly my doubts were on MacMurry. No response to several letters. No information on his activities. In this regard I'd gone through both the Iranian Press Attaché, and Ali Alizadeh, the Embassy's Economic Counsellor. I'd gotten zilch. No one knew anything about such an undertaking. The State Department's Iranian Desk was equally unhelpful. "Why don't you try the Canadian Foreign Office in Ottawa? We don't have anything on that sort of thing."

The Canadian Embassy watchdog referred me to the Scientific Advisory Office where I was informed in due course that the company was privately owned and in no way connected with Canadian governmental operations. At that point, I said, the hell with it. The whole thing had probably been a pig in a poke, the Shah had beheaded MacMurry, and rest in peace.

I had just about decided that weariness was the only argument for spending the night in Tehran when we taxied past a line of assorted aircraft. My eye was taken by a dun-colored DC-3, and as we swung by I saw emblazoned on its fuselage in black letters—Weather Operations Ltd. The sight did wonders for my spirits. I half expected to see a red head stuck out the cockpit window, red cylinder in hand, waving.

The next day it was Rod Hickam, Commercial Attaché at the Embassy, who unearthed MacMurry and group for me. The concierge at the Tehran Hilton had been unable to find any listing for the company, and I had turned to Rod as the one solid contact I had in the city. "It's not so much hush, hush, old buddy," Hickam quipped with Cheshire cat smile, "as it is cous cous."

"What does that mean?" His office, airy and high-ceilinged, looked out on the well-shrubbed embassy compound, a blending of cyprus and eucalyptus, with the mountains for background.

"It's one way of doing business out here with the government, particularly if the business is something as exotic as cloud seeding. The company has a contract with the Tehran Regional Water Board, so that's the umbrella it's hidden under." He grinned at his metaphor. "If the experiment doesn't work to the Board's satisfaction, or to that of the Ministry of Power and Water, under which the Board serves, the contract will run out and the whole thing will be chalked up to research And if someone like John Erikson should write about the lack of positive results it can be said that the forward looking Shah is willing to try all new technologies for the benefit of his people."

"And what about the results?"

"Wel-l-l-l, couple of things." Behind Hickam's easy-going, round-faced blandness, I knew there was a lot going on. "A year ago last fall when old MacMurry arrived in his gooney bird, this region was six years into a drought. Water was rationed. Sugar beet crop was practically non-existent. Government was having to pay the farmers a subsistance allowance to stay alive. By spring of last year the snow pack on the mountains was said to be the heaviest anyone could remember. Catchment basins in the Sefid Rud, Karaj and the Latian were filled to overflowing. Sugar beet crops turned out to be the biggest on record. Allah or MacMurry? I don't know. Neither do the Iranians. Now old Mac's winding up a second season. I've heard tell they've had so much rain and snow in the mountains where he operates that they've begun to worry about some of the dams holding. Word is they made him halt operations for a month, but that's mostly rumor, so don't quote me. In fact, don't quote me at all."

"I think I read somewhere that the area from Turkey to Pakistan has had an unusually wet winter."

"Could be. I'm just telling you how it is here."

"Sounds interesting. Has MacMurry got an office somewhere, a telephone?"

"Sure. He's in a new building on a new street called Kormanshah Boulevard. I'll give you a number, but better go direct. He's got an American rep, Sam Catton, to mind the store and keep the Water Board boys properly tuned."

"Isn't MacMurry here?"

"Oh, he's in and out, I'm told. Running around the Middle East, trying to sign up other thirsty clients. Don't know if he's here now or not."

"Do you know Catton?"

"Oh, we've met a few times socially. Couple of weeks ago the Ambassador threw a cocktail party and made a point of inviting Sam. He'd hardly gotten a drink in his hand when Clara, the Ambassador's wife, rounded on him and started giving him hell for making floods. I thought he handled her rather adroitly. She comes on kind of hard."

"Speaking of adroitness, aren't you people somewhat interested in the possibility that MacMurry might have something?"

"Sure." Hickam leaned back in his chair and put his meaty hands behind his head. "But there's not much we can do about it until we

60

know whether he's making the track record over those mountains, or nature is doing it."

"Somebody must be keeping records."

"Oh hell, they've got rain gauges all over the place—inside the target area and out, but the Water Board's not saying what they prove, not until. . . ."

"Not until they've got ten years of statistical reports to shuffle."

"Or maybe not until we see whether they renew MacMurry's contract when it expires next year. That would be pretty good proof of something."

I didn't add, why don't you invite fellow American Sam Catton to drop by for more than a drink and ask him. I'd do the dropping by on Sam instead.

Kormanshah Boulevard's newness was such that part of it was still unpaved and much of its building area was open to the breezes. This made it a spacious espalande over which the cab drivers could practice for the International Stock Car races. "Look, you silly son of a bitch," I cut loose with every decibel I could summon, "You slow up, or I'll cut your goddam throat!"

He didn't understand a word, but the sound indicated a reduction in tip and the look in my contorted face, thrust over the back seat, accompanied by my doubled fist conveyed the message. He slowed, his unshaven, dark, seamed visage, locked into a sulk, his yellowish brown eyes peering straight ahead. The leap from the camel's hump to the magic of the internal combustion engine took some getting used to, the switch having produced the highest highway casualty rate in the world.

"Over there." I waved toward the only building on the block with an exotic-looking antenna on its roof. It fitted Hickam's description: "A two-story villa with a meat market on the first floor," he'd said. I thought he'd been kidding on that, but he wasn't.

I gave my would-be executioner the exact number of rials for his pains, and we did not part friends. Now it was he who raised his voice in anger, and I needed no translator to tell me the thrust of his observations.

The building was a stucco affair with a flat roof and a walled balcony on the second floor. I was wondering if I should enter through the meat market, which was closed, when I spotted a small sign extending from the side wall and beneath it a side door. The

61

writing was in English and Arabic script. The English said: TRWB, and underneath in very small letters, Weather Operations, Ltd.

The side door was open, and I went in and up a dust-filled stairwell to the top landing. There was nothing on the door to tell me that I had arrived. I knocked, gave the knob a twist, and followed the door inward. The room was spacious, occupying much of the entire floor. There were several desks, files, the usual office assortment. Off to one side in a cubicle I spotted the Weather Satellite Tracking equipment. I did not spot MacMurry.

Seated at a desk backed by the balcony window was a comely Iranian lass with black olive eyes, an authoritative nose and an overripe mouth. She was taking dictation from a man who had swung around toward me as I'd made my entrance.

I had several immediate impressions—compact, contained, no wasted effort. He was a bit on the short side. His blue slacks had a sharp press and he wore a solid maroon tie to light up his short sleeve white shirt. The compactness was there in his solid forearms and the bulk of his tapering shoulders. He would hit a mean golf ball. Square, tanned face, close-cropped pepper and salt thatch, and mustache to match. They served as the well-formed setting for a pair of very alert, somewhat small, brown eyes. He reminded me for a moment of an NFL head referee—the very fit middle-aged man, keeping up with those ten years his junior.

"Sam Catton?" I said.

"Why, yes." His voice had that clear baritone assurance, a hint of a welcome smile curled one end of his wide mouth.

"My name is John Erikson. I'm looking for Doctor MacMurry."

He moved toward me. "He should be here shortly. Can I help?"

We shook hands. "I think so. I'm stopping through on my way to Karachi and—"

Catton had been trying to plug in his memory. "Didn't you do that article on us after the Water For Peace Conference?"

"That's right. At the time Doctor MacMurry invited me to stop in and have a look so I could do a follow-up. I'm a little late, but I thought I'd do just that."

"Well, fine!" He showed me a set of even, white teeth. "Maybe I can fill you in a bit before Mac shows up. How did you find us out here in the boondocks? Embassy?"

"Rod Hickam was good enough to solve the mystery." He led me across the room to the largest desk. Where he sat me down, I, too, had a view of the mountains.

"Like something to drink? Peri can fix you a cup of coffee or tea." He was smooth and polite, but I sensed something veiled in his manner, as though, having sized me up, he was backing off. He was pleased to show me on the wall map the five-thousand-square-mile target area over the Elburz where the seeding was taking place and the three catchment basins in the Elburz where the benefits of the seeding were being collected, principally by run-off from the built-up snow pack. He had no hesitation in explaining that the seeding season lasted from mid-October to mid-April. Within that period the weather systems that passed through were highly seedable. He showed me photos received by the tracking station. They were of great benefit, he said, in anticipating weather. In the generalities of the operation, he was fluent and informative, but when I pursued specifics he shied away. It became a matter of my question, a partial answer and then a question to me and me fighting to get the seeding thing back on the track.

Later I realized he had drawn more from me on my own work and activities than I had drawn from him on the activities of Weather Operations. At the time I thought, the hell with it, I'll wait for MacMurry. But I am nothing if not direct, and I wanted him to know how I felt about his evasiveness.

"You realize I learned more about what you people are doing in five minutes at the Embassy than you've told me." I was exaggerating, of course.

"Oh?" His eyes widened a bit, and he smiled. "What did you learn there that you didn't learn here?"

"For one thing, you had to stop seeding for a month because of an over-abundance of precipitation."

"What else?"

"I thought I'd come here to ask you questions. It's obvious that you don't want a very perceptive article written about what you're doing here. Maybe because you're not doing much of anything."

"Well, it might be a bit too soon." He ignored the sarcasm.

"I got the impression from MacMurry that any time wouldn't be soon enough."

"That was nearly two years ago, I think. It's possible he may have changed his thinking a bit. After all, we're working for the Iranians.

They pretty much call the shots on who says what."

"Well then, maybe I'd better go have a talk with their Minister of Power and Water."

"I dunno whether Zahedi would see you, but it's worth a try." He was calm and unflappable, and I was feeling the effects of jet lag.

"Isn't MacMurry trying to interest other countries in what you're doing here? How can he do that without publicity?"

"Oh, there are ways, and there are ways. Official inquiries, that sort of thing."

I decided I wasn't going to argue the point further. And I didn't have to, because from somewhere below came the sound of an engine being accelerated and then silenced.

"I think that's Mac," Catton said. "No flight today."

"Too much water?"

"No," he gestured with his head. "Not enough clouds." He was right, it was a bright jewel of a day.

MacMurry made an entrance, generating his own storm cloud, his voice rising up the stairwell ahead of him, proclaiming angrily, "I told you I don't give a bloody damn if you are commander of the plane! Paul Dufore is the Met! He selects the cu; not you! Not Stein! Not anybody but Paul!"

There was a rumbling unintelligible response.

And MacMurry bellowed, "Be goddamned to your contract! I'm telling you if you can't obey . . .!" The door slammed open and the man himself strode in, garbed in rumpled khakis and breathing fire. His companion, similarly dressed, followed behind, and later I would be introduced to him as Captain Liam Ganin.

Although my eyes were on MacMurry, my impression of Ganin was that, if anything, he was slightly amused by the blast.

MacMurry took me in, and I saw the struggle for recognition intruding on the conflict at hand. I didn't wait for him to wrestle my identity into focus.

"Doctor MacMurry, John Erikson, from Washington," I said, moving across the room toward him, hand extended.

He made the connection before I reached him, the scowl transformed into his foxy smile. "Well, now! Well, now!" he pumped my hand and grabbed me by the shoulder. "It's good to see you, laddie! Come to have a look, hey? Good! Just the man I want!" He peered past me. "I see you've met Sam. Has he been telling you all about what we're doing here, hey?"

"Filling me in a bit." I emphasized the "bit."

"Oh, I'll bet he has! All lies, hey Sam?"

And Catton replied lightly, "Whatever you say, Mac."

MacMurry and I dined that night at an Armenian restaurant on Takit Jamsid Road. He did not invite Catton to join us, which gave me an opportunity to learn more about the relationship. Although what I did learn came out in the course of a wide-ranging dissertation on the success of his venture and optimistic projections on new cloud-seeding contracts to come.

As for Catton: "Ahh, Sam is quite a laddie. When I set up here I knew I needed someone who could do more than mind the store. You have to keep the local chiefs happy. Wine them, dine them, pat their arses, otherwise you'd get nowhere. You understand? Sam's great at that." He grinned. "More, he's an American, which gives me representation in your capital when I want it." He winked, lifting his glass.

"What's his background?"

"Oh, the best. He knows the Middle East, the sub-Continent. He speaks Arabic, Farsi—the language here. He's worked for a number of big firms out in these parts. Bechtell, Litton. He's got contacts. He's a savvy public relations type."

"How did you latch on to him?"

"Oh, I have a few friends on both sides of the border. We were introduced. He liked the sound of something new, even if he had to meet my price."

"You said public relations. There doesn't seem to be any. No one back home, no one over here knows anything about you. I can understand the reluctance here, but—"

"Look, man! I hope you're canny enough to know what I'm up against. With a very few exceptions, every water expert and Metman, in your bloody country and mine, hopes I either fall on my arse or break it. I'm going against the entire academy." He spread his hands as though he was going to wring someone's neck. "Do you think I could make any statement on the basis of a single year's work! They'd hand me my head and rightly."

"But this is your second year."

"Aye, that's right, laddie," he beamed cagily. "And you're here as an act of Divine Providence—although Sam doesn't see it like that. He wants to keep everything bottled up until next year when we renew."

"Have the Iranians indicated they're going to?"

"Have no fear, they know what they've got, and at a price they like."

"I'd like to know what they've got, too."

"Well, you come flying with us tomorrow, and you'll find out right enough."

"But apparently your man Sam doesn't want me to write about it."

"Be damned to what Sam wants! I'm chief here! What Sam refuses to see is that this is only one contract. I'm close to bottling up a couple of more. The right piece by you in a national publication or in your newspaper column could be just the thing to push the pen across the line."

"Maybe you should have hired me to do your PR," I joked.

"I'll do better!" He laughed. "I'll sell you stock in the company!"

"Better wait till you take me flying."

Later, I realized that until the flight, and the two that followed, it had been more the wild-eyed independent quality of MacMurry's nature that had attracted me than any solid acceptance of his cause. Because of his credentials he wasn't someone the atmospheric scientists could simply scoff at, although they could ignore him. He had too much background of achievement, although not specifically in the field of weather modification. I'd been around the "scientific community" long enough to fully recognize the character of the power structure. All too often instead of being enlightened and far-reaching, it was narrowly proscribed. So seeing a Canadian heretic, daring the cannon's wrath, red cylinder in hand, had appealed to me. Like most, I have always admired the bona fide rebel, willing to put his money where his mouth is, at the risk of his professional neck.

After the flight, however, I knew something else about Angus MacMurry. Behind the sound and fury, he could make rain.

That next morning I had been a bit surprised to find Sam Catton waiting at the airport. Like me, he had camera in hand, and I supposed he would use it as a part of his job to photographically record the results of the mission.

He was easy and gracious, introducing me to Everett Stein, who, with Paul Dufore, the meteorologist I had previously met at the Washington conference, made up the technical end of the four-man crew. Stein—gangling, bearded, bespectacled—had that remote and studied air of the young scientific intellectual. His job was to fuse, prime and eject the Weathermaker with a ramrod-type plunger through a short metal barrel, extending from the belly of the aircraft.

"He's our real weathermaker," Catton quipped.

"What he means," MacMurry added, "is that he's the laddie who makes it all work, and if he's not careful he can blow us all to kingdom come. Isn't that right, Ev?"

Stein had nodded non-committally and moved away to join Dufore, who was unloading a couple of crates from the Land Rover.

We took off from Mehrabad in the still cool air of early morning, Ganin at the controls, his overweight co-pilot Stanley doing the gear-pulling and flap-milking. The old work-horse DC-3 ambled along the runway and became airborne at its own pace, engines accelerating in tune. It was quite a transition from the swift impersonality of jet flight—leisurely, a more humane movement, and, as any old pilot like Ganin knew, the bird was the finest piece of aeronautical creation since Kitty Hawk.

Ganin guided the plane upward, traversing the russet-hued flanks of the mountains until he had gained ascendancy over the range, and as he eased the plane on to a northerly course, it was possible to gaze across a great ragged expanse of white-capped peaks and dark declivities between. A short distance above lay the base of an overcast that extended to the horizon. It was not solid and standing behind the pilots, where MacMurry had suggested I might enjoy the view, I watched Ganin continue his climb upward through the cloud columns.

He had not spoken to me since our introduction in the company office the day before. Now as pilot in command, he opened up a bit, turning his head to announce, "We don't often have company."

"My luck!" I had to speak up to get my voice over the pound of the engines.

"This will be a good seeding day."

"How can you tell that?"

"We'll be on top at about eighteen thousand. Can't ask for anything better than that."

"How do you determine your run, particularly if you can't see the ground?"

He and his co-pilot exchanged knowing grins. "Oh, we drop cloud markers, red and blue, and just fly between them." He swiveled his head around, looking up at me with amusement. "I'll show you when we get there."

Before we got there Sam Catton tapped me on the back, presenting me with a portable oxygen bottle, hose and attached mask. "Better try this on, John. We're getting up where it's thin. Once we level off, Mac says come on back and see how Paul and Ev get set up."

Mask in place, bottle hooked to ɔelt, I watched Ganin bring the plane over the last cloud battlement into the bright-hard blue. He leveled off above the jumbled sea of cloud, and because of its closeness there was the feel of great speed.

He, too, had gone on oxygen. Now he lifted the mask from his face. "You see that pile of cu over there?" He pointed off to the right banking the plane toward the designated outcropping. "The Karaj basin and dam are right under it." Before the mask went on again I had the benefit of the smirk.

When we reached the appointed spot he began circling a wide rent in the cloud cover and down through it I could see a large body of water cupped in arid folds. At one end there was a dam with a white geyser of water hosing out of the spillway. Ganin and Stanley exchanged nods, and thumbs up signals. I bobbed my head in recognition of his unexplainable expertise, a form of Irish navigation yet unknown to me. I was sure he'd enjoy talking about his ability to locate objects on the ground by the shape of cloud tops, at the neighborhood bar. I added my thumb to the mutual-admiration club and went back to join Mac and the others.

Dufore, who replaced me in the cockpit, acted as the target selector and Stein, in the cabin, played bombardier. From the charts Catton had shown me and the diagrams MacMurry had scribbled the night before, I knew the shape and dimensions of the 5,000-square-mile target area.

And for the next hour as we traversed it, MacMurry, his mask off more than it was on, explained the flight and bombing procedures that Dufore and Stein carried out in dropping Weathermakers into selected cu.

When drop-time came, a red light flashed on the panel above the ejecting tube. Stein, kneeling, would have a cylinder resting in the tube, and on signal he'd activate the plunger—and it was bombs-away with only ten seconds to detonation. As an explosive device, the Weathermaker had the impact of a 30mm. mortar round.

The rather easy-going manner of the operation impressed me, but what really hit home were the results. MacMurry's film had been one thing, but to see individual clouds transformed in the space of twenty minutes from tame fair weather cumulus into towering anvil-headed nimbus, mushrooming up in slow motion and then extending outward to absorb lesser formations, was something else again.

"Get the glaciation! Get the glaciation effect, man!" MacMurry kept shouting at me as I moved about shooting film from all angles.

Catton was shooting, too, but busy as we both were I had the impression that he was disturbed by my presence and actions.

When, on instructions from MacMurry, Ganin took us back down through the cloud deck we broke out over the mountains in heavy rain and snow showers. We flew over the three catchment basins and their snaking rivers in heavy rain and snow showers. When we left the mountains and flew over the crop lands, we flew only in rain. And when we finally came in and landed at Mehrabad we were out of the rain showers into the sunlight, and we could see the dark hanging spill of the rain, tapering off over the mountains.

I stayed a week and went on two more flights with the same results. One afternoon MacMurry and I drove into the mountains and visited the Karaj and Latian dams. There, I talked to engineers, sharp Armenians, about the unusually high water-levels. They showed me figures on their anticipated run-off from the snow pack. I examined rain-gauge data both in and out of the target area. And over Caspian caviar, toast and vodka, MacMurry explained his method of targeting and furiously debunked the biggest bugaboo of the technology—if you make rain in one place you dry it up in another.

"It's bullshit! And there's not a meteorologist worth his salt who doesn't know it! It's the old business of telling a lie long enough to get it accepted as truth. You've got twenty-seven or twenty-eight states in your blooming country with laws prohibiting cloud-seeding for that very reason! Look you, man, what's happened down-wind of our target area? Are they getting less than their normal precip? They are not! In fact, they get some spill-over, because we can't turn it off like a spigot quite yet. Pakistan is down-wind of us. The major systems that come through here head there. Have you heard of any drought in West Pakistan?

"You have not!

"Everything to the East of us has had the wettest winter in a decade. Nothing we have done here has had any effect except right here!" He used his finger to stab a hole in the table. "And I'll tell you why!"

Now his finger was a barrel pointing at my nose. "In any weather system there is only so much moisture. In a smashing downpour you may get ten percent of the total. Ten percent, mind you! All right with the Weathermaker, I can double that amount. I can get a hundred percent over the normal, which still leaves eighty percent in the system! Now who in hell has dried up what! Clouds have life-spans like everything else, and anything nature or Angus Mac-Murry puts on the ground from one of them is going to have no effect on what it puts on the ground someplace else!"

"Can you prove it?"

"Prove it!" The nostrils of his beak flared. "The proving is in the doing, and I'm damn-well doing, where no bloody bugger can shoot me down! Look, do you realize we can computerize the chemistry of a cu, of any cu? We can take any cloud and find out what's in it, how much can be taken out of it and what you'll have left. The hit and miss of this business needn't be there, but it's being kept there by the power types who, for whatever their reasons, don't want to see the technology come of age.

"A blind idiot could tell you that while water levels sink, demands for water grow and global drought is spreading. One day it's going to get bloody serious. If we can show here what can be done, then it won't be so serious and that's why I want you to write about it now. Now!" He gave the table a whack for good measure, spilling vodka and scattering toast.

Before I got to the writing, I went back to see Rod Hickam and asked him if he'd line me up a meeting with Minister Safed Zahedi.

"He may not choose to see you, old buddy."

"You tell him I'm anxious to do a big take-out on the Shah's forward look into the realm of Weather Modification."

"How does it look to you?"

"I'll send you a copy of my article."

"Don't be coy."

"To someone who's not a meteorologist, it looks impressive, but I want to talk to some people back in the states before I commit myself. Meanwhile, why don't you ask Sam Catton to let you go out on a mission?"

"Would you believe I've made the request several times and been turned down—politely, of course."

"By Catton."

"And the man you want to see. Experimental work, possibly dangerous and so forth."

Hickam had called me that afternoon to say that the man would see me the next morning. When I arrived at the ministry, a nondescript cement-faced ziggurat on Firdausi Boulevard, it was not an Iranian functionary who met me to guide me through the labyrinth, but Sam Catton. He read the reaction in my face. "Sorry, Erikson," he said with a deprecating smile, looking very sharp in a charcoal pin-stripe. "The Minister called and asked me to be on hand. I thought I'd save you the surprise by meeting you here."

"Thoughtful of you." I was swiftly debating whether to call the whole thing off, but as he led me through a dimly-lit foyer, with marble floor and dome above, I calmed down. Nothing could be served by letting professional pique get in the way of my purpose. I have always tried to operate on the theory that any contact, no matter how disappointing, adds something to the total and is therefore better than no contact at all. Zahedi might have wanted Catton present to backstop anything I might ask that he'd prefer not to answer himself, or to make sure that anything I might write about the meeting could be corroborated or denied by two sources. Or so I had reasoned, but found I was wrong on both counts.

The Minister was waiting for us in a board room with two of his underlings. Unlike many of his countrymen, who have a greyish aspect, he had a nut-brown complexion. It went nicely with his black hair, shrewd black eyes, full black mustache and expensively-tailored black suit.

Catton made the introductions smoothly. The Minister's grip had all the pliancy of hard wood. Although he had a nob of a nose and a heavy-lipped mouth that added to the impression of physical bulk, there was no doubt of his toughness inside and out. Hickam had told me that in his youth Zahedi had been a dedicated Marxist, a leading light in the Tudah party. When the Shah, with CIA assistance, had broken the Communists, Zahedi could have gone to jail or have been shot. Instead, the young ruler had converted the peasant firebrand to his own cause. And here he was, an important minister. Not a bad success story.

"Mistair Erikzon, my English you will excuse, please." His voice was a hefty baritone. "Mistair Caatton, he will act as the interpreter, yes?" He gestured for me to be seated.

The interpreter moved into the chair beside me, Zahedi's two young Turks sat facing us, and their boss sat at the end of the table.

It was a dandy con job. For half an hour I sought answers and got the Iranian runaround. Sam funneled questions and answers in Farsi and English, enjoying a fine linguistic exercise which added up to— no comment.

Finally, I decided to stop wasting our time. "Please inform His Excellency that I know my readers will have a question." I kept my eyes on the Minister's own attentive black eyes.

As Sam translated he got the message and nodded for me to continue.

"They will wonder why the head of such an important ministry would be willing to spend so much money on such a revolutionary program without having any idea of what he was getting in return for his rials."

Zahedi blinked and waited. Sam rattled away in Farsi.

The Minister grunted, showed me the gold in his teeth, and barked like a seal. His reply was swift and good natured. "His Excellency says he'll be interested in seeing the answer you supply."

I had let Catton drive me in his Mercedes up the long length of Pahlavi Boulevard from the city's center to my hotel because he made the offer, and because I knew that would be easier on my nerves than a taxi ride.

Until the end of the ascent, which took us up past newly-built villas amidst the graceful greenery of newly-planted trees and shrubs, we did not talk shop. Mostly it was remarks on Tehran's rapid growth, Washington in the springtime, and whether the newly-elected

American President could do anything about ending the war in Vietnam.

But once Catton had swung into the hotel drive and come to a stop where we could view the towering impact of the mountains, he got down to it. "I know how anxious you are to write about what Mac has shown you, but believe me, John, you'll be doing him a favor if you hold up."

"For how long?"

"Zahedi would like a year. He said he'll give you a real interview if you'll wait."

"Nice of him. Is that what he told you?"

"Yes. Being premature could lose us a new contract."

"Why?"

"It's a matter of psychology. You don't understand these people. I do."

"Bullshit!" I snapped. "MacMurry doesn't think it will lose him anything, and I don't either. Good news never hurt anyone. There isn't any better psychology than that."

"You were not good news to Zahedi." A hard line had come into his voice; it matched the look in his eye.

"Look, do you believe in this thing or don't you?"

"You have no idea how much. But there's too much at stake here to have it jeopardized by badly-timed publicity." He sounded very convincing.

I opened the door. "Thanks for the ride, Sam. Oh, one other thing. That snow job we just went through with His Excellency—when I write about it, do you think I should explain that I know Zahedi speaks English as well as you speak Farsi? Hickam told me." I had the satisfaction of leaving Sam Catton looking momentarily glazed.

Angus MacMurry and I bid each other farewell at the airport, he on his way to Athens and a meeting with the Greek Minister of Agriculture, and I heading for Pakistan.

I had told him of the meeting with Zahedi and Catton's concern, and he had shaken his head impatiently. "John, man, pay no heed to Sam. He's spent so much time in these parts he thinks the way they do. He's good in his way, and he's looking out for my interests, but this is just a start here—just a start." He looked out over the milling crowd and added, "I can feel the winds of time blowing hard on me. What I've found says, yes! to the world—where there is so much of bloody no!"

That was the last we had seen of each other, not because either of us planned it that way, but because of an important Senator who asked me to call on him directly after I got back.

As for the article I wrote, I knew that none of the official scientific journals would touch it, the self-righteous explanation being that the piece lacked the necessary proven statistical data. However, I wanted a general audience anyway, and *Viewpoint* was happy to give "Where Rainmaking Is a Success" a big ride in its May, 1969, edition.

Then, just when the reaction from the groves of academe, as well as inquiry from the interested, began to mount, the call came from the Senator. As chairman of a special subcommittee on the environment, he was not interested in cloud nuclei and silver iodide over Iran, but in the use of herbicides and defoliants in Vietnam. As he put it, I was the only man on earth capable of leading an investigating team to Saigon for the committee. And I, like a goddamned fool, believed him. Momentarily my thoughts skidded down that wretched track.

*

In the brief ride from the hotel my thoughts had cut a long swath through a past that now seemed very close. But now, it was the cab driver who jarred me back into the present moment. "M'sieur, voulez-vous me répétez le nombre de la maison?"

It took me a moment of head-clearing to answer. "Ahhh, four fifty-three—quatre cinquante-trois."

We had turned into a suburban street, lined with solidly middle-class homes. But what struck me was the number of cars lining both sides of the block and the scattering of their passengers heading toward a single dwelling, about mid-block with an open front door. The flow was in both directions, for some were departing the house as others entered. The driver brought his cab to a halt in front of the place, flipping the meter handle. We sat there for a moment, he waiting for his money and me caught with a knot in my gullet.

"Is this four fifty-three?" I asked stupidly.

"Oui, M'sieur, quatre cent cinquante-trois."

As I fumbled for my wallet I had the feeling that I wasn't going to be staying long. "You—ahh—attendez moi, s'il vous plaît. Oui?"

"Cab! Taxi!" Both the cabbie and I turned toward the caller. A man in a hurry, his arm raised in signal, was coming down the walk from the front door, past the latest arrivals. I should have been bowled over, at least momentarily, but somehow at the moment I wasn't, I suppose partly because I had been thinking about him and partly because I already had a deadly suspicion of what I had arrived at. It was no cocktail party.

He came toward us, passing neatly between two closely parked cars. Six years didn't seem to have made a dent in him.

I opened the door. "Be my guest, Sam." I said.

He was the one who reacted, lips parting, eyes digesting recognition. "Erikson! John Erikson!"

He entered the cab, gripping my hand. "Damn! It was good of you to come." The stillness in his face that I remembered had momentarily broken down.

"I've been up north fishing. What have I come to?" I asked with an awful presentiment.

He stared at me and then said bluntly, "Old Mac killed himself two days ago."

Even though I was somewhat prepared for evil tidings, it was a fist slammed into the gut. "I didn't know he had a family," I said blankly, trying to pull the situation into proper focus. "What is this—a wake?"

"Something like that. I've been traveling. I didn't hear about it until late last night. I've had a devil of a time getting here." He rattled the words out. Close to, he looked worn around the edges.

"I don't know anyone. Do you want to take me in and introduce me?"

His eyes held me for a moment and then he smiled wanly. "You'll do better on your own. I'm not exactly welcome in there."

"Oh?"

A horn honked behind us, a car wanting to pull away. "Go ahead," I said to the driver. "Allez! Go around the block."

Sam quickly supplied the proper French. The driver threw up the meter bar, and we jerked forward.

After he made the turn, I said, "I did hear he had some mental problems and his business went bust. At least that's what Ganin said."

"Ganin!" He came up straight. "Where did you run into that bastard?"

"In Sept Iles. He flies for the power company. What happened to Mac?"

His glance was not friendly. Something hard glittered in the weariness. "It's a long story. I hadn't seen him in over two years. He became paranoid, everybody was out to destroy him. I was a CIA plant, the real villain of the piece."

"That syndrome, eh?" I said absently, still trying to absorb the impact of the news.

"Yeah." He smacked his hand down on his leg. "Poor devil, they drove him over the wall."

"Who's 'they'?"

"I'm too damn sick and tired to talk about it now. The whole rotten story is coming out in a book I've written." He looked at me. "Maybe you should have written it."

"Am I going to have to wait till you get it published?"

"No, no. I'll fill you in before that, but I've been about three days without sleep, and I'm full of jet lag. Do you have any idea where I can get a hotel room? Everything seems to be booked. Holiday or something."

My suggestion was not the result of premeditation, it was spontaneous reflex. "You can probably have mine. I'm at the Dorval Arms, and I'm heading back to Washington sometime tonight."

That brightened him up a bit. "Hey, that would be a real plus, friend."

"Dorval Arms," I said to the driver, deciding a funeral reception was not in my plans.

Catton sat back with a sigh and closed his eyes. I considered the options.

"Any idea why he did it?"

He didn't open his eyes. "He'd been in and out of mental hospitals since '73. Laurie, his daughter, told me he'd been released about a month ago, and they thought he was really coming out of it. He had an offer on one of his patents or something, and he'd sold it and made quite a bit of money, enough to pay all the bills. Then, bango."

"Just like that."

"Pretty much, I guess."

"It's hard for me to see him in that light, I mean as I remember him."

"Time marches. Things happen, people get changed. I've found memories can't stand up against certain realities."

"Let us sit upon the ground and tell sad stories of the death of kings," I intoned.

He cocked an eye at me. "Yeah." And then he lapsed into silence, or so I thought until he began again, "Laurie said he got a letter with some aerial photographs. Somebody trying to sell him some wilderness real estate up north, she thought. Got him all steamed up. . . . Ahh, I dunno. He left no note, nothing, just a hole in his head."

His muttering left me ramrodded like a plebe at his first meal. I sat there bug-eyed, my thoughts zinging around in an empty skull, trying to get a fix. Too much was coming at me too fast.

Catton sat up. "Hey, I left my bag at the airport. Why don't we swing around that way?"

"Hotel is on the way. We'd better stop there first and nail down the room. I have to check on some baggage that didn't arrive with me. Give me your claim check, and I'll pick up your bag, too."

"Well, that's good of you, but when's your flight out?"

"Not till around nine-thirty. You can get some rest, and then you can fill me in on the past."

"That goes for you, too, friend." The look was both quizzical and penetrating. It matched his slightly accusing tone. "Mac wondered why you dropped out of sight."

Dropped was certainly the operative word.

When we arrived at the front desk there was a sizable jam of the newly arrived, demanding their rooms. I gave Catton the room key and told him to move in; we'd straighten out the switch when the traffic thinned out.

"I really appreciate this," he said, meaning it. "Look, in my bag there's a copy of my manuscript. Read it over while I'm sleeping, and I won't have to answer so many questions." His curling grin hadn't changed either.

On the way to the airport I had two intertwined considerations to disentangle: how could I get a look at the photographs MacMurry had received, and should I fill in Catton? One reason for doing so would be that in spite of how the MacMurry family felt about him, Catton would have direct access to Laurie and that might in turn produce the photos. Why I should think they had any connection with the shots I'd taken at Lake Poitrine, I didn't really know. The reaction they had produced, hunch, nerves, imagination, the inter-relation between reflections and events? It didn't matter; I just knew I wanted to see them. But the question beyond that, with regard to Catton, was what could he contribute to the next move? I was damned if I knew that, either. As the cab pulled up before the terminal entrance, I decided the course I chose would be determined by what arrived on the three o'clock flight from Sept Iles.

As it happened, nothing arrived for me. The inquiry sent by the airline that morning had brought a completely negative report. There was no record of the chest, no record of its having been ticketed or shipped.

"And my baggage ticket?" I held it up for the junior office manager to see. "I suppose it was never issued either."

"Mr. Erikson, I'm sorry." The young man, too, was annoyed at the inefficiency of the cargo section at Sept Iles. "We'll continue to check on it. Most of our key people are off today. I'm sure it'll turn up. It's only a matter of time."

"It's something I've run out of, along with my patience."

"When is your flight leaving?"

"I suppose there are no ranking airline officers on duty today."

"I'm afraid not, sir, not with the holiday." He was probably wondering what kind of nut is this who wants to make a federal case out of some lost fish!

"I'll be in touch." I said.

Before I gathered up Sam Catton's over-night bag, I put in a call to the Sept Iles operations office. I got Maurin. Some of the superciliousness had been bled out of his manner. "There is nothing definite, M'sieur. The search continues, although the weather is becoming poor again, a new area of low pressure coming out of James Bay."

"What do you mean by nothing definite? Is there something indefinite?"

"Only the rumors, M'sieur. It is not good to repeat the rumors, n'est-ce pas?"

"You repeat them for me, and I'll be the judge."

We went through a long pause. "There is word that some fisher-man up on la rivière Moisie saw a flash in the sky and heard a detonation about the time Picard was flying in the vicinity. But you understand M'sieur, it was most probably the . . . the lightning, the thunder."

Before I reached the hotel again I had made up my mind that if there wasn't safety in numbers, there was at least some degree of assistance—a need that was becoming overwhelming. I was cutting Sam Catton in. His contacts in higher places might be better than my own, and in any case, I didn't figure I had a damn thing to lose by confessing all. Pete Scott had had a rule on that one, too: *"You know Ben Franklin once said that three people can keep a secret if two of them are dead. Well, you can be dead, if you have a big secret and you're stupid enough not to let it out."*

I wasn't sure how stupid I was, but I did know that next to MacMurry, Sam Catton would grasp the essentials of my meteorological horror story quicker than anyone else in the neighborhood.

I found the lobby of the hotel even more crowded as I passed through it. And having become very conscious not only of traffic to the rear but also of my fellow man bearing down on me from every direction, I went slithering past the festive throng like a chameleon on his way to a convenient crack in the wall.

Catton was oblivious of my gentle knock.

"Hey Sam, open up. It's your roommate!" Trying to arouse him without arousing everyone else in the corridor was something for a ventriloquist's act. For me, impatience was the order of the day. "Sam, wake up!"

I rattled the knob. I pounded on the wood, and when I paused to see if I could hear him stirring, the silence and emptiness of the corridor suddenly became an enlargement of the silence and the emptiness within.

A strange sensation of lightness possessed me. My hand went automatically back to the knob in a futile reflex. "Sam!"

I gave weight to my grasp, pushing inward. The door yielded slightly. The pause before I put my shoulder to it was not so much to gather strength as to register a kind of inchoate recognition of what I was going to find.

He'd fallen in such a way that his body had blocked the door, and what I saw first was his bulk and the blood it was lying in. To my surprise, though, I could detect a faint pulse.

Inspector Galland possessed a high-domed forehead, with a furry grey matting of hair to frame his tanned baldness. Bulky of frame, with large hands and quick gestures, he had pouched blue eyes, a Cyrano-like beak and a sardonic mouth in a perpetual slant. He'd seen it all, and he'd heard it all many times, but he had that one quality necessary to a good police officer—patience.

He was patient with me, leading me gently for the tenth or twentieth time through my actions during the past two days. He understood my state of shock, but the question was, did he understand all of it? Were his queries aimed at satisfying doubts as to whether I had shot Sam Catton; or if my story was true, whether perhaps I had been the intended victim?

On this last I had no doubt whatever, and as we sat in his office in the gathering summer eventide with a thunderstorm moving in, I struggled to keep my thoughts and impressions from becoming a pile of spaghetti.

Throughout his interrogation, his subordinates had been checking on my account of my movements, and from time to time the phone would buzz and he'd get a bit more of verification or lack of it. Now he put down the receiver to a sizable crack of thunder and managed a fleeting grin, nodding toward the window. "Coincidence seems to be the order of the day. That was the hospital. Your friend is still alive."

"Well, thank God for that!" My voice sounded as though someone had used sandpaper on it. "Anything on his condition?"

"No. Very serious, of course. But at least that is something . . . being alive, I mean." His tone was light, and I wasn't sure of his meaning.

"Yes."

"It does not appear from his personal effects that there is a Mrs. Catton."

"Not that I know of. But it's not something I'd know with any certainty."

"I understand. A chance meeting. . . . You know, what strikes me is that there is so much of that in this whole thing. Picard, the pilot, is missing." He spread his hands in a *comme çi, comme ça* gesture. "Your scientific colleague, Dr. MacMurry, a suicide, and now this— this attack after a meeting of coincidence." He got up from his desk and moved to close the window as the wind puffed in and the rain began to splash down. "What do you make of it?"

I knew what I made of it, all right, but if I told him, where would that put me? "Like you said, Inspector, a very nasty coincidence. What else can I make of it? If robbery was the motive, I realize it could have happened to me instead."

"Exactly!" He returned to his desk, and turned on the lamp. "But it doesn't appear that robbery was the motive. No money taken, nothing of yours taken, not even your camera equipment. He opened the door to a knock, probably thinking it was you, and then someone shot him . . . bang, bang."

"And you wonder if there would be any motive in shooting me?"

"If your story is correct, M'sieur Erikson, it is a possibility to be considered, no?"

"I suppose so . . . I haven't given the idea much thought. I was going to check out and. . . ."

"I understand that. But if you give the circumstances some thought, can you see any reason why someone should wish to shoot you?" He grinned, raising his hands, "You see, we don't like having our visitors shot, particularly on a long holiday weekend, and if you are in some danger, it might be best for us to give you some protection—at least until you return to Washington. Two Americans shot in a single day could be very embarrassing."

I appreciated his wry sarcasm. It helped me to keep from confessing all. "I can't solve it for you, Inspector. If Catton makes it, perhaps he can."

"Ahhh, bien." He palmed his dome. "In the meantime, we will continue to explore the realm of chance and coincidence. It would have been so much easier if you had shot him."

In retrospect, I could hardly say I hadn't been given my chance to tell all. Perhaps it was the knowledge that Catton was still alive that dissuaded me, plus the fear of the reaction to my explanation. At the moment it was greater than the fear of an assailant who had tried and missed. I knew my reasoning wasn't logical, particularly because I had been anxious to bring Sam into the thing. But Sam wasn't a Canadian policeman, and being judicious was never one of my strong points.

The storm swept in, and amidst the flashes and the cloud-ripping bombardment, rain slashing at the windows, Inspector Galland finished his interrogation. Enough of my story had checked out that he felt free to release me, but if there was to be an inquest he would expect my return.

"You will be on the nine-thirty flight to Boston and then to Washington?"

"Yes, but I'd like to check at the hospital first."

"Of course." He looked at his watch. "I can arrange to see that you get a ride there, and you can do us the favor of delivering M'sieur Catton's bag for us. Let's hope he will still have need of it."

"Amen to that, Inspector."

In parting, the Inspector had given me his card and said, "M'sieur Erikson, if for some reason you should need to contact me, you may feel free to do so . . . at any time." The rueful, rather sad, expression that accompanied his farewell indicated that he strongly suspected that I was being foolish.

Riding in a police car offered brief reassurance. It was one thing to sit in the safety of the Inspector's office and try to convince him that all the joinings of the case were built on a series of coincidences, and still another thing to go purring through the rain-soaked streets in the early darkness, courtesy of the Canadian Police. But when the protection was withdrawn, I could start walking backwards, perspiring freely. It was true that at the time I could cling to one fairly solid conclusion: whoever had shot Sam had mistaken him for me. My would-be assassin undoubtedly believed he had carried out the assigned hit and would be far from the scene. I'd be safe until he read the morning papers or viewed the late news on TV. By then I should be in Washington and, with luck, talking to people who could act.

We paused at the hotel, where I recovered my gear and paid my bill. The management was not unhappy to see me depart. I had brought them an unwanted and unexpected uproar. Even in this do-your-own-thing age, the Dorval Arms did not like the idea of its guests being shot, particularly if the guest was not a registered guest —or something.

At the hospital, the police driver bid me adieu, and a gentle-faced nun, Sister Fleurette, asked me to wait in a small room adjacent to the entrance foyer. I watched her move up the corridor, a graceful lady in white, her pointed cap giving her a medieval aspect. Then I sat down with Catton's compact bag on my knees. He had said a copy of his ms was within, and I quickly located it and transferred it to my pack. The title on the Manila envelope was "How They Killed the Rainmaker."

When Sister Fleurette brought the doctor, he didn't tell me anything I didn't already know. My friend was under intensive care. His survival remained in doubt, but he was strong physically, and if no further complications developed, he might come through.

Sister Fleurette relieved me of the patient's belongings. I said I'd call in the morning. She smiled and assured me that M'sieur Catton was in the hands of le bon Dieu and the staff of the Good Shepherd Hospital, and those were very good hands indeed. "Que Dieu vous benisse, M'sieur."

There was a pharmacy across the street from the hospital, and I made for it in the deep hush of summer eventide—daylight nearly smudged out, the rain drops pattering on the leaves. Storm gone from without while storm rages within. And who lurks in the shadows to snuff me out?

Evidently no one, for the moment. I reached the drugstore, breathing a bit hard. I would have to steady down, have to keep reminding myself that the hunter was home from the hill—at least for the evening. But reason said that could be all wrong, too. I stepped on reason. Right now I had to make a phone call, and I had to have all my wits about me—not to mention my luck.

The phone rang for a long time, and I was about to concede that my luck was out for the evening too, when the receiver was lifted.

In the "Yes?" there was inquiry wrapped in cool silk.

"I'm sorry to be calling at this time. My name is John Erikson. I'm from Washington, D.C., and I just heard the news about your father. I happened to be in town, and I wanted to call to convey my sympathy and my respects." It came out, sounding like a cross between a telegram and a high school recitation.

"That's very kind of you, Mr. Erikson." The coolness turned to warmth. I liked the tone.

"Would you be Laurie?"

"Why, yes." A note of faint surprise.

"When I visited your father in Iran, he mentioned you." I was full of old wives' tales. That brought a pause, and I wondered if I'd hit a barrier. "I did an article on his work out there," I said quickly, "and we saw quite a bit of each other."

"Oh yes, you're the writer! *Viewpoint Magazine.* I thought I recalled your name."

I took a firm grasp on my luck and pushed it. "It's good of you to remember. I realize this is a very bad time to intrude, but I wonder if I might stop by and see you."

"I'm afraid I'm here alone at the moment. My mother and my brothers are at the church, seeing about arrangements for tomorrow, and—"

"I certainly understand, but I must go back to Washington tonight, and there is something I think you should know. It's a matter I can't discuss on the phone. It concerns your father's business."

"His business!"

"Yes." I was hoping her curiosity would override the occasion.

"I don't understand."

"I realize that, but if you'll see me I. . . ."

"Mr. Erikson, my mother has had a very difficult time, and. . . ."

"If I could come and talk to you right now I could explain." I stressed the "you".

We shared a long pause, and I terminated it. "Miss MacMurry, I have a cab waiting. I'll be there directly."

I had no trouble locating a cab at the hospital, and during the ride I mentally replayed the nuances of her voice. Undoubtedly, she was suffering a tragic loss though none of it had surfaced in the conversation. Perhaps her permitting me to barge in was an indication of her guard's being down even though she had sounded in complete control of her emotions. Her father's voice had had a somewhat harsh quality. Hers was pitched in a softer quieter range, but nonetheless I had detected a connection—maybe it was in the tinge of Nova Scotian accent. Magnetic, to my ear.

The idea of arriving travel-pack in one hand, camera case slung on shoulder, was not appealing, but neither was holding the cab. It would cost a fortune, and I was fresh out of fortunes. I went up the short walk, noting that except for the outside door light, the house appeared to be in darkness.

Not so. When she opened the door to my knock, the light in the hall was behind her, and she stood before me, a rather tall young woman with a magnificent crown of auburn hair. I couldn't determine the color of her eyes, but their gently fluted cast in the somewhat concave structure of her face gave them a slightly oriental look. We took each other in, and I got far the better of it. Laurie MacMurry, whatever her antecedents, was a helluva striking-looking woman, and for someone whose attention had been diverted from the female sex for so long, the realization had a strongly positive effect. I grinned at her. "I'm really not the man who came to dinner. I'm just between flights."

She smiled faintly. "Come in, please. You can put your things there if you like," pointing to a corner with a chair.

I followed her from the hallway into what must have been the living room, and I like the way she moved. There was only one lamp on in the long, heavily paneled room, and I still couldn't determine the color of her eyes.

She gestured for me to sit down and sat down across from me, not interested in my appearance but the reason for it—so she could bid me a fast farewell. I decided to dispense with the apologies and condolences. "Thank you for letting me come."

"What is it you wished to tell me, Mr. Erikson?"

"I saw Sam Catton this afternoon. . . . He was the one who informed me about your father."

She placed her hands on her knees. "I see." Her face was largely in shadow, but she accepted the information with no particular reaction. Good enough.

"We met by accident. He was staying at the same hotel. That's why I called you. Actually, I came to Canada to see your father." All my lies contained tissues of truth.

"Oh?"

"Yes. Your father received some photographs . . . I wonder if I might see them?"

She stared at me and then shook her head. "I'm afraid you're not being very clear."

"I realize it's a bit complicated. I hadn't been in touch for years."

"Yes. I know that. Dad thought you had done such a fine job. He wondered what had happened to you."

"My intention was to explain. Right now I'm involved in an investigation, and oddly enough the photographs which Sam said your father received might have a bearing."

"A bearing on what?" A wariness had come into her voice.

"I know about the suit, the accusations."

"What's that got to do with some aerial woodland pictures? Do those photos have anything to do with my Dad being hounded to his death!" The MacMurry fire was up.

"I don't know," I said, "but if I could have a look. . . ."

"Just who are you an investigator for, Mr. Erikson?" She was on her feet now, the graciousness gone, suspicion and hostility on the rise.

"Believe me, I had great admiration for your father." That was as far as I got in my explanation. I heard the front door open, muted voices accompanied the sound of its closing. In the foyer I saw three people, two men and an older woman. Mrs. MacMurry and her sons had returned.

"Excuse me." Laurie moved quickly across the room.

Mrs. MacMurry was a long, angular woman, bereaved and in no mood or condition to receive a stranger. For some reason, all I could think of was the thin woman of Innis McGort. The two sons, Edwin and Morcar, were obviously older than their sister, tall, lean men who favored their mother.

Laurie made the introductions, trying to smooth the way by explaining who I was and how I knew her father. Then I made the damnfool mistake of mentioning Sam Catton. His name slipped out of me before I could think.

Mrs. MacMurry had large luminous eyes shot with inner pain and weariness. She glared at me. "Haven't you done enough to us?" It came out in a loud, despairing sigh.

"I'm sorry. . . ."

"The nerve of that man, coming here this afternoon! He helped to ruin Angus! Helped to kill him!" She brought her handkerchief to her mouth and her eyes filled.

"Mother," Laurie said. Edwin moved toward her.

"Your wretched CIA—what do they want with us now? Why did they send you?" She began to cry.

I felt a great helplessness, knowing it was futile to reason.

"Mother, Mr. Erikson was a friend of Dad's," Laurie interjected gently, putting her arm around her.

"Friend! He had no friends, not from that place!"

Edwin took over and guided his mother out of the hallway, throwing back at me a furious look that was all MacMurry.

"I think you'd better leave, mister," Morcar growled.

86

I did so, full of turmoil from the effect I had on Angus MacMurry's widow and the defeat I'd suffered when I was sure that five more minutes with Laurie would have brought a look at the photos.

On top of that, I had hoped to be well enough received that I could use the phone to call a cab. Instead, I'd been evicted, bag and baggage, into a suburban neighborhood where all the streets looked the same and nothing was familiar. Maybe I could locate Polaris and find my way to the nearest shopping center.

After several blocks of fuming, the impact of the encounter faded enough that a new perception came to me. I was not only lost in the wilds of suburbia, I was also openly exposed and extremely vunerable. Quickening my pace didn't do any more than jangle awake the damaged nerves in my spine, sending that old unwelcome ache down my left leg. The injury had long been quiescent, but, like its mental counterpart, it was always lurking in ambush.

It was eight-thirty, yet the street had a much later, gone-to-bed feel to it. In the darkness I imagined that the occupants of the facing rows of close-set dwellings were taking their ease in the plots behind their homes, swatting mosquitos and talking about the holidays they were about to go on. Many of them were probably already gone, for it seemed that a number of the homes were vacant. None of these perceptions were of any benefit to me, other than that I had suddenly become acutely observant of my surroundings. I could hear the distant hum of traffic, and it seemed that ahead, above the house tops and the tree tops, the darkness showed a pinkish stain, and that was the direction to follow. But the sound was deceptive and the sky's discoloration was equally so. Several cars passed me, heading in the opposite direction.

As I reached the crossing to a new block, I paused and looked back to see the headlights of a vehicle moving in my direction. I could tell that it was moving very slowly, as though the driver was looking for something. It took no reading of the entrails of dead birds to foretell that I was that something.

Instead of crossing the street, I went around the corner, prepared to drop everything and run for it as best I could. It was a bad turn. To my left lay a school yard brightly illuminated with overhead lights. It had all the wattage needed to put me center-stage, in full glow. I legged it to the other side of the street, but the shafts of pain knifed down my thigh, slowing me down.

I hadn't known this physical impediment in over a year, and then only after six sets of hard-fought tennis.

But this wasn't any tennis match. The car checked at the intersection and then turned. Even without headlights there would have been no trouble in spotting me. I had absolutely nowhere to go. Nowhere to hide. For an instant, as the driver angled toward the curb, everything within me congealed. My instinct was to run up a low bank of lawn toward the nearest house, howling for help. Instead I dropped my bag, and moved, not away from the car but toward it, clutching the strap of my camera case, ready to slam some very valuable photographic equipment against the side window or whoever was behind the glass. Through some inexplicable alchemy, the hag of fury had mounted the boney horse of desperation. I wanted to get at my would-be slayer, even if my only weapon was a Hasselblad 500.

"Mr. Erikson?" It was not the voice of doom, but the sweetest sound in the world.

My own response was an unintelligible "Ahhh!" And instead of attacking the vehicle, I let it hold me up, somehow noting that a Volkswagen bug no more fitted the character of an assassin's chariot than did a red-headed driver named Laurie MacMurry.

She had leaned across the interior and opened the door. "Hop in, and I'll give you a lift." In the glow of the inside light, I could see she was trying to conceal her amusement at my reaction.

"You kind of caught me between the wind and the weather," I explained, trying not to sound like a man who had run a very long way.

"You were going in the wrong direction," she said as I retrieved my bag and in wondrous relief managed to get my dunage and myself into the car.

"All my words of thanks will never measure up, but thank you fair lady, thank you!"

She laughed at my words, a soft clear note in the sudden peace and stillness of the evening. Then she put the car in gear and we moved on.

"I must apologize for my mother, but I think you can understand."

"Of course. It was a lousy time to pay a visit."

"We're going to the airport?"

"That would be nice." Sitting beside her, taking in the line of her profile, her hand fastened over the clutch knob, I felt a swift attraction for her—part relief and part being picked up instead of being picked off, being chauffeured by a nifty-looking somebody. But there was something else, something magnetically warm, something intruding on the past, that I suddenly welcomed.

She looked at me, knowing I was staring. "Is there anything wrong?"

"No! No, no, not at all. I was just feeling very grateful for your being such a good Samaritan."

We drove in silence for several minutes before she responded. "I'm afraid there's more to my coming after you than gallantry, Mr. Erikson. I'm anxious to know more about the investigation you mentioned. Whose investigation? Why?"

I was in for more backing and filling, and I didn't like the idea a bit, not with this lady. "Perhaps I oversold it. It's my own investigation. I was interested in your father's work. I wanted to know what had happened to him. The need for the technology he developed becomes more important every day. In the future it will have to be used."

"We know that's true enough, but. . . ."

"You say we. Are your brothers involved?"

"No. Edwin is an aeronautical design engineer and Morcar's an accountant." She spoke quickly, wanting to get back to the point. "But why are you investigating *now?* Why did you wait so long? Where have you been?" Her tone was almost accusatory.

"It's rather a long story. I was out of the country for a long time. I got deflected by other things. I lost track of your father. You can say the recent attention on spreading drought brought me back to searching for him."

"A pity you were so long at it." She said it quietly, sadly.

There was nothing I could say in reply. I considered asking her about his decline and fall, but decided this was no time for her to have to explain that.

"And how do the photographs you wanted to see come into it?" She wasn't going to let me off the hook.

"Perhaps they don't," I said, truthfully for once. "But when Sam Catton told me about them—well, I do a lot of photography myself, and I wanted to compare them with. . . ."

"But they have nothing to do with weather modification, with cloud seeding." She glanced at me, and I decided she had what could only be described as an elegant nose; thank God the sons had their father's beak.

"Who sent them to your father?" The technique of answering a question with another question is one effective form of escape.

"I don't know." She shook her head, and I liked the way she did that too. "He didn't keep the letter. My mother said it was some sales campaign—you too can own your own lake in the Laurentians. That sort of thing always annoyed him. And because of his health he had an even more angry reaction."

"Then you don't think it had any direct bearing on . . . on what happened?"

She shook her head again, and in the reflection of outside lights I could see that the luminosity in her eyes had become more pronounced. "No." Her voice had a torn quality. "Dad had been failing for a long time." And then, "Why! Was that what Sam Catton told you?"

"He told me he was not welcome, and I understand. . . ."

"Never mind that. What exactly did he say about the photographs that made you feel they were so important?" She had recovered control and an air of determination returned to her probing questions.

"There's something I've got to tell you about Sam," I said, unhappy with my premeditated decision but knowing the news of his present condition would occupy her thoughts and our conversation until we reached the airport.

"Is he really in the CIA?" She said it, hoping that it wasn't so.

"I think not, but he is in the hospital." And then I told her.

She was appalled, hardly able to speak, and I knew that part of the effect was due to the personal loss she was suffering.

"I'd rather not have told you, but you'd read about it or hear about it," I said lamely.

"No, no, it's all right. It's just that—oh, I don't know, everything is getting to be too much. What's the point in all this savagery? Why would anyone want to shoot him! For his money, his watch, maybe a gold ring. Is that what a life is worth?"

"The thing to concentrate on is that he's alive."

"Yes, and so was my dad!" The bitterness broke through.

I didn't say anything, and she concentrated in making a turn across the traffic into the airport entrance.

"I'm sorry," she said, "I didn't mean to get female and irrational."

"I don't mind your being female. It becomes you. As for being irrational, I'm the one to apologize to you. I haven't even told you how deeply sorry I am about your own loss."

"If you keep it up you'll have a sobbing woman on your hands."

"Look, I've been presumptuous as hell, right from the telephone call, so I'm not going to change the impression. I'd like to give you my phone number and when you feel like it, and if it wouldn't be too much trouble, you can give me the word on Sam, collect."

She brought the car to stop at the terminal entrance, "Yes, I'll certainly do that." She looked at me.

"And what about your investigation? Is there anything I can tell you or send to you about dad's work that you don't already know?"

"Not now, Laurie. Maybe later."

Sitting in the dim light, she seemed as intent in looking at me as I had been earlier in watching her. "I'll keep you posted," I said. "I'm glad we've met and sorry it wasn't sooner."

"And the photographs . . . you still haven't told me why you wanted to see them."

"I don't want to be clever with you . . . or deceptive. I thought they might have something to do with cloud seeding."

She held my eyes with her own, not sure but wanting to be. "Well, all right. You can satisfy yourself that they don't." She reached down beside her seat and brought up a Manila envelope. "You can take them with you. I don't think there's any need to send them back."

The surprise in my face was apparent even in the half-light. She laughed, a delightful sound. I resisted a very strong urge to take her face between my hands and, as the old folk song goes, *kiss her ruby lips*.

"Thank you," I said, "thank you for everything. And one other thing. My name is John. Yours is Laurie. Can we put it on that basis?"

"Of course." We shook hands. It sounds corny and terribly passé but I didn't want to let her hand go.

After I climbed out of the car, I stood on the curb and watched her drive away, the Volkswagen a puttering pumpkin coach merging into the flow of airport traffic. At the moment I wasn't about to try to analyze my feelings. In fact, one of my troubles had been too much self-analysis. Maybe in meeting Laurie MacMurry I had turned a corner. I didn't know. I did know her presence stayed with me right on board the plane and up to cruising altitude.

Then I had a look at the photographs her father had received before he'd shot himself. The scene they offered drove everything from my mind but the fact that I was looking at some familiar aerial views of René's Lac Poitrine and its surrounding terrain. There were a half-dozen shots taken from different angles but at approximately the same altitude. They were black and white, before and after. Three appeared over-exposed because everything in them had a greyish-white aspect. No doubt the accompanying letter which MacMurry had destroyed gave an explanation. But they begged the question; had he in some way been involved? Or was it enough for him to be told how the technology on which he had risked his professional career had been subverted to being a killing agent. Somehow my memory of the man made me feel he must have had prior knowledge and that the sender of the photos had used them to push him over the brink. Since everything appeared to be centered in La Belle Province de Québec, it followed that if the Weathermaker had undergone further development, MacMurry would have had to have been in some way connected. I knew he had applied for global patents of the product. Had he sold them? I very much doubted that. He had also said there was a secret chemical process in the manufacture of the Weather-maker. Could it be duplicated? I wanted to bail out and go back and ask his daughter to give me the answers. After a while, I took out Sam Catton's MS, hoping I'd find some clue in it.

*

I found no clue. But sadly the explanation that clarified Mac-Murry's plunge was not an unfamiliar story—a theme about as old as mankind. Yet, in our own time in which science has become the god of affluence, one could hope that the rigid mentality that beset the age of Galileo had become a bit more open, a bit less mired in the concrete of its own absolutes.

And, of course, I of all workers in the ecological wilderness should have known better. I think it was Ashton Lee who had once dubbed me the *"polluted man's Cassandra."*

92

The Iranians had given every indication that the contract was to be renewed. A week before the official signing Zahedi had called in Catton to inform him that the Shah in his wisdom had decided against it. No explanation, despite a track record that indicated an unheard-of 90-percent average increase in the precipitation within the target area. The ways of the Shah, however, were no more inscrutable than those of the Cypriots.

. MacMurry had landed an interim "show us" contract with the Makarios government in Cyprus in the spring of the year when the passing weather systems were weak and nothing much in the way of rainfall could be expected. But Cyprus had had no rain in months; reservoirs and catchment basins were down to cracked mud. The important cereal-bearing portion of the island could not now bear much of anything; the fruit crops were particularly in danger. Desperate conditions required desperate measures. Bring in MacMurry. He brought rain when RAF weather predictions, long and short, said no rain. The Archbishop sent his blessing. The radio stations in Nicosia, Famagusta, Limossol and throughout the island, including the Turkish enclaves, played "Rain Drops Are Falling" every hour on the hour. It was too late to save much of the cereal crop, but the results obtained, including an unheard-of two inches of snow on the Troodos Mountains in April, brought the offer of a four-year contract, to commence in the fall. In September, when MacMurry and Catton arrived in Nicosia to sign the contract and set up operations, fresh from the shock of the Iranian rejection, they were informed there had been a change of personnel in the government and a change of mind. No contract.

Within this same time period, the Agricultural Director of Greece, a noted agronomist and career civil servant, had been following MacMurry's work in Iran and then in Cyprus, first with much interest and finally with conviction. As a result, he had recommended to the Government of George Papadopoulos that a cloud-seeding program be instituted over a man-made lake north of Athens. Prospects for a contract appeared excellent, he wrote to MacMurry in June of 1970. In July he telegraphed that negotiations would begin October 1st. MacMurry and Catton arrived from Cyprus on September 30th to learn that the Greek dictatorship had suddenly gone sour on the whole idea. The Agricultural Director had decided to take early retirement.

Three strikes, and all in a single month. Within another thirty days, six additional countries—in the Magreb, the Middle East and the Subcontinent—completely lost interest in MacMurry's proposals whereas prior to that time enthusiasm had been extremely high; at Rawalpindi and Madras preliminary negotiations toward contracts had already been conducted.

Weather Operations, Ltd., was suddenly without a client or the prospect of one—the tap had shut off. Both MacMurry and Catton were sure pressure against the firm had been exerted from behind the scenes. MacMurry believed the source lay within the WMO—the U.N.'s World Meteorological Organization, which was then directed by a Soviet academician. Angus argued that the absolutely closed ranks of the international meteorological bureaucracy could exert enormous pressure throughout the world to halt any weather operation outside its approval. After all, there wasn't anything less predictable than weather. And it wouldn't take all that much to claim that the Weathermaker was messing up the atmosphere, or that Mac-Murry was simply a confidence man hiding behind a scientific background. Further, the Soviets had been involved in serious Weather Modification research and development for nearly half a century. They were now perfecting the aim of their artillery batteries by firing shells of silver iodide into clouds, for the purpose of suppressing hail. And they were not about to allow a Canadian rainmaker take the ball away from them.

Sam Catton had a different villain—the State Department, via the Nixon Administration, egged on by the U.S. scientific and meteorological community. It was a suspicion supported by his own contacts within State. It was nothing he could use as evidence; suspicions developed out of inferences made and hints dropped. And what had really alerted the bureaucracy and encouraged it to attack? John Erikson and the article he had written, said Sam Catton. And this was the underlying reason he had not wanted the piece published. His nose was sensitive, his contacts spread wide, so he could perceive what might happen. And now it had happened.

In the final analysis, it didn't make a damn bit of difference to MacMurry who had shot him down, one power bloc—or another—or both. He was tough enough and sharp enough at the time to know he would only be wasting his energies seeking proof of Byzantine dirty work. What he had to find was a way around its reach. He had to attract public attention on a large scale, so the opposing vested interests could not block him.

He brought his plane and staff back to Canada where he promptly fired Ganin, having learned through Catton that the pilot had attempted to work his own deal with the Iranians, setting up a competing cloud seeding operation. Next he put Catton in Washington and with his aid began establishing contacts in Spain where there was a serious drought in the southern provinces. But it was no good. His name had become mud everywhere—in Ethiopia, in Jordan, even in Libya and Algeria.

The following summer, with the company nearly broke, there came what MacMurry saw as his opportunity to go public. Devastating forest fires had hit Alaska. The fires raged out of control, and the loss in timber mounted toward catastrophe. Through a friend of Catton's, MacMurry and Sam went to see an Under-Secretary of the Department of the Interior. MacMurry laid it on the line. At no cost to the U.S. Government, he would seed the present weak weather system moving in over the fires. If he put sufficient rain on the fires, he would expect a contract. He would also expect a team of official meteorological observers on board his plane during the demonstration flight, along, with of course, representatives of the press.

The Under-Secretary liked the proposal. He thought it sounded "sexy" and the Department needed something like that to win a few bows. As he said, "What can we lose? It won't cost the taxpayers a nickel."

It would cost MacMurry an estimated ten thousand dollars to carry out the operation which included flying aircraft and crew from Montreal to Anchorage.

"Time is everything" was his only comment after obtaining the necessary bank loan. Time passed: two days in which MacMurry and Catton met with middle-level civil servants from various DOI branches and the Bureau of Atmospheric Research; two more days of internal backing and filling, and then, two more on top of that, as the fires spread and MacMurry raged, threatening to go to the press. This had brought the announcement that according to law any contract let by the Department must be done on a bid basis. MacMurry announced he was withdrawing. Catton begged him not to, because a stipulation had been included that the bidders must have had prior experience in seeding over forest fires, and only Weather

95

Operations was so qualified. Three days later the award went to a firm that did an annual hundred-million-dollars worth of defense business with the government, but had no previous seeding experience over forest fires. Reason: it was the low bidder by two hundred dollars in a 75-thousand dollar contract.

Against Catton's advice, MacMurry went to the press, but by that time there wasn't much to the story. In the ten days since he had made his offer, the fires had destroyed over thirty million dollars worth of timber and were burning themselves out. The AP carried a short three-paragraph item on the wire under the heading "Canadian Rainmaker Claims U.S. Foul."

MacMurry returned to Montreal, where the pressure rose as the bank balance descended. He had insulted so many of his more traditionally-minded colleagues that his efforts to find consulting and lecturing assignments came to little. Sure of his course of action, as only he could be, he had cut himself off from other areas where his expertise had been recognized, and since then the word had got around in scientific circles that he'd lost his balance altogether. The rumor was that the Iranians had gotten rid of him because he had actually retarded precipitation. Poor man, needed psychiatric help. Same sort of thing happened to old Bentley. Once his detractors would have added that he was a lush and a homosexual. But since both of those conditions had by now become accepted as normal, they skipped that. Although MacMurry could no longer afford Catton, Sam, who had taken over as the PR director of a major petroleum association, continued to represent the company's interests where and when he could.

In a year's time, MacMurry's world became Kafka-like. He battled and thrashed about against a power he knew was there but could not expose—a faceless power with which he could never come to grips or even identify by name, rank or serial number. Nothing he could prove. No one whose throat he could get his hands around. But *they* were there ready to block his every move. He knew that above all else, and the symptoms began to show.

Catton received instructions not to call the Canadian office on the company line any longer. MacMurry knew it was bugged. Next came the suspicion that the mail was being opened before delivery, then the word that he was certain he was being watched often followed.

Worried, Catton went north. He found a dramatically changed

man. The volatility in MacMurry's nature had become bent, the balance was gone, extremes of temper outweighed judgment and perception. The things people said to him no longer meant what was said—the words had an ulterior purpose.

Laurie and MacMurry's wife Anna were equally worried, and with their help Catton somehow talked the ailing scientist into going fishing with him. In the week they spent in the quiet of a lake which lay cupped amidst hills of birch and black spruce where Arctic Char were eager to take a fly, Catton managed to penetrate MacMurry's hard wall of outrage and to restore some reason. By the time of their return, Sam had convinced him that the only way to retain sanity was to drop the weather business altogether and pick up the other sciences where he had excelled and would find acceptance once again.

The turn-around was brief. Catton was no sooner back in Washington than columnist Jack Anderson broke the story that cloud seeding was being used as a weapon of war in Vietnam and had been since 1967. Its purpose was to flood the infiltration trails and damage crops yield in Laos and North Vietnam. The code name for the operation had been Intermediary Compatriot. It was a CIA undertaking.

MacMurry went wild. He called Catton, shouting they had both been wrong! It was not the WMO or the Russians, not the National Academy of Science or the meteorological fraternity, but the Nixon Administration and the CIA! "By bloody hell, I've got them! Now I'll show the bastards! They stopped my work to wage their bloody war!"

He brought suit against the CIA and the Department of Defense for 100-million dollars on the basis of patent infringements, maintaining that his Weathermaker had been stolen, his technology duplicated to wage war while the power of the U.S. Government had been used to halt his own peaceful and beneficial efforts. Catton's attempt to reason, to talk him out of what he saw as a futile and costly battle which he could not possibly win, was shouted down. "By the balls of hell, nothing on this earth will stop me!"

But he was stopped, and Catton described the seemingly inevitable results in his clear, terse style.

At the outset there were scattered press reports of the rainmaker who was bringing suit. The CIA was becoming fair game for anyone who had a beef, no matter how exotic the claim. All the rest was a slow wretched grind down to nothing; the business bankrupt, the debts like piled snow drifts. Through Laurie and her brothers the family home was secured, but all else was gone. What was lost was not only the case but MacMurry's sanity as well. When after three years, the case was thrown out of court for lack of evidence, Mac-Murry turned on Sam Catton. It was he who had been the CIA mastermind behind the whole thing. Catton saw it as the last pitiful outcry of a man destroyed by a bumbling power-structure whose own turn had come with Watergate and the consequent exposure of the CIA's abuse of its own mandate.

Catton's last chapter was a damning indictment in which he revealed through his own quiet investigation considerable tangential evidence to back up MacMurry's contention that the CIA had indeed been responsible for the destruction of Weather Operations Ltd. It was not evidence that would stand up in court, but few readers would doubt its accuracy, partly because they would not want to doubt it. And the motivation, as Catton put it: "Any covert mission as globally sensitive as weather control in a war as globally unpopular as the war in Vietnam, could not afford to have that same control used overtly for fear that its popularity and public acceptance might in someway point toward its covert use."

Once upon a time, I wouldn't have bought such a rationale. After all, Angus MacMurry hadn't invented cloud-seeding, and pyrotechnic flares used by Dr. Joanne Simpson on fair-weather cumulus clouds off the coast of Florida had produced dramatic results which had been featured in "Science Magazine." But with the knowledge of the facts that had been revealed since then, I could see it. MacMurry had pioneered dynamic seeding, and his Weathermaker had been officially declared to be the world's most powerful cloud-seeding generator. Catton's explanation made a wretched kind of sense, particularly considering what had happened to cloud-seeding since it had been used by the military in Vietnam.

*

I sat back, eyes closed, hurtled comfortably through the night. There had been Congressional hearings focused entirely on the negative—fear of weather or climate control as the ultimate weapon, and then a Senate resolution to outlaw the science as an instrument of destruction. Further conclaves held in Stockholm and Geneva, championed by the Soviets as well, brought forth resolutions to outlaw weather as a global weapon. As for the beneficial uses of cloud-seeding in the U.S., the science had gone puttering along as it had for twenty years, a kind of non-technology in which sparsely-funded government programs operated by frugal functionaries carried out the same "research" studies, and the handful of private operators such as Irving Krick continued to increase precipitation in varying small amounts for the farmers, ranchers, and utility companies who, out of need, recognized their worth.

No, Sam Catton's account offered no clue on how the weather-modification invention and expertise of a crazy Scots-Canadian had been converted into the latest ultimate weapon that had done what I had seen at Lake Poitrine, but I surely had an understanding of the connection.

If I had been on the scene, could I have made any difference? In Catton's eyes, indirectly at least, I was the villain. But, hell, did he think the CIA, the White House or whatever, wouldn't have known of MacMurry's activities in Iran without having John Erikson to tell them about it? Ahh, they knew. Old Hickam had been sitting there and sending in reports. But perhaps, in the eyes of the mighty, my article had alerted the public to the fact that after all these years the pig-in-the-poke of rain-making was no longer a hit-or-miss, half-assed meteorological boogeyman or a dangerous piece of atmospheric con-artistry. And it was not an acceptance the faceless decision-makers were ready for, particularly after the flash floods in Rapid City, South Dakota, had killed 240 people. Hadn't some real pro seeded two thunderstorm cells and brought it all down? That, of course, had been swiftly hushed up, and I hadn't been around to report it. That was something I'd better start doing right now.

Only one piece of information had come out of Catton's sad tale that intrigued me. I learned that Laurie MacMurry earned her bread as an instructor for the Mountjoy Instrument Flight School, of which she was also a part-owner. I couldn't picture her in the guise of René Picard, but the underlying air of competence and orderliness which I had sensed in her during our ride to the airport, translated easily to the cockpit! I could see her in that exacting role, although the few female aviators I had previously encountered had seemed rather masculine. What Laurie exuded was something quite different—something in the MacMurry blood perhaps. The thought brought me back to the immediate issue.

Who had ruined her father was one matter, but who had driven him to suicide was another. . . . Or were the two the same? It was about the ugliest thought I'd had in a very long and ugly day. It was a day that wasn't quite through with me. When I reached my apartment in Alexandria, I put in a call to Sept Iles. "M'sieur, je regrette . . . they have located *l'avion*. The remains are burned, it is said by explosion. . . . Non, M'sieur René has not been recovered. L'avion fell into the lac, it is very deep."

And the bell, it tolls for thee. . . .

*

Worn as I was, I didn't sleep very well that night. The deaths of two men I had known but briefly but whose individual qualities had made an indelible impression, haunted me through the small hours in a manner that was despairingly familiar. They had had in common a special vigor, a hold on the spirit of life and of living that deserved far better than cruel and sudden extinction at the hand of human idiocy. And there was the vision of the third man, Sam Catton, lying in his own blood but still alive, still alive. Hang on to that. The fact was, I was supposed to be the third man, and hell, I'd already died once, so screw that road to nowhere. I'd concentrate on the profile of Laurie MacMurry. What color were her curtained eyes? I finally drifted out toward a far distant beacon and to sleep.

At seven I called Ash Lee's home and woke his wife, Jan.

"Hello, darling," she yawned. "Where are you, and wherever it is I wish you were here. I'm hungry and. . . ."

"Not for me!" I practically shouted. "This is John."

"Of for godsake, John! What the hell are you calling here for, at this hour? Ash isn't here!" The inviting warmth had turned to dry ice.

"Jan, forgive me, but where is he. I've got to talk to him right now."

"You and half of Washington. I don't know where he is. I suppose he's on his way back here from wherever he's been. Now do me a favor and hang up!"

"Jan, listen—!"

I listened to the click that meant our love affair had ended. And so started a new day—Air Quality Index—foul!

My darkroom was a converted cul-de-sac that had been somebody's idea of a dining ell. While the coffee was perking, I developed the shots I'd taken from René's plane. Over a breakfast of juice, toast, and coffee, I compared what my camera had produced with the photos Laurie had given me. They were interchangeable, the only differences being in altitude, angle, and clarity. All the "after" shots had the same whitish aspect. It was damn little evidence to show anyone. In fact, it wasn't evidence at all, simply a means by which I hoped to attract and hold the attention of Mark Feldman, Deputy Assistant to the President's Science Advisor. I had chosen Feldman as my first contact not only because he was a direct source to the top —and could command immediate attention—but also because we had known each other professionally for a number of years. He owned autographed copies of my books *The World of Birds,* and *Man Versus His Environment.* During his tenure on the Hill as Press Aide for the Senate Interior Committee, we had frequently talked over environmental issues.

Later, when he'd become an Assistant Under-something-or-other in the Bureau of Land Management, he'd been helpful as a contact and a source of information.

After my long absence from the Washington scene I had found him properly titled and carpeted in the grey keep of the Executive Office Building near the White House. His ascension had done nothing, as far as I could see, to change his quietly thoughtful manner and steady approach. He was not impressed by the bureaucratic pomp about him, even though he was a part of it.

As I approached the EOB, coming down the steps off of Pennsylvania Avenue in the early morning brightness, I had the feeling that I was moving toward a sanctuary in that ancient structure with its four stories of columns. The stone courtyard between the street and the old world entrance could have been a drawbridge.

I had taken a bus from Alexandria because I believed it would make me less open to attack. "Assassins of the world, bugger off!" I muttered as I reached the portcullis.

With hair cropped short and aquiline features cut long, Mark Feldman bore a lean and scholarly look. His clothes, the papers on his desk, his office appointments, everything about him indicated orderliness, attention to detail, no wasted motion. As we shook hands he looked me over, "Well, John, tell me what it's all about. But first —care for coffee" His voice was wonderfully low and calm.

"No, thanks, Mark, a shot of adrenalin might help though."

"You do have a slightly harried look." He smiled faintly, "What can I do for you?"

I knew he'd hear me through without interruption, and he did. Then he sat studying the two sets of photos, and the silence drew out, and during it I suddenly felt completely drained. I'd said everything I could say, and he was busy trying to assimilate it, or maybe figuring whether to call the paddy-wagon.

Finally he took off his glasses and gave me his steady dark-eyed attention. "You never saw the green-colored rain come down."

The statement surprised me. "No, just the results of it."

"So actually we can't be positive it happened like that."

"What Picard said, I would trust."

"You've assumed that the cloud was nucleated, in some fashion. Seeded. But there's no proof."

"What about the photographs before and after, the ones Mac-Murry received and the ones I took?"

"That's not really proof, John."

"It's proof of something, chum." I could feel perspiration starting to rise.

"I know all about MacMurry, his background and his claims. He was into other things beside weather modification."

"Well, what has that got to do with—look, MacMurry hasn't anything to do with the point of this. René Picard knew what he saw, and we both saw the results."

"But you have no results with you."

"Exactly! And that's why I've come to you. The President should be briefed. He can tell Trudeau, and a special biological warfare team can get in there right now!"

His response was not immediate. He was back at the photographs again. "Yes, this phenomenon you describe is really Ottawa's business."

Internally, I sensed what a slight breakfast I'd had. "I guess I didn't make myself very clear, Mark. For Christ's sake, don't you realize what I'm talking about!"

He ignored my outburst. "I know you were high on MacMurry's

operation in Iran. You'll recall I was interested in your article at the time, but later when we got a report from the Iranians, we began to have serious second thoughts about his expertise and his claims. We found. . . ."

"Mark, will you tell me what in the name of hell MacMurry's reputation, or lack of it, has to do with what I've been talking about?"

He put his glasses back on. "John, I don't honestly know what these photographs mean."

"And all I'm asking you to do is to make a move to find out."

"Yes, I understand."

"Well, that's progress." I got up and began making footprints in his thick, beige carpet. "Look, are you worried that I might have lost my marbles?"

"There's no need to ask that."

"Well, then I don't get it. I've come to you in desperation. I know what I saw. I know what's happened since. I know someone in *the White House* should be clued in, and you sit there putting me off, worried about poor old MacMurry's credibility. Why?" I sat down again.

He didn't blink. "John, I'll have to present your story to my boss, the Director. I'll make a report on it, and we'll discuss it. But you should know Dr. MacMurry's name is an anathema to him, he—"

"Mark, leave MacMurry's name out of it. Leave everything out of it but what happened at Lake Poitrine. All you have to tell him is that a killing agent came down in the form of rain—there's nothing new in that with tons of hydrocarbons coming down everyday! In this case it was purposely induced by persons unknown. Those persons unknown have got to be found, and the agent they used has got to be put back in the bottle!"

"I find it difficult to believe that a nerve gas or a toxic substance could wreak such total havoc." He said it as though the thought presented an additional problem.

"So do I. Two days ago I would have said it was impossible, but neither of us is an expert. How soon can you call your boss?"

"He's tied up in meetings all morning, and he's leaving for the Chesapeake this afternoon."

"You can't pick up that phone and speak to him right now?"

"No, I'm afraid I can't, John."

"Don't you see this as an emergency?"

"It could be, and I'll do what I can as soon as I can. Why don't you call me Monday about noon."

I left, feeling like a gutted hare, knowing the steadiness and orderliness I had come to admire in Mark Feldman had not been attributes that stimulated whatever quality of character it took to take quick and direct action. Our go-round had revealed what really lay beneath the calm and thoughtful manner. He was incapable of action without command from above. He was a civil servant hewn of lard.

I strode past the White House and Lafayette Park oblivious of traffic, of my fellow pedestrians, of pickets protesting the high cost of contraceptives. I could have been shot, run over, disemboweled, or beheaded, for all I cared. I was not only torn with outrage at my failure to alert the troops, but also my lack of perception in failing to realize that Feldman was a solid without real substance. By the time I'd reached my office, all I'd worked up was a sweat.

Annie took one look at me and said, "Oh, my God! I'll bring you a coffee."

"And a doughnut," I snapped, going into my office.

I sat at my cluttered desk and took heart at the sight of disorganized scramble of papers and periodicals. There must be something good to be said for such messiness after where I'd just been. "It means I'm an active fellow," I said aloud, "and one strike never was a ball game!" I slammed my fist on a copy of the Congressional Record for good measure.

Annie came in with the coffee and doughnut. "Everybody's been trying to reach you."

"Tell everybody I'm not here." I relieved her of the grub. "Thanks, you're wonderful."

"Max Wilk says you owe him two columns. Dr. Richardson called to ask when you were going to have the Redwood piece."

"Never!"

"My, you are grumpy. It must have been a nice trip."

"I'm still on it to everybody but Ashton Lee or a call from Montreal. And would you get me Bud Goss?"

Among the faceless who are the countless cogs in the vast machinery of government there are on the staff level a scattering of real pros. They are probably the reason why the whole damn thing hasn't come unstuck and float away in the Potomac. I had thought Mark Feldman belonged to that category. I knew that Bud Goss did. I had the feeling he'd been around Washington since L'Enfant had laid it out. He knew both sides and both aisles of the Hill, the inner and outer workings of legislative committees, their makers and their movers, the key department heads and the people worth knowing on their staffs. Now, like Feldman, he had recently moved into the executive branch and was a special assistant to the director of ERDA—the Energy Research and Development Agency. The kind of energy I'd run into in Quebec was not exactly ERDA's business, but Bud Goss would know whose business it should be, and I knew he'd have no hesitation in picking up the phone once I'd spelled out the message.

The intercom buzzed and I lifted the receiver. I heard his secretary say, "Just a moment."

"This is Goss," came the standard greeting.

"If not, I wouldn't be calling you."

"Hey! I've been looking for you. I've got a hot tip for you."

"That makes two of us. Can I come up now?"

"No, I'm just going into a meeting."

"Lunch."

"I'll have to break one."

"Can you? It's important."

"I like important lunches. I'll see what I can do."

"When?"

"You sound uptight."

"And then some."

"Okay. How's La Cave sound? You know where it is. Noon?"

"On the dot."

"Hey, I can hardly wait." There was a lift in his tone. Drama had always appealed to him.

In spite of tension, turmoil, frustration, and weariness—in that or any order—I managed to concentrate on the overdue requirements of my syndicated column and had one batted out before it was time to head for La Cave.

As I made for the door, passing through Annie's office, she handed me the usual stack of pink slips recording the calls she'd fielded. "Keep up the good work and I'll give you a raise."

"That'll be the day."

"It will indeed. We'll celebrate, and you can buy the champagne. Equal rights, you know."

"I never should have given up that job with Senator Howard."

"He's a dullard, and you know it. He won't get elected again."

"That's what you said last time."

I had been checking through the call slips as we batted it back and forth.

"Who's this one?" I said, holding up a blank with her check mark on it.

"Oh, I wanted to tell you about that. I think he called twice, once before you got here and then again about a half hour ago. He wouldn't leave his name. He wanted to know if you were in town, or when you were expected back. He said he'd call again."

"How did he know I was out of town?"

She gave me her puzzled look. "I don't know. Maybe he *didn't* know."

"You didn't recognize the voice?"

"No, but he seemed to have some kind of accent, and that's why I knew he had called back."

"Annie, if he calls again, you tell him you've heard from me, and I won't be back for a week. I've gone to Ottawa."

"Ottawa! Is that a good place to go?"

"The best, and see if you can get a name and number out of him."

"When will you be back? Not from Ottawa. I mean from lunch?"

"I don't know." She'd set loose a bee in my bonnet. "Look, how would you like the afternoon off? Make it a long weekend."

"Well, my goodness! What a way to treat a girl. What about the backlog?"

"Re-type the epic I left on my desk and take off."

"What about all the rest?"

"It's Friday, and that will have to wait till Monday. Now stop arguing before I change my mind."

"You're a good boss." She blew me a kiss.

I took the elevator down to the second floor, then I used the fire stairs and made a side exit into the back end of the PMI parking lot. I didn't question my actions. Unknown callers with accents could mean anything in Washington, but I was ready and willing to err on the side of playing shake-the-tail, or something, for my safety and Annie's, too. I wasn't going to leave her alone in that office, a prey to my worries or something that could end all of hers.

I hailed a cruising cab on E street and headed for lunch with Bud Goss.

Goss had a unique, catch-me-if-you-can idiosyncrasy that defied medical analysis or parallel. He was the only man I knew with three separate wardrobes of clothing. One was for his non-alcoholic dietary period; the next was for his two drinks before and pie after lunch phase, and the third attired him during his Falstaffian interval when the drinks were seemingly without number or particular brand, and the food and desserts were woven around and through the alcoholic base. The metamorphosis usually required about a year, from water-wagon to waterwagon. Throughout, while his size was increasing, one characteristic remained constant: he played furious tennis on week-ends and often in the evenings. His salad days had long since passed. That he hadn't dropped dead, either swelling or shrinking, was in the nature of a medical anomaly, for in whatever stage of compression or decompression, all his systems remained unalterably "go." His wife Marian, calm lady that she is, had given up trying to prevail on him to choose plateau on which to level off. I had once asked him the inevitable—"Why? What for?" And he had replied with gusto (he was in phase three) "Because, as the mountain climber once said, it's there!"

Since I hadn't seen Bud Goss in quite some time, I wondered which period of muscle-building he was in and whether I would recognize him. The interior of La Cave didn't help. It lived up to its name by being barely illuminated.

As I stood in the foyer, peering uncertainly into the gloom, he hailed me from the bar. I knew he was somewhere past his monastic phase. "Johnny, steer to port!" he called.

I did so, and he stood to greet me, appearing almost as wide as his grin. "My boy, come join the wicked."

He was looking beamish and fit, his broad features somewhat florid.

"Have you just joined them yourself, or have you been dwelling in their midst for a while?"

"A slight dabbling, nothing strenuous or untoward. What will you have?"

We had a drink, and he brought a second to the table.

Since the manager was an old poker playing friend, we had a place set apart from the general hubbub. As soon as we'd ordered, he fixed me with knowing eyes and said, "You're hungry to spill. No need to wait for the soft-shell crabs. What has someone done, polluted the Tidal Basin?"

I told him what someone had done, not going into great detail about MacMurry, other than to mention his work, his suit, and his suicide. By the time I'd concluded, he was finishing the last of his peach Melba. In fact, throughout my recital he'd concentrated on filling the inner man as though it hadn't been filled in a long time. If I hadn't known better, I'd have thought he was deaf to all but the joys of gourmandizing.

With his big nose, compacted mouth, and tufted blond eyebrows, he sometimes bore a trollish aspect, and he assumed it now as he threw down his napkin and burped. "This place is all right for a confessional" he said, "but no good for Q. and A. Let's go sit at the feet of the statue of honest Bob Taft."

"Mad dogs, Englishmen, and Bud Goss," I said.

"I think better in the shade of the great Ohio Republican. Besides the squirrels don't understand my patois."

"Are you CIA or CIO?"

"Both. Come on. Enough of this cave dwelling. The heat's good for you, it'll purge all the carbon monoxide you've been ingesting."

And so we actually went out into the heat and humidity of Washington at mid-day and walked several very long blocks to sit on the low marble wall bordering the bronze statue of the late Senator, backed by its rectangular carillon tower. Limp oak leaves above shielded us from the sun, but nothing could shield us from the humidity.

"Pretend you're taking a sauna," he said sitting down and spreading his pale blue jacket on his lap, his forearms tanned and powerful.

"Now let's see your snapshots." He examined them one at a time and then returned them to the envelope. "They won't stand up in court," he said.

"The point is they were taken by two photographers, me and someone connected with the results," I said, remembering I'd said the same thing to Mark Feldman.

"I realize that, but number one on the score card is that you want action on this thing from the top, and your exhibit A will only confuse my boss, and I think he's the man to handle it. He and the President are old golfing buddies. I'll probably want you to brief him after I do. Now tell me something: how come you didn't take your tale to the Environmental Protection Agency? You undoubtedly know Russell Train."

"Couple of reasons. I'm persona non grata with EPA, ever since I did a series on the Tussock moth out in Oregon. The only thing that will kill the moth is DDT. EPA wouldn't give permission for its use. Land owners went to court. I went out to see the damage, about fifty-million dollars worth to seven-hundred-thousand acres of Douglas firs in Oregon, Washington, and Idaho. I came out on the side of the affected."

·He looked at me and wagged his head, "My, and I thought you were on the side of the angels. You do like to challenge the mighty."

"I like Douglas firs. The forest is a watershed which supplies surface- and ground-water to a helluva lot of animals and people. Without spraying there's no measuring the eventual loss. Under proper control, the DDT could do the job and do a lot less damage than the moth. It's taken a couple of years for them to make up their minds on the problem. How much time do you think they'd need on what I've just told you?"

"I think there has got to be a certain amount of irony in this." He tossed a twig at a squirrel. "You come out in favor of the poison to kill the moth to save the forest. I remember you went to Vietnam to prove almost the opposite. Now here we are, and a piece of sky that falls with some kind of poison kills everything that it touches. Does that mean we're going up in the world or down?"

"Technological advance, they call it."

"Yeah. Whose? Got any thoughts on that?"

"I've had some very nasty thought about it. They tie in with MacMurry's charges."

"Oh crap, don't fall into that one." He snorted. "Everytime someone farts now, they point the finger at the CIA. Hell, they're not capable of pulling everything. I know. Some of my best friends work for the Agency."

"Maybe you should ask them. Ask them how it went in Vietnam."

"Cloud seeding in Vietnam's a helluva lot different than what you've just told me. I'd have done the same thing. Flood the infiltration trails, save G.I. lives—if saving their lives doesn't offend the anointed in our midst."

"Look, I said it was a nasty idea because I don't have any other. Maybe it's the work of some separatist group in Quebec."

"That's one helluva way to separate." He hauled out a large white handkerchief and blotted neck and face. "Lousy air-conditioning in this place."

"I'm waiting for the tower bells to chime."

"Patience. Let's go back over the track. You don't really know how that stuff came out of the cloud, even if you think you do. You only know what it did. That's the first solid point in this whole business."

"There are others."

"Never mind, never mind! That jet could have been doing a buzz job. Your friend what's-his-name could have busted his neck flying in bad weather. It's happened to the best of them. And Sam Catton —whom I happen to know—could have been shot by a hold-up man."

"And these photographs MacMurry got before he shot himself?" I held up the envelope.

He shook his head. "You've got a one-track mind. To someone brand-new to a story they wouldn't want to accept in the first place, the pictures are a turn-off, and it doesn't matter who got what and when. I'm trying to pursue a clear line of development. If my boss is going to call the Oval Office and the man there is going to contact the man in Ottawa, I want all the ducks lined up before I stick my neck out. Now shut up while I boil your yarn into something that will sell. Part one is the effect of what came down, which because of the lost specimens can't be proven. Part two is the need to get more right away. Part three is who did it, do they plan to do it again, and that may or may not include all the nasty things that have been happening around you personally. I don't think I need tell my boss that part."

"Well, you'll have to be the judge. In the meantime. . . ."

"In the meantime, you'd better watch your butt." He shoved a blunt finger at me. "You could probably use a bodyguard."

"Are you available? I figure the sooner some official action can be taken on this thing, the longer I'll stay healthy."

He stood up. "The big thing will be to find the bastards who peed green poison, before they take a leak over a nice populated area like this."

"That's one good thing about this weather. No clouds. Pray that it continues."

"I'll pray for you instead. Go into hiding somewhere where there's air-conditioning, and give me a call in about an hour."

"I hope I've told you all you need to know." I stood up, my shirt sticking to my back.

"If you haven't, you can tell my boss. I'm sufficiently impressed as it is. Let's have lunch sometime when we can talk about tennis or tell lies about getting laid."

Behind and above us the carillon sounded. Startled, we looked at each other and laughed.

I returned to the Press Building, but not by side alley or front door. Instead, I made a scuttling kind of entrance via Costain's Restaurant lobby exit, checking for loiterers. Seeing no one who fitted the TV description, I joined a pack of elevator riders and ascended to the safety of the Press Club on the 13th floor.

A call to my office raised the answering service and verified that Annie had departed. There had been no return calls from Feldman, Lee, or points north. I spent the remainder of the hour in the club library on the second floor, far from the Friday cocktail lunch-hour throng in the bar, grill, and dining-room below. I did a bit of at-tempted homework on chemical poisons, but the Press Club is not the National Science Foundation. My major success was in passing time in a cool atmosphere, but as the appointed hour approached to make the call, I became keyed up with expectation.

So was Bud Goss, but not with expectation: "Jeezus, man! Why didn't you tell me that MacMurry sued the DOD for a hundred million! My boss was Under-Secretary of the Air Force at the time, and it all came down on his neck! All I had to do was to mention that Canadian bastard's name, and he took off! He didn't want to hear about anything connected with him!"

"Oh, crap!" It was the best I could summon, the air going out of me like a punctured football.

"Well, it sure hit the fan, friend." His voice had a wry, disgusted twang.

"And I did tell you about the suit."

"Not the DOD, you didn't! You said the CIA!" he snapped. "There's a difference, pal."

"Okay, okay. . . . What do I do now—punt? Do you know anyone at the White House, beyond the third-assistant latrine orderly?"

"Well, I've been busy trying to put my teeth back in." His voice subsided but the annoyance remained. "What about you writing me a one-page memo—no rain-making, no nothing outside the facts. I'll put it on his desk Monday morning and try to start over."

"I appreciate it, but I feel a very great urge to move right now. Who do you know over there whose got some clout?"

He let out a long sigh. "I suppose the best guy is Grant Salisbury, if you can reach him. You know him, don't you?"

"We aren't exactly kissin' cousins. Met him a couple times."

"Well, take his number down and tell him I sent you."

We left it that we'd both attempt to make contact with Presidential Assistant G. A. Salisbury, and, failing that, we'd try to figure another route. A Friday afternoon in July made the possibility for meaningful contact extremely thin. How thin was proven by the Salisbury connection, which was no connection at all—the man was on vacation.

On my return call to Goss, his pleasant-voiced secretary informed he had been called suddenly into a high-level conference, and there was no telling how long it would last—possibly as long as the energy shortage.

I decided to return to my office and the hell with it. I'd leave the lights off and lock the door between my office and Annie's. If anyone tried to storm the place I'd scream for help and jump out the window. An eleven-floor drop on a hot afternoon might cool me off.

I didn't remain long on the premises—only long enough to engage in some quiet Socratic dialogue without benefit of the sage. "All right, Feldman was my bad judgment. Goss was bad luck. Suppose you called Getler at the Post, or maybe O'Leary at the Star?"

"Hello, Mike, I got a hot story for you. Somebody up in Canada made some green rain that killed everything it fell on. Proof? Well, I lost that somehow, but if you want to go up there with me maybe I can find the place and show you and you can see for yourself. How do I know about it? A dead pilot saw it happen, and he told me about it and took me there. I got some pictures from the air of the place. But the guy who can tell us how it was done shot himself and now somebody is out to shoot me. . . . What's that? How long was I in that hospital in Da Nang? Why, about six months." End of dialogue.

And that sure as hell was about how it would sound to a newsman. The thing was that barring a Bud Goss, the only qualified person in the town capable of accepting from a scientific point of view what I had to say, and of concluding that I was not on cloud nine, had to

112

be both informed and open-minded—not an easy combination to find.

"Doctor Paul Weigal," I said aloud to the solemn emptiness of my office. The phone rang as though I'd hit the jackpot. It made me jump. I let it ring, waiting until the answering service earned its fee, then I carefully lifted the receiver. "Mistair Erikzon, where is he?" The voice was heavy with a gutteral quality, the accent definite but not definitely placeable—German, Austrian, Swiss, Eastern Europe, KGB?

"He will be out of town until next week, sir," came the dutiful response.

"You informed me of that earlier, but you said he would return. Where is he? I need to reach him. It is important."

"I'm sorry, sir. I don't know."

"You don't know, and you are his secretary!" It reminded me of my conversation with Muriel Morgan.

"No sir, this is the answering service. Would you like to leave your name and telephone number? I'm sure Mr. Erikson will be calling in."

"Where is his secretary? Where can I reach her?"

"I don't know, sir. She's gone for the weekend."

The caller didn't leave his name or telephone number, but I had that screwed-tight feeling that I had been listening to the voice of my would-be executioner. It took me five minutes of fruitless mulling as to whether I should have come out behind the answering service to challenge him to a duel. Then I placed the call to Dr. Weigal, Director of Weather Modification Research for NOAA—way the hell and gone out in Suitland, Maryland.

The Doctor was a quiet elderly gentleman, low key and seemingly never upset by the *Sturm and Drang* that went on about him in the multitudinous bureaus and satrapies that comprised the National Oceanic and Atmospheric Administration. I had once written a lead that although the Creator was given credit for having put the earth and the fullness thereof together in six days, NOAA had stepped in on the 7th to claim dominion over sea and sky, and God had better mind his p's and q's. In Doctor Weigal's case, at least, it was an exaggeration. He moved quietly and unobtrusively, and consequently so did weather modification research, the winds flowing around him counter-clockwise and toward the center. Nevertheless, our relationship had always been pleasant. He would know what I was talking about and perhaps I could galvanize him into taking sudden—if unusual—action.

When I learned from his secretary that he was attending a fog-dispersal conference at the Mayflower Hotel, I felt a bit of luck had come my way. Connecticut Avenue was a damn sight easier to reach than Suitland, particularly since my car was parked in Alexandria.

I entered the hotel from the 17th Street entrance and walked the long, carpeted avenue past the line of conference room doorways, looking for the concert-chamber where all the fog was being dispersed. My luck held, for I spotted the Doctor's distinctive shock of white hair, topping his long, lean frame, hard by a conference room entrance. He stood in the midst of a large puddle of attendees. Somebody had called a ten-minute break between lectures—another break for me.

Dr. Weigal was talking to two colleagues when I became the third.

"Ahh, John Erikson," he smiled in greeting. "How nice of you to stop by. This is Doctor Globmassfrass (a heavy black beard) and this is Professor Schmorgnift (his was blond)." Or so the names sounded. "Mr. Erikson, gentlemen, whose column I'm sure you read, believes it is possible to save both the environment and the economy. Isn't that right John?"

It took ten minutes to disentangle myself from that one, and I could see that the Doctor was enjoying himself. He had a wry sense of humor and a youthful grin to match. He knew his two overly-serious companions would rise to the bait and bear down on me at least until the next lecture was announced.

I didn't wish to be rude, but when the buzzer sounded, I was. I interrupted Blackbeard in full cry. "Doctor, I realize how pressed you are for time, but I came here specially to see you. I wonder if we could talk for a minute. I'm sure you gentlemen will excuse us, a matter of deadlines." I smiled at Blackbeard, hoping to erase his baleful stare.

The pair took a somewhat miffed leave and joined the others drifting back into the conference hall. I managed to disentangle the Doctor from the herd by insisting that what I had to tell him could best be done over a glass of iced tea. My salesmanship and his curiosity won out against the next speaker, who Weigal realized would not be telling him anything he didn't already know. So we repaired to the coffee shop, which at the hour was all but deserted.

With the Doctor, my approach was somewhat oblique. "Have you done any studies lately on man's inadvertent modification of the weather?"

"Not since our last year's report, John. Why? Do you know of something new?"

"Are you monitoring the rate of incidence?"

"You mean how many fewer tons of proto-chemicals came down in rain and snow this year than did last year?"

"Not so much the amount as the effect."

"Well, as you know, it's a cumulative thing."

"Ordinarily, but there are cases where the results have been very swift."

"Some years ago, of course, but environmental controls are helping to eliminate that sort of thing. What have you got in mind?" He smiled benignly, blinking his pale-blue eyes at me behind thin-rimmed bifocals.

"Look, there is no argument, is there, that pollutants rising into the atmosphere nucleate in certain types of clouds and come back down again in precip?"

"Why, of course, not." He wrinkled his forehead, puzzled that I would ask a question whose answer was so obvious to both of us.

"Then why is there any argument about seeding clouds to do the same thing to increase precip?"

He smiled knowingly. "The problem is in the yield, how much you get, where you get it, and what you do to the cloud structure in getting it."

"All right, but you don't deny that cloud-seeding is here to stay."

"Not if I want to hold on to my job," he laughed. "No, I won't deny that, at least from a research point of view. I think at latest count there were some forty-four continuing projects, principally in the West. But you know all this."

"I know about a forty-fifth project, Doctor, where the rain came down greenish in color and killed everything it touched, including fish in a lake."

The faintly-amused expression faded and before he could recover and start asking the obvious questions, I began supplying the answers.

Throughout, he didn't touch his iced tea. He sat unmoving, his eyes fixed on mine, his aquiline face immobile. I concentrated on René's description and our joint experience at the lake. I left Catton out of it and René's crash—everything but the scientific aspect and my loss of the specimens.

When I concluded, he picked up his glass and drank most of the contents, then set it down, gently blotting his mouth with the paper napkin. "Hot, isn't it?" he said vaguely, and then, "John, how do you know the precipitation was man-induced?"

I had anticipated the question, in fact had aimed for it. "Because Angus MacMurry was either in some way involved or knew about it."

He stiffened and said with a startled expression, "MacMurry! But the man is dead . . . God rest his soul."

"Indeed he is, Doctor, and his death may be connected with what I've just told you."

"But John," and I could see both doubt and rejection rushing in, "Angus MacMurry has been in a mental hospital, he—"

"Not at the time of his death, and just before it he received these photographs." I had removed the shots from the envelope, and now I handed them to him. "And these are ones I took." I passed them over and sat back to watch his reaction. He adjusted his glasses and examined each photo with care. "Notice that all of mine have that coated quality and two of his don't," I said.

He made no reply. When he had finished his examination, he put them in a neat stack and handed them back to me. Then he took off his glasses and blew on them as though what he had seen had clouded the lenses. His napkin served as polishing cloth. When he had his glasses on again, he finished the last of his iced tea and gave a long sigh that brought his narrow shoulders forward. "Poor Angus, he had so much promise," he said. "He should have stayed out of weather modification."

"I thought he did pretty well at it, Doctor."

"Oh, he made a lot of claims, but he never had any real statistical proof, nothing he ever showed us, nothing we could examine, always secretive."

"You should have read the article I did on him when he was operating in Iran."

"Oh, I did, John, I did, and with great interest, but as you know, the Iranians decided to drop him, and so did everyone else. He went too far, too far and too fast, poor man."

I had not come to discuss Angus MacMurry's cloud-seeding abilities. "I think the important thing, Doctor, is that before he shot himself he was somehow a part of a forty-fifth operation whose results are, at least, terrifying."

"Yes, I understand, John. So you say, so you say." He looked down at his folded hands resting on the table, and then he lifted his head. It was his turn to startle me. "Whom do you plan to see about this?" he asked. He observed my surprise. "Oh, I realize this could be very serious," he added.

I choked off a sarcastic "Bully for you!" and instead said, "Doctor, I came to you not only because I realized you'd understand the technical feasibility of what's happened, but also because your boss happens to be the Secretary of Commerce and his boss is the President, and the President can pick up the phone and call the Canadian Prime Minister, and then the proper agencies could be alerted on both sides of the border."

He was back to looking bland and professorial. "John, as you know, the U.N. Conference on the Environment passed a resolution to outlaw Weather Modification as a weapon of war, and Senator Fell, whom I'm sure you also know, was one of the prime movers. He chairs the subcommittee on Oceans and International Environment. I should think he would be most interested in your account, he—"

"And you're not, Doctor?" I had to bite my words to keep my voice level down. The egg-beater in my stomach was churning.

"Of course! Of course I am!" His hands jerked off the table into his lap, and reddish blotches colored his cheeks. "But I can't contact the Secretary, he's—he's somewhere in the Midwest, I think. However, Senator Fell is close to the President, and I'm sure he knows you and will see you."

"Doctor, the Congress is observing its Thursday to Monday recess, and on a hot Friday afternoon there's not a corporal's guard of Congressmen on the Hill. Couldn't *you* contact the President's Scientific Advisor?"

"John, I'm sure you'll get more mileage out of the Senator's office even if he's not there at the moment."

"Doctor, you amaze me! I've just told you a god-awful horror story. I think I've made the picture clear, and you don't want to act on it. Would you mind telling me why?" I couldn't keep my voice down, any more than my blood pressure.

I'd gotten his own up. He pursed his thin lips and shook his head, frowning, thoroughly upset. "Let's just say that, like Angus Mac-

Murry's claims, your account lacks sufficient credibility. I'm a scientist, I have to deal in facts. You have none, nothing tangible. The photos don't really show anything, at least to me. If you had. . . ."

"Are you suggesting I made this all up!"

"I'm suggesting you need proof, John, which you lack. And since I know that you, too, went through a bad period a while back, it would be well for you to obtain proof before you can expect action on a higher level. And now, I'm sorry, but if you'll excuse me, I have to get back."

*

On the taxi ride up to the Hill, I somehow managed to get a rope around my thoughts. It was strike three with a vengence, but then this was no ball game. Except that the kindly, benevolent dean of the atmosphere had just kicked me in the groin. He'd given it to me there, because to believe me meant he would have to step out of his GS 15 slot and take action—which if it turned out unprovable or had been hatched in the mind of a nut would leave him with scrambled eggs all over his impeccable record. To disbelieve me was to avoid getting involved. The old sonofabitch was out to protect position, sinecure, and forthcoming pension, even if a piece of sky fell and killed everybody under it. Again, the error reflected on me for not recognizing he would fly true to form.

Well, at least he'd given me an idea, even if it was his intention to pass the buck. It was not the noble Senator, fearing the advent of climatelogical warfare—while the learned scientists disputed the benefits of cloud-seeding that sent me winging Hillward but his chief counsel, Jeff Horn.

Horn was not one of my favorite people. But I knew he possessed two characteristics that by reflex action had brought me in his direction. If everybody else in the Congress had gone home, Horn would still be there. Somebody had once said he was so cheap that he would not rent an apartment, but lived in the old Senate Office Building. Secondly, I knew him to be a tough, irreverant type who, if the fancy suited him, would storm 1600 Pennsylvania Avenue without benefit of protocol. He stood in awe of no one and diplomacy was not in his vocabulary. It was known that his boss Senator Fell, more a pillar of salt than of strength, kept him on the payroll and tolerated his overbearing manner because, as the subcommittee's counsel, Horn was adept at making the Senator look good despite his limited knowledge of the oceans and the atmosphere.

Ordinarily I wouldn't have gone near him, but I'd had enough of scientific types. All I needed was someone who would get the message and carry it. And at that hour of the day, my choices were limited. I was now looking for anybody who wasn't afraid of getting wet in a pissing contest. Horn fitted the description.

The lofty corridors of the Parthenon-like Old Senate Office Building have always impressed me with their vaulted grandeur. The cool, marble floors and mellowed rosewood doorways supply a sense of tradition and august serenity—even if it's all a stage setting. Under the dome of the arched and pillared foyer, the police guard seemed to be carved of wax. The hall I entered was empty and still. The legislative process was at rest. Maybe Jeff Horn would be gone, too.

But he wasn't, nor was his tall, dark-haired, secretary. The name plate on her desk said Trudi Proyer.

"Well, hello!" She had looked up from her nail-finishing job with surprise. "I didn't think there was anybody else alive in this place."

"I'm the sole survivor."

"What can I do for you, survivor?"

"If your boss is behind that door, you can tell him John Erikson has stopped by for a cup of tea."

"Oh, he wouldn't like that. The tea I mean. Is he expecting you? He and Mr. Rosen are having a meeting."

"He'll be surprised to know I'm here, and he'll wonder why I want to chat with him."

She smiled, showing me some nice teeth. "I'll see."

She could have done it by inter-phone, but instead, she rose and went to the closed door so I could observe the grace of her going away. I was pleased she was wearing a skirt and not the usual tight slacks. She knocked on the door and let herself in. I sat down and took in the familiar outer office, with its wall-to-wall clusters of photographs of the great man posed with other great men, all smiling, all pals together, all autographed.

Trudi was back, quickly the faintly dopey smell of her nail polish returning with her. "He'll be glad to see you in about five minutes."

"Good for him."

"Would you like a magazine? I think we have the latest *Playboy.*" She looked toward a table bearing an assortment of publications.

"No thanks, I'll try something dull like this." I had spotted a Congressional-hearing publication on the end table beside my chair, one with the title "Atmospheric Research Control Act." The testimony had been taken before the Subcommittee on Oceans and Atmosphere of the Senate Commerce Committee, and it was all about a bill "to authorize and direct the Secretary of Commerce to plan and carry out an experimental research program to determine the feasibility of and the most effective methods for drought prevention and alleviation by Weather Modification." I could hear MacMurry's booming laughter and his derisive summation: *"Ahh, for twenty bloody years they've trotted out their bills and never passed a one! The same bloody nonsense, not operations but experimental research! Research, indeed!"*

I found the "indeed" on page 296, under the title "Weather Modification and Food":

> There now exists marginal capability in some types of weather control, but steady improvement or more than marginal operational usefulness is by no means automatic. It was to this, the necessary sharpening of effort, that we addressed our attention in previous years by stressing:
> The need to overcome the existing fragmentation of Federal programs in weather modification now scattered amongst numerous Federal agencies; the need for greater emphasis on research in the physics of cloud formation and on the science and technology of rainfall augmentation; and the need to confront legislative and public policy issues governing the proper use of a new technological capability which has the potential of doing harm as well as good . . . ,

It all sounded sensible, but what it summed up was two decades of pinwheel-spinning.

"My God, Erikson! You look like a man reading his will! Horn stood hulking in the doorway. Trudi giggled.

"Hi, Jeff," I held up the hearings. "Love's old sweet song always brings tears to my eyes."

"Well, drop that crap and come in! Come in! Glad to see you."

Horn had a melon-shaped face with big myopic eyes, made more prominent by the bags beneath and by the magnification of his horn rims. He was quite bald and with his dangling nose and over-size lips his appearance was somewhat beagle-like. At least in momentary repose. Once he opened his mouth and his tobacco-charred voice sounded, the resemblance leaned toward a bloodhound in full cry.

"I can't imagine what the hell you want out of me, unless it's a drink," he said, having to clear the smoke out of his throat as he reached for his cigarettes. "You know Mike Rosen, here, don't you?" He nodded at Mike, who was seated in a captain's chair which was tilted back so his feet could rest on the edge of Horn's paper-strewn desk.

We exchanged 'hi's', he gesturing with his cigar, a short, roundish man with a square face, carrying too much weight and, in his small, bright eyes, too much self-importance.

"Sit down, Erikson. Take that chair or lie down on the couch if you like."

"Thanks." The large, green-carpeted office was rich in paneled wood and solid furnishings. The high windows let in deflected light which penetrated and exposed the layers of smoke being gently currented by the air conditioner. Both men wore short-sleeve shirts, collars unbuttoned and ties pulled aside.

Horn plumped down at his desk and lit his cigarette. "What can I do for you, chum?" he asked through the smoke of his exhalation.

"Well, what I wanted to talk to you about is confidential."

"You don't say." He sat back in his chair. "What happened, somebody get the clap?"

"Beats me."

"Well, okay, what's on your mind? What do I need to know that's confidential that everybody else doesn't know already?"

I didn't reply. I looked over at Rosen.

"What he means," Rosen said, "is that he wants to whisper in your ear privately. Maybe we should get Jack Anderson in."

"Anything you've got to tell me about what goes on here," Horn said, "you can tell Rosey." He hunched over the desk, leaning on his arms.

"This has nothing to do with what goes on here, Jeff. I didn't stop by to waste your time or mine, or to play touch football."

He gave me a long, mournful look. "You always were a hard-ass. Hell, let's have a drink. It's past the hour, whatever the hour is, and it feels like a long time since lunch."

Rosen stood up.

"Where are you going?"

"I can sense when I'm not wanted," he said good-naturedly. "Come on, sit down! The bar's open." He swung around to a low mahogany cabinet, one-half refrigerator, the other half stocked with liquor. "What's yours, John boy?"

Against my better judgment I said, "Bourbon".

"Spoken like a true son of the South. I suppose you want your usual rat poison," he glanced around at Rosen.

And so the drinks were made, and during the making I had time to decide whether I'd cancel my plan, insist that Mike Rosen depart before I explained my presence, or go ahead and brief the pair of them. I rejected the last. It was obvious that trying to penetrate the glibness of their joint personalities would be more difficult than taking on Horn alone. Also I was sure Rosen would leak; he had the look of a water soaked sponge. Further, if I let Horn dictate the ground rules, psychologically I'd be at a greater disadvantage, and I'd had enough of disadvantages for one day.

"To all the ass any man can handle," Horn toasted.

"And yours is waiting," Rosen intoned, glancing toward the door to the outer office.

"Don't get cute, Rosey," Horn said. "Drink up and confess," he said to me.

"I'll drink up and thank you." The strong bite of the honey-brown liquid went down hotly. "But as I said before, and I mean no offense, I came to see you privately. If you can't see it that way, I'll enjoy the drink and be on my merry way."

Horn gave me his witness-stand stare. "You're a stubborn bastard. How long will your confessional take? Rosey and I are busy."

"Maybe ten minutes."

"Rosey, go take ten." He kept his eyes on me and his glance had a disturbing quality, because his expression remained constant, revealing nothing but the penetration of his magnified look.

Rosen took his feet down again and arose. "Crap. What have you got to sell, Erikson?" he said. "The missing eighteen-and-a-half minutes, or are you really Deep Throat? I don't like drinking alone," he added, crossing the room to the connecting door to his own office.

"And don't forget to close it," Horn called, stubbing out his cigarette. He stroked his bald pate and then sat back, drink in hand. "Okay, now that you've insulted my friend and broken up a perfectly happy happy-hour, what's your problem?"

For the fourth time that day I related my problem. Only this time, having grown wise in the telling, I left out the summons from René. I was simply in Sept Iles catching salmon in the Moisie River. I left out loss of specimens. I had only seen the results of the rain, through René taking me to the lake. I omitted all mention of MacMurry, Catton, and events in-between. It didn't take long to tell, but after a couple of minutes into the telling, Horn had withdrawn his stare and was busy making notes. When I was done, he dropped his pen and reached for his glass.

"That's a helluva yarn for a late Friday afternoon," he said, finishing off his drink and reaching around to bring the bottle on to the desk. "Help yourself to another," he gestured.

"I'm fine, thanks."

He refilled his glass, adding a handful of ice. "All right, Johnny, who or what made the green rain come down?"

"I haven't a clue, but I figured somebody better start looking into it."

"Yeah, and why come to me?" He was back to the penetrating stare.

"The Senator. The Senator knows the President."

"Who else have you tried this on? You sure as hell didn't come here first."

"You're the fourth—no, fifth." I thought of my attempts to reach Ash Lee. I told him of my day.

He grunted and made derisive noises. "Jeezuz, haven't you been around this town long enough to know better?"

"Evidently not. Bud Goss tried to move on it."

"That's what you think. Why the hell didn't you go see someone in the DOD? It'll be bucked down to them anyway."

"Better it came down from the top. National Security Council, whatever. There is the Canadian connection." I had finished my drink. The bourbon had relaxed me, and I reached for the bottle.

"Yeah, there's that. You know your story sounds like a crock."

"Maybe that's the way it sounds, but it's the best one I've got at the moment."

"The only poison I know about is in that bottle, but whoever heard of quick-killing branch water? Sure your canuck friend wasn't drunk?"

"He might have been, but I wasn't, and I think you'll agree

123

somebody had better pick it up from here before we all get wet."

"Only ten-percent chance of rain forecast for the weekend, the man said. Well, okay," he had a gulp of his drink while a newly-lit cigarette got some rest in a crowded ashtray. "Can you be here Monday morning at nine? The Senator will be back from sailing, and I'll get you in to see him before he gets confused."

"That the best you can do?"

The stare grew more fixed. "Considering, I think that's pretty good. What do you want me to do, call the Pope?"

"I'd settle for the President, maybe Dr. K., or one of his top people."

"Look, Johnny baby, I think I'm doing pretty good as it is. From a legal point of view, you don't have a case, you have a piece of cheese. I don't mind sticking my neck out, because it's too tough to chop. I also realize whatever happened up in your fishing-ground was either some kind of goddam fluke of nature or somebody testing something nasty. Either way, I figure it'll hold till Monday. No one works on the weekend, not even mad scientists."

"And if by some chance you're wrong about that?"

"If I'm wrong, it'll be a helluva boon to the umbrella business." He broke himself up on that one, having to set his drink down, half-choking on the smoke in his throat. "Rosey!" he gargled his stentorian summons. "School's out! Come join the happy throng!"

*

I suppose it was the fuel in the two bourbons that pointed me toward the Pentagon, as a last resort. That, plus all the rest. My earlier assumption had been that Ashton Lee and SRG would handle all necessary communication in that direction, for I had no desire whatever to have any contact with the DOD and more particularly with Major General Robert Kilbourne of the Air Force who had been a colonel when I had last seen him in Vietnam. Nevertheless, because of his position in chemical research, it was Kilbourne on whom I called at the end of a very ragged day.

Before the connection went through, I was half hoping I'd find he had left, and in some sequestered corner of my mind I was reflecting on how desperate I must be to allow myself to make the contact.

He was as surprised to hear my voice as I was reluctant to hear his.

"Erikson! John Erikson?" Like the voices of a lot of big men, his was in the upper register.

"Yes. I wonder if you have any time. It's very important."

There was a long pause and then he said, "It must be. How soon can you get here? I'm leaving in twenty minutes."

"I'm on the Hill. I'll be there as soon as a cab can deliver me."

"Come to the River entrance. Captain Frank will meet you."

On the way to the Pentagon, I forced myself not to reflect on past relationships. When I had last seen Kilbourne, he'd been in command of the 14th Air Commando Squadron at Bien Hoa, in charge of the herbicide- and defoliant-spraying operations carried out by our Air Force in Vietnam. His troops had jokingly referred to him as "old 2-4-5-T." Now he headed up an R&D operation aimed at defending the U.S. against CW, not to be confused with BW—biological warfare—and since the Soviets have an unsurpassed capability to conduct chemical warfare, Kilbourne was a busy fellow. I sought to concentrate on how I would present my oft-told tale to him.

Captain W. E. Frank was youthful and lean and smart appearing. His pale blue short sleeve shirt with shoulder epaulets, nameplate on right breast, silver wings on left, and dark blue uniform slacks, gave him that I-belong-to-the-team look. He guided me through the identification point and up two flights by escalator, then down several long corridors between paintings of aerial scenes from old wars, past honey-brown office doors capped with imposing titles like Deputy Assistant, Assistant Deputy, Vice Under-Director OOZZZ.

The Captain and I addressed ourselves to the possibility of a break in the weather and the ease with which the uninitiated could get lost forever in the maze of angling halls of the defense establishment—both comfortable clichés. Throughout, I was questioning my sanity, damning Horn and his bourbon, and wondering just how I was going to manage with Kilbourne. On this last, he must be having similar thoughts.

We did a sudden column right through an open doorway into a long, narrow outer office. It was bright with fading afternoon sunlight and two secretaries anxious to give up their typewriters for the week-end. Both managed to look up and smile.

"If you'll wait just a moment, sir." Frank did a neat left-oblique through a connecting foyer into what I could see was a far more commodious suite. His return was immediate. "Come right in, sir." He stepped aside as I came right in.

The brightness seemed magnified by the bigness of the room, the bigness of the desk, the flags on either side backed by draped windows. The air-conditioned scene was dominated by the officer behind the desk; not that there was anyone else present. He was the type that exuded a force that demanded and attracted attention. His size was undoubtedly a part of it, and the bulk that went with the height was solid. His skin was smooth and tight, a handsome coffee-colored hue. It went nicely with his blue uniform, the command pilot's wings, and the pastiche of ribbons. Major General Robert Kilbourne was a black man who had fought his way up the military ladder the hard way— the only way a black of his vintage could—by flying over, around, and through the color barrier. He hated my guts, and it was strictly mutual. He didn't come from behind the desk as he studied me across an uncrowded room, his eyes polished obsidian, his strong features expressionless. I remembered that in looks he had reminded me of the singer Paul Robeson in his prime. It had been more than five years since we had seen each other. The only apparent changes were a neat bush of mustache and his advance in rank.

"Good afternoon, Erikson," he said, not moving. "Why don't you sit there?" He indicated a Moroccan-leather piece, one of a cluster of assorted furnishings that graced the room. "Captain Frank, I'd like you to remain," he added.

He waited until I had sat down before he settled into his massive, high-back throne. He placed his folded hands on the desk top before a yellow memo pad. "What can I do for you, Erikson?" he said. My eyes on the reddish stone of his class ring, I recalled that the first time he had asked me that there had been some warmth and genuine interest in his voice. Now the query had all the warmth of metal.

"Someone has developed a substance that comes down in a rainfall which kills everything it touches, animal and plant life. I've seen the results. I thought you people should know about it." I kept my eyes locked on his and attempted to match his tone and manner. I sensed that the Captain, who had taken a chair close by, had reacted.

After a moment, Kilbourne glanced down at his hands. "Hadn't you better start from the beginning?"

"I plan to. I just wanted to make sure I had your undivided attention."

His eyes came up, animosity flickering to the surface. "Suppose you address yourself to the claim. Captain, please take notes."

"If you want to tape this, it's all right by me. Just flick the button." I nodded at his desk where I was sure such a button existed and may have already been activated. He made no reply, waiting for me to start.

Again in the telling I made no mention of MacMurry or Catton or the loss of René and the specimens. I did stress the jet that had nearly killed us in order to indicate that the killing rain had been man-made.

Throughout most of my recitation, Kilbourne had concentrated on making his own notes in a big, slashing hand.

When I'd finished he put down his pencil and said, "Captain Frank, see if you can locate a sectional chart of the Bagotville and Quebec areas."

Frank left us and Kilbourne came back to me. "You know, of course," he said after a moment, "that there is no known toxic agent, bacteria or virus, that can do what you have described."

"The operative word is 'known'. Somebody has proven that we don't know enough."

The way he looked at me I suspected he was waiting for me to add: 'We do our killing more slowly and selectively with defoliants and herbicides and nitrogen oxides.'

"I'm surprised you didn't collect some evidence, since you say you were on the site." His inflection told me he meant he didn't believe a goddamn word of it.

"I thought of it. I also thought I might contaminate myself. There was the thirst factor, and then there was the Lear jet."

"How do you know it was a Lear?"

"Picard knew." I could feel a sense of ugliness rising out of the bourbon dregs, and I figured it was my turn to ask a question. "You people are the experts. Have you ever come across anything remotely like this?" The accent was on 'you.'

The glitter in his eye measured me. Was I being a wise guy? The electricity generated out 'of our past association short-circuited around us. Kilbourne kept his balance, disconnecting his glance from mine and plugging it into the element of oil paintings that had been brought in from the corridor to break the monotony of the far wall. "I know about acid rains coming in on weather systems from Britain and the Benelux," he said, "dropping four thousand tons of sulfates on southern Norway last January, which was inadvertent. Do you have any proof, one way or the other, that what you claim wasn't inadvertent?"

Before I could decide whether I'd show him the photographic proof, Captain Frank swept into the room, bearing maps and suppressing his excitement.

Kilbourne got the sectional chart spread out on his desk top and studied the details for a moment. "Would you indicate the site of the contamination?" he said without looking up, swinging the map around to my side.

"I can't be exact. The area is full of lakes and swamps on a high plateau, but I think somewhere in here."

He had come around the desk to stand beside the Captain, who was concentrating on my finger. "The lake is shaped like a woman's breast; at least that's how Picard saw it." But I couldn't see it on the map. "It's probably too small to be indicated," I concluded, lamely.

"Where can we reach this man Picard?"

Kilbourne went back to his own side of the fence, where his push-button communication console was ready to perform.

And now we'd come to the bitter bit. "I don't believe we can."

"Why not?" I had his full attention.

"Because when I tried to reach him, I was told he'd crashed. They found the wreckage in a lake, and not the lake we're looking for."

Now his stare put wrinkles in his forehead. He blinked at me, the muscles in his jaws flexing. "I recall you seem to have a faculty for that sort of thing, don't you?"

"What's that supposed to mean?" I was aware of a wildness starting to surge within.

He gave some thought to his answer before he offered it. "I admit I find it difficult to look at you Erikson, and not remember Major Gregg. I can't help thinking that if it weren't for you, he'd probably be alive today."

Somewhere in the torment and depression of past agony, I had dreamed such a scene or thought it or played it out in my subconscious. Only in it, my reaction was to get my hands on his throat. Maybe the events of the present were so interrelated with the events of five years ago that my seeking out Kilbourne was as much to face him as it was to gain his assistance—as I had previously sought it. At the moment I didn't dwell on the psychology of it, for my response was pure venom-loaded reflex: "And I find it difficult to look at you, General, and not think of my wife! I can't help thinking that if it weren't for you she'd probably be alive today."

I did not stand on the order of my going, but left the place under a full head of fury, leaving Kilbourne and his startled aide to clean up the débris.

*

A shower is not only a good place to wash away the soil and toil of the day but also a good place to take stock of its results and decide what next. In my case there was damn little stock to take. I'd capped a day of solid failure by making a goddam fool of myself just when I was beginning to attract some positive attention. Calmed down, I knew full well that although Kilbourne had been indirectly involved in Nan's death, his was not an act of intent. It wasn't his act anyway, it was mine. The hell with it! If only he hadn't goaded me!

As for what was next, there were a number of options, and I was rinsing them off, along with a mixed sense of weariness and frustration, when the phone ringing brought deliberations to an end.

At the moment there were too many people I wanted to hear from to prevent my answering. Slopping water and suds, I made for the beckoning sound.

"Hello! Yes!" There was expectation in my opening.

"Hello, yourself," came the deep toned response. "This is Ashton Lee of SRG" he quipped

"My God, Ash, where the hell have you been!" Utter relief laced my roar. "What kind of think tank are you running where you can't be reached."

"Oh, I can be reached. I'm reaching you right now. I'm here."

"If you don't fire that goddamned witch you call a secretary, I'll have her burned at the stake! I tried to call you from Montreal and —"

He had an infectious laugh. "Jan says she forgives you, so you'd better forgive Muriel Morgan. Besides, she only does as I tell her."

"Well, pal, you've got one lousy way of telling when somebody needs you the way I do."

"What are you doing now?"

"Getting the rug wet. I came out of the shower for you."

"Jan says come out for dinner. I'll give you something long and cool to cool you off."

"I love your wife, and I'll accept the long and cool of your hospitality if it's strong."

"Come along, you old reprobate," he laughed.

Driving out along the George Washington Memorial Parkway in the early eventide, ascending the flank of the bluffs that border the Potomac, I could not help but think that had I spent the day in bed, I would have been no further behind in the action I was seeking. Still, I had had no way of knowing when Ashton Lee would return. I could only thank God that he had. Things would start happening now.

Fact was, I began to suspect they had already started, only in an unfriendly way. By training, habit and inclination, I am acutely observant of my surroundings—even when my thoughts are elsewhere. Most ornithologists are. It wasn't that kind of bird, however, but a beige van that appeared to be following me. Due to past circumstances, I had been on guard when I had departed Alexandria, and I had spotted the van some distance behind when I had turned off St. Aphas Street. I noted it again when I stopped for the light at Fairfax and King. The vehicle took none of the bridge turn-offs to the city as I skirted the river, and it was still chugging along behind as we rose up the parkway.

By the time I reached the Georgetown Pike-Route 123 exit, I knew two things about the van, neither of which was comforting. When I slowed down, it slowed down. When I picked up speed, it picked up speed. The traffic was well thinned-out at the hour, but still heavy enough that the van could remain back in the pack.

As I swung off at the exit and followed the two cars ahead of me up the climbing turn, I could feel tension rising within me. This was going to prove my suspicions one way or the other. There was no intersecting traffic on to the highway. Ahead, the light was green. There was an Exxon station on the far left corner. I made for it, and had just completed the turn and crossed the on-coming lane when the van popped into view. I pulled in beside the gas pumps and nearly hit one, with my eyes riveted on the rear-view mirror. The light had gone red and the van and several other vehicles halted.

"Fill it up," I said to the attendant, wondering what I was going to do if my follower decided to fill up, too, and shoot me while I waited for change. I had been so anxious to prove a point I hadn't considered trapping myself in doing it. From where I sat I was too far distant to get a look at the driver or to see if he had someone riding shotgun. If such were the case, to step out of the car would only make me a better target. Aside from that, the angle was wrong to decipher the van's license number. The light changed. The traffic moved. I hunched down instinctively as my nemesis moved with it and went on up the highway disappearing into the rancid twilight. I caught only an indistinct glimpse of the driver. The gasoline attendant had to say "That'll be five-fifty" twice before I reacted.

I was not exactly surprised to spot the van again, this time parked off the Pike just beyond the CIA headquarters entrance where it intersects with Dolly Madison Boulevard. From his vantage point he could follow me, whichever route I chose.

I had nothing in front of me and about two seconds to make up my mind after I passed the lights at the CIA turn. I made it up and was doing about sixty when I angled off on the Pike's secondary branch. But I was up to seventy when I passed the van, which hadn't moved an inch. The road was narrow, the surface not too good, and only a congenital idiot would be doing eighty on the heavily-shaded incline. I was doing worse than that when I topped the rise. My pursuer was not in sight as I crested and started down the backside. My foot came off the accelerator and hit the brake with care. I made the right turn into Goose Run Road, sounding and looking like a candidate for the Grand Prix. I knew the road intimately, for I had once lived on it, and I hauled my compact around into the oak-clotted entrance of the Telford's drive coming to a gravel-spitting halt. Through the trees and foliage I could see a small section of the main road, and momentarily framed within the vegetation I saw the beige van as it zipped by. There was a certain perverse satisfaction in proving my suspicion had been correct and that in the best tradition of the Agency, I had shaken my pursuers.

Ash Lee's house sat on a low bluff hidden by trees and Virginia creeper vines. It was reached by ascending a steep, curving macadam drive, which I had cursed many times in winter months, but now gave it my blessing for its twin features of concealment and grade, the latter requiring the shifting of gears which warned the inhabitants of an approach.

The house was low-slung ranch style, with sliding glass doors, lower level, sun-deck topping it, and a swimming-pool. The view was contemporary urban, a mix of trees and house tops, looking off toward a great beyond development called "Evermay". Old Thor, the family wilde-beest-cum-German Shepherd, came to greet me, barking and wagging at the same time. I squatted down to have a chat with him, ducking his tongue and grabbing him by the scruff with one hand, patting with the other.

"Listen, you silly fellow," I instructed, "you go sharpen your teeth on a good bone, and if anyone comes around here, you give it to them right in the kazoo. Hear?"

"Hear what?"

I looked up to see my smiling host standing in his front door. He wore white slacks and shirt, which accented his pencil-like thinness.

"How good a watch dog is he, really?" I stood up, continuing to rub Thor's topknot.

"Depends on what you want him to watch." He came down the stone walk to meet me. We shook hands. "How have you been?" The question was lightly put but the glance was observant.

"Impatient." I said accusingly.

"Tell me something new," he laughed. He laughed a lot, not only because he was an optimist, but also because he was out going with a broad sense of humor, and he enjoyed most people. "Why do you want a watch-dog?"

"You give me a drink, and I'll tell you."

"What have you got in the envelope, pictures?"

His very lean face with its close-cropped pelt was framed by jug-handle ears made more prominent by his thinness, but his features were evenly and finely formed, the pale blue eyes lined up straight beneath a high forehead.

Thor followed us up to the door and wanted to come in. "Thor, you go catch a gombeen man," I said. "Bite his ass off."

"Whatever are you talking about?" Jan stood in the doorway. I had not seen her in the gathering dusk.

"I'm talking dog-talk, madam, and I hope you won't sic him on me for my early-morning bugle call."

"Time heals all wounds, you silly man." She took my hand and I kissed her cheek. She smelled delicious. Where Ash was light complectioned and tall, she was dark, small, contained but never fragile. He was extroverted, restless and always on the move. And where he came on strong, she was dry-witted and warm. The perfect couple.

Before I had lost Nan, we had been neighbors.

"Where are the kids?" I asked, noting the silence of the house, noting it because I was worried more than anything else.

"All visiting for the weekend. You two go out on the porch and give the mosquitoes something to eat, and I'll bring something for *us* to nibble."

"Come get your drink first." Ash led me into his den.

I waited until we were seated on the deck in the humid but acceptable after-glow of the long day before I explained my interest in Thor's talents as a watch-dog.

"Of course, the first question is why would anyone want to follow you out here?" Ash sounded slightly amused.

"That's the second question. I just answered the first."

"Well, we've had a lot of robbery and vandalism hereabouts. No reason I can't call the police and report a suspicious vehicle. Pity you couldn't get the license number. At least we can give them type and color."

"I'm for that. But more to the point I want to explain what this is all about, and I don't want to do it in front of Jan."

"Best we go denward."

"Look, I didn't start the day off very well for her. I don't want to add insult to insult."

"Oh, come off it," he laughed. "I'll explain. We're not going to eat for a while anyway."

With Ash there was no need to hold back on anything, but before we started I tried to give him hell. "I want you to realize that if I'd been able to reach you two days ago from Sept Iles this thing might have been solved by now! But because you've got an unliberated conch shell holding down your fort—"

"John!" he interrupted, "Muriel Morgan doesn't make the rules."

"Well, whoever does ought to change them!"

"They can't be changed, not with the guidelines under which I have to operate."

"Christ, man! When are things so secret that you can't be found and talked to?"

"Since things that are supposed to be secret have become so public. Now stop your ranting and tell me what it's all about." He grinned at me. "I promise to listen."

"Turn on your tape recorder and don't intrude."

After my day of convoluted recitations it was a relief to tell it all honestly and to know that I had the right audience. When I'd finished, he had a long look at the photographs, using a magnifying glass. Then he sat back, leg lifted, hands locked around his knee, thinking. "What the hell could it be?" he finally muttered.

"Some fast-acting derivative of dioxin, or Kepone, maybe?"

"No, I don't think so. It's got to be more sophisticated, something that would nucleate—act as a nucleator."

"Silver iodide is the nucleator. Couldn't the toxic substance be impregnated in it?"

"Off hand, I don't know. Whatever it is, it would have to be very delicately managed or it might contaminate whoever was putting it together."

"How come René and I didn't get contaminated?"

"I suppose because the lethal effect is brief. But it's no good wasting time with guesses." He stood up. "You made your mistake coming back here, although I don't blame you," he added quickly, smiling at my instantaneous reaction. "We've got to get some more specimens *tout de suite.*"

"I can leave right now," I said.

He ignored my offer. "Question is, who should be informed?"

I snorted. "Bub, I spent the day trying to inform half of Washington."

"Who?"

I told him who.

"Well, I can understand most of the reaction." He had made us another drink, during my cataloguing. "And so can you, if you just calm down. Nothing is too impossible to believe today until you face someone with it and expect them to do something about it. Proof positive is what you need. Here, try some of *this* proof and see if it improves your disposition. I'm sure that bringing MacMurry into it made it all sound like oddsville to Feldman and Weigal, or at least it gave them an easy out."

"Maybe you think you're telling me something I don't know."

"Kilbourne, of course, was the right man to go see. It's just too damn bad you have to keep carrying a stupid grudge around."

"You might tell him that, too."

"No, I'll tell you something else you should know. Bob Kilbourne has been going through a very rough period, the kind you should be able to understand. He had twin daughters whom he doted on. They both died of sickle-cell anemia about a month ago."

That news did put the damper on the hot plate that Ash had been firing up within me. I had a taste of my drink. "I'm sorry to hear it. That shouldn't have to happen to anyone . . . even to Kilbourne."

He stood looking down at me, measuring me. "I've got one more thing to say about this, and then we'll move on to the matter at hand. You blame yourself for Nan's death, and you blame him because you don't want to blame yourself, but neither of you is guilty of anything but damn-bad luck."

His words punched holes in me. I held the mug-like glass pressed between both hands and stared at the ice. I wanted to rage at him and tell him to mind his own goddam business. "Look," I finally said, "I've had enough for one day, let's stick to the matter at hand."

"Okay," his voice became light again. "I'll call Kilbourne later and fill him in on our plans. He may offer some valuable input."

"What are our plans?" I looked up at him, feeling some of the tightness starting to ease off.

"I'd say an early morning departure for Sept Iles. I'll notify our flight operations. How does an eight o'clock take-off sound to you?"

"All right, but wouldn't we be ahead of it, if we left tonight?"

"We've only got one flight crew. After flying me around and about, they have to have at least one night's rest. We're going to louse up their weekend anyway. Also I want to bring along our two best chemical and bio people, Richardson and Chung. It may take a bit of doing to reach them."

"You'll need a float plane or an amphibian to get into the lake."

"I'll have our pilot make the arrangements. I'm sure we can lease something up there that will float. Now why don't you go out and help Jan baste the goose or whatever, and I'll see what I can line up."

He smiled at me, eager and ready to go, after God knows what kind of a week he'd put in. There was assurance in the directness of his manner, in his movements and in his expression; he was a man who knew what the hell he was doing.

"Before I go make eyes at your wife, one question. Have you ever heard of anything like this?"

"In a word, no. And I wish I never had. It seems it's my lot to keep hearing about new and ultimate weapons. This one sounds more selective in an obscure way. If you lived in the desert, you'd be pretty safe from it, wouldn't you?"

When I bid the Lees farewell about eleven o'clock, I had an almost euphoric feeling. Complete acceptance and positive action had me on the other end of the seesaw. Although Ash had not been able to reach the pilot and the two wizards from SRG, word would be waiting for them to meet us at Page Airways at seven in the morning. He had had no luck reaching Kilbourne either, but had left word for the General to return his call on an "urgent" basis.

As we walked down to my car in the still darkness, Thor wagging along behind, Ash said, "There's one thing we haven't gone into and that's your safety."

"Old Thor hasn't growled once."

"No, let's not kid about this."

We stood beside the car. "You're right, and I don't feel like kidding. What do you suggest?"

"What about staying here tonight? I spoke to the police about the van. I can call them again and ask them to patrol the area."

It made good sense, but at the same time I wanted to pick up my camera and some clothes, and that was my excuse for turning down the offer. So often a man's fate rides on a decision which at the time does not appear to be of great magnitude. At the moment I didn't think it made much difference whether I spent the night in McLean or Alexandria.

Ash did not push it. "Give me a call when you get home," was the way we left it.

I had no real sense of premonition beyond an awareness that it was a long ride home, that I would be on my guard, and that in the darkness the van would be hard to spot, but then, so would my own car. I found how wrong I was on this last as I came down the parkway incline from Point Lookout. It's a rather sharp drop which at its base crosses a deep gorge. At some point a car had gone off into the gorge and after that cement guard rails were erected to protect the incautious. I thought I was being very cautious. The traffic was thin, a couple of cars ahead of me, nothing behind. Nothing behind until the juggernaut arrived.

It came without lights, moving so fast that I didn't see its bulk until it was almost on me. Instinctively I knew it meant to run parallel with me and then, with superior bulk and speed, slam me over the guard rail into the gorge. I had no time to reason. I simply reacted, my foot nearly driving the brake pedal through the floor. The action jack-knifed my body, the shoulder strap and my forearms keeping me off the wheel as I fought against a couple of laws of physics and the car's tendency to skid wildly under such sudden deceleration. At almost the same instant, I was clipped by the passing van, the glancing impact wrenching me around so that I nearly lost hold of the wheel.

My sudden braking had spoiled my would-be killer's aim, and he was by me, swerving back into the passing lane as my right fender shrieked along the cement pilings, losing paint and contour.

My shout was as much from rage as from relief. My foot came off the brake. I hit the clutch and shifted into third and then gave the accelerator the same treatment. Seeing the bastard moving away safe and sound did something visceral to me. The nearness of death, the recognition of survival, was too new for rational thought. I was still reacting as I gave chase. When I heard the siren and saw the flashing lights behind, I thought, thank God! Now I'll get some action. I did indeed. I got pulled over and thoroughly lectured by two unfriendly officers of the law, who gave me a ticket for doing 90 in a 55-mile-an-hour speed-zone. And it made not one iota of difference to these impressively suited and hatted and holstered protectors of the innocent that I could demonstrate a couple of crumpled fenders and a tale of murderous intent. I was the speeder. I was the guilty one, and it was a good thing I was obviously sober, but I'd better lower my voice or they'd add to my bill by hitting me with charges of verbal abuse of an officer, or maybe I'd like to spend the night in the slammer and do a little cooling down. Hmmm?

If what I had told them was true, and it was apparent they were highly skeptical, I could file a report on form 1040 D–22Z, or something. But in any case, doing 90 in these days of restricted speed limits was a serious no-no, and it was going to cost me so as to make sure I didn't do it again, even if somebody was out to kill me. As for the van, they did call ahead to another patrol car to be on the lookout for it and suggested that if located the driver be held for questioning.

On this last, I demanded and, wonder of wonders, got an escort home, right to the foot of the street where I parked my car because some thoughtful troll had swiped my assigned spot in front of the condominium. The pair bid me a formal goodnight.

"May all your flats be multiple," I muttered my own good night, as they drove away, red eyes rotating slowly.

My apartment was on the second floor of what was once a three-story private home. When it was converted from well-to-do Federal to utilitarian-modern, at least the original facade was kept intact, but the remodeling required a new stairwell, rising from the small entrance foyer. I approached with the utmost caution, reaction from the near-miss beginning to savage me.

Due to the realities of life in the after dark jungle of the outer-city, the front and back exits to the house were equipped with an alarm system triggered by anyone trying to force the locks. Only we condominum owners had the proper keys. Even so, and with the outside and foyer lights shining brightly, I let myself in by careful degrees, making sure to stand clear of the door as it swung open.

I don't know of any way to go up a flight of stairs—except quietly —without being exposed to someone waiting at the top, and since my entrance for all my care had not been sound-proof, it was a matter of holding my breath and treading softly.

What was true of entering and climbing, was also true of hoping to find my apartment as vacant as I had left it. My willingness to proceed was based more on the belief that the van-people had made their bid for the night and wouldn't have one of their number staying up late to greet me, than any act of courage on my part.

Once I was inside, and sure that I had my place to myself, I simmered down to a tremble. Ash had asked me to call him once I was safely home, and I knew by now I had knocked a hole in his sleep. My interlude with the police had been time-consuming. It was just after twelve-thirty when I dialed his number and got a busy signal. Hell, he was probably alerting the 82nd Airborne. By one o'clock I was sure of it; six tries and six busy signals was enough for one night. Fact was, he didn't seem ever to rest. Well, he could call me, and I could swear at him for disturbing my much-needed sleep.

Before I lay down, I did some furniture-moving, blocking my door with a solid, 19th-century highboy. It was the only extra precaution I could think of. In the doing of it, I learned I had not escaped the van's hit unscathed. The twinges of back and leg pain felt in Canada rose out of hiding. I'd be stiff and limping in the morning. Aspirin and a hot tub were required. I took the aspirin and substituted a heating-pad for the tub, too weary to risk drowning.

I had thought to fall asleep at once. Instead, I lay in the dark and saw Major General Robert E. Kilbourne looking at me. We had something in common now. My loss was older than his, but now I could sympathize with the poor bastard, as certainly I never could have done before. It wasn't that I had anything against the military in general or the Air Force in particular. The Vietnam meat-grinder was not their fault. They brought dedication and loyalty to a stinking job and men like Kilbourne's friend Major Gregg had died in carrying out the demands of the politicians. I had represented the latter, thinking at the outset that my cause was scientifically just, but later I had come to realize that behind the assignment was a larger political determination which was to make the military look bad in the pursuit of a goal so proscribed that it was impossible to attain. I realized, too, that Kilbourne had seen me as an instrument of that determination; yet he had been compelled by higher authority to cooperate and supply me with assistance. Behind his can-do military bearing, his feelings toward me had been apparent which had only stimulated a reciprocal attitude on my part. Then when it had all come down around me, as Ash had said, I blamed myself but I wanted someone to share the blame, and Kilbourne's blind act had made my blind antagonism possible.

"And now, and now," I muttered. "What's any of back there got to do with Lake Poitrine and people who want to kill me? Nothing. Go to sleep and think about nothing."

Nothing until I began to dream. Mark Feldman, lean, long-nosed and horn-rimmed was lecturing to a packed auditorium. I noted he had a tic in his cheek. He appeared uncomfortable behind the lectern. "The U.S. defoliant and herbicidal program began in South Vietnam in 1961," he said. "By the time the program was ordered suspended on April 15, 1970—as John Erikson, whose work was instrumental in the suspension, can tell you—five million acres or about twelve-percent of South Vietnam had been affected by the spraying.

"There were five purposes behind the effort to clear base perimeters of protective foliage against infiltration by the V.C, to clear lines of communication to prevent ambush, to expose North Vietnamese and Viet Cong infiltration routes, to expose the enemy's base camps, forcing him to move and to destroy the crops planted to sustain him.

"I'm really not in the position to say whether this was a necessary program—at least until I've received a go-ahead through channels from the Deputy-Assistant Under-Secretary—but Mr. Erikson is here, and perhaps he would be willing to comment."

"There are four herbicidal-spray materials," I said, standing with my back to the Taft Carillon tower while Bud Goss rose up to play to a forearm shot in careful slow-motion. "They are agent orange!" he declared, slamming an orange tennis ball past me. "Agent purple!" Moving swiftly now, he back-handed a purple ball toward Feldman, who ducked.

"Agent white and blue!" He hit a white ball to his left, a blue one to right, grinned hugely and made a deep bow toward Feldman and the lectern.

"Each drum is marked with its own colors," I said, climbing up on a metal drum that began to teeter. I struggled to keep my balance, while trying to explain.

"Orange is the most prevalently used. It's commonly known as 2-4-5-T or Trichlorophenoxyacetic Acid, one of the Polychlorinated Phenolic family of chemicals." I was proud of the smooth way in which I had been able to pronounce the mouthful, but the drum was going over, and I had to concentrate on gliding. I maneuvered above the audience, knowing it was all a trick. When no one paid any attention to me I called to Feldman, "Over to you, over to you."

"When the aerial spraying was first begun as a test," he took my cue, "it was used in the vicinity of Saigon along road canals east of the city. The purpose was to increase visibility to expose the V.C. Then the area of spraying was enlarged to cover a two-hundred-mile strip from Saigon to the coast, and it went on growing from there."

He was quoting from my report, and I didn't much like the way he was doing it. I swept down and landed on the lectern, blocking him from the audience but finding the perch more unstable than the metal drum. I knew I'd have to be quick. "By the time I arrived with my mandate to investigate," I said, rotating my arms, "serious Congressional and State Department concerns had arisen—both humanitarian and political."

"Cut the crap, Erikson" Jeff Horn ballooned up out of the audience, thrusting his cigarette at me, trying to upset my precarious equilibrium. "There wasn't anything humanitarian about it at all. It was pure politics. The boys in State were worried we'd be accused of using germ warfare, like in Korea."

As he spoke, I was frantically trying to duck his on-coming ciga-rette. I didn't succeed and the lighted stub made contact with my forehead just as I fell off the lectern.

I came awake with a convulsive jerk, automatically attempting to rid my forehead of the burning sensation. It was a mosquito, not a cigarette, I flailed at. In any case, the instinctive effort brought me fully back to consciousness. Eyes closed, I took several deep breaths, exhaling slowly. Then I assumed the sponge position, Yoga-fashion, concentrating on relaxing my body from the toes up. But my mind wouldn't relax, and I lay listening for unfriendly sounds in the night. Hearing nothing more menacing than the hum of the air-conditioner, I let my thoughts pick their way through the debris of my dream, and then permitted myself to reflect on my Vietnamese past. I knew it was the wrong way to go, but at the hour I hoped such reflection would put me back to sleep—hopefully not to dream.

It was true that in large measure politics had lain at the heart of the Senator's desire to send me forth. But I knew the use of sprays in South Vietnam had grown three-hundred-fold in five years. Serious scientific concern began to be raised over the effect on the ecology of the affected area. Over a half million acres of crops—rice, manioc, beans, sweet potatoes—had been subjected to spraying. Rubber plan-tations had also suffered damage from wind-blown spray, as had mangrove stands along the estuaries.

I recalled that Bud Goss had argued with me, before my departure to Saigon, that both the Joint Chiefs and the National Security Council had spent a great deal of time reaching a decision—which at the time President Kennedy had approved—that defoliants were a useful weapon. I could hear Goss saying, "Look, the idea is to save *our* guys, not theirs! If our guys say defoliants are needed, that's good enough for me. We're in a war, and I can't help wondering what side some of your friends are on."

A war, indeed. Briefly I had become a part of it. Briefly, but forever. I began explaining to myself what had happened, lecturing like Feldman. "The flying, until my last mission was done in C-123s. We'd fly in an element of three. Each plane carried a thousand-gallon tank with thirty-six nozzles on wings and tail. It was very low work, done at tree-top level, no higher than 150 feet and flying slowly, almost at stalling speed. It was hairy and hazardous. Aside from the flight crew there was a spray operator who sat at a console in the tail section, regulating the spray. He could do the releasing in five minutes at three gallons an acre, or dump the whole load in thirty seconds when under fire. We were under fire during six of the ten missions I flew in the C-123. When you unload like that, when you drop a thousand gallons of 2-4-5-T in a confined space, it's going to raise hell with everything it hits. But when you see the tracers coming up from the brush, when you feel the plane taking hits, you can understand the reason for dumping because your immediate survival is involved. Evaluation of long range ecological affects get swallowed for the moment in the accelerating roar of the engines. . . .

"They called it "Operation Hades . . . A food denial program . . . A food denial program. Hold it there, "I sighed to myself and my invisible audience. "Knock it off, and go to sleep."

But sleep wouldn't come. I was caught in a different kind of current, too strong to swim against. From exposition of past events, I was drawn into a scene that was craved into me with all the irrevocability of a loved one's name on a tombstone:

I sat across the desk, looking over an enlarged name plate at Colonel Robert E. Kilbourne, USAF. He wore a khaki short-sleeve shirt, displaying powerful forearms. He looked up from the order I had brought bearing the Corps Area Commander's signature.

"I thought you were all through here, Erikson." He said, flatly, keeping his eyes on the paper.

"Not quite, Colonel. One more ride and that should do it."

"We don't send our C-123s up there. You know that."

"Well, I don't mind going in a chopper, a Jolly Green, a Buff, or whatever."

"We don't send choppers up there except to pull our people out. It's a very bad place, Erikson. Why don't you let it rest? You've got everything you need to show how bad a job we're doing here."

"You've got it wrong, Colonel. My job is to tell it like it is from —"

"You don't *know* how it is, Erikson. You don't really know what it's like, and you never will."

"From a scientific point of view I know pretty much what it's like. I have a report to make."

"Well, go make your report, and leave us alone. I've given you all the cooperation I can."

"Colonel, I've got my orders and you've got yours." I nodded at the paper he was still holding.

"Erikson, I don't mind risking your neck," his voice was hard, his anger barely contained. "But I hate to risk the life of a good officer on an unnecessary mission just so you can take pictures to prove your point."

"But that is the point, Colonel. I do need the pictures."

The thing that put an end to the remembered scene and brought me fully back to the lonely darkness of my room was the sound of crying—a distant mewing.

A child?

I lay listening. Nan's ghost had come to haunt me. She had begged me not to go to Vietnam. I had never seen her like that before. Never! . . . she knew, she knew, goddammit!

Now I could hear her sobbing, ugly sounds torn from her throat. I could see her, her head lowered, defenseless. The top of her head, the hair neatly parted down the center, long dark hair mantling a bowed head. The gentle curve of her stomach. Pregnant women are always unpredictable. Humor them. Feed them strawberries and champagne, but don't give into their moods, not on important things. They'll be all right in the morning.

"Please, John! Don't go! Oh God, don't leave me! Don't leave me!"

The explosion was a monstrous sound. It blasted me from my nightmarish hauntings and left me lying sweat-soaked, momentarily stupified. Somewhere I heard glass breaking. The bed was shaking; the child's crying had become a terrified shriek. Above me on the ceiling a pinkish stain formed and grew and began to undulate. Something blew up, that was all I could think—but that's not right. Then I was out of bed and at the window. My foot touched a piece of glass, and I jumped back, swearing. I had trouble avoiding the breakage while getting the window raised and the screen up. I could hear doors opening and other windows going up and the excited voices: "What's happened? What is it!? Somebody call the fire department! Call the police!"

At the foot of the street by the curb a large clot of flame lighted the pre-dawn darkness, sending up a heavy column of smoke. The still air was laced with the acrid smell of explosives—dynamite? Cordite? Gelagnite? I watched the flames and heard the growing sound of the neighborhood issuing forth. I turned on the lights, hopped into the bathroom to examine the cut foot, plastered it with a large Band-aid, found bathrobe and slippers, shoved the furniture away from the door and went out to join the gathering throng. It was a shattering way to finish a bad night's rest.

The police swarmed in, sirens wailing. The fire department arrived, sirens competing, a mass of trucks complete with hook and ladder, clogging the length of the street. A pair of ambulances made for the scene as the firemen moved swiftly, killed the blaze and cordoned off the area. A crowd gathered like locusts. The last to arrive were television crews and their gaggle of inquiring reporters: "Sir, where do you live? Did the explosion wake you? What did you think when you heard the explosion? Do you know who was in the car?"

A bit later I stood next to the network man giving his report to the station's news desk. "Bob? This is Max, at the scene in Alexandria. We're getting some good stuff. According to the chief there's at least one fatality. . . . No . . . unidentified so far, blown to hell and gone. The destruction was so complete, what's left of the car is mostly pieces. Parts of it are all over the place. . . . What's that, Bob? . . . no, there's no identification as to the owner of the car. They're looking for license plates, registration. Be hard to find. . . . Say again. . . . Well, from what I've picked up there are two possibilities. The victim could have been starting the car which triggered the bomb, or somebody could have been placing the thing and it went off by accident. . . . Yeah, well, I overheard a couple of the cops saying that it might not have been the owner that got it, but somebody trying to steal the car. They've had a lot of thefts in this part of town. . . . No, that's right, since no one so far has claimed ownership. I'm ready to do a take whenever you say the word."

Slipping through the vocal throng, thoroughly shaken, I returned to my building. In some recess of my mind I noticed that spectators of any violent incident become buoyed up, excited, the women's voices shrill bird calls, the men talking loudly, laughing a lot, a form of gaiety of unity in survivorship. *We made it while some poor joker has been blasted into unrecognizable clots. We were there to see! We were there! And we're still here, all alive and well. How about a Bloody Mary to welcome the new day? Fantastic idea!* As the intended victim, I was unable to enter into the spirit of the thing.

I sat on the bed and struggled to bring order and calmness to my thinking. I remembered my registration had not been in the car because after the police had given it careful scrutiny in my encounter on the parkway, I had put it in my coat. The chances were that it would take some doing to locate what was left of license plates, probably not before daylight, if then. Also, the car behind mine had had its front end blown off. At the moment my reason for not wanting to inform the police of ownership was recognition that to do so would only get me tied up in a ball of investigation and make me the object of media inquiry. The result would be a drastic delay in the planned flight. I knew that without me there could be no flight. Three times now, twice in a very brief period, an attempt had been made to kill me by shooting, wrecking, and blasting. Why was my death so important to them? For the same reason's René's was. Because I knew where their hellish experiment had taken place. I was the only one who could lead others to it to obtain proof. That was the quality of my reasoning at that hour and under these circumstances. And that eight o'clock take-off had better be set back right now, before someone had a more successful crack at me.

I had awakened Jan yesterday at seven. Today I'd awaken her husband at 4:30. At least that's what I tried to do, but after three attempts and no connection, I called the operator and asked for assistance. She gave it a try and a computerized voice gave back the message: "The number you have called . . . 281-9253 . . . , is temporarily out of order."

"Sweetsuffering Jesus." I went over to my pine commode bar and had a straight slug of bourbon out of the bottle. I'd no sooner set it down than the phone rang. The sound jerked me around as though I had been hit, illustrating the condition not of my reflexes but of my nerves. I had the receiver in hand before the thing could ring again.

"Ash!"

"Hey," came the soft rasp. "This is Goss. Are you okay?"

I let out a gibbering sigh. "God! What are you doing up?"

"Proving that insomnia has some benefits. I've been watching the very very late show, and they just broke in with a news flash. I'm sorry I woke you but—"

"Hell, you didn't wake me. It's a big block party. If I'd known you were watching, I'd have waved."

There was a pause. "I don't think I'm exactly in your court, but I thought you should know about Ash Lee."

There was a ringing in the wire and a ringing in my head, and the two of them had suddenly been pulled so tight they were going to snap. "What! What about Ash!" I was shouting again.

"His house burned down. He and his wife Janet are in pretty bad shape. Evidently, the dog barking woke some neighbors. The details were pretty skimpy." I was unable to answer him. My voice froze in my throat.

"They were taken to Fairfax Hospital. I figured you'd want to check."

"Yeah, thanks. Look Bud, I . . . I may want to call you back if you're still up."

"Sure. But I'd better call you, so we don't wake Marion."

"Right. Do that, say fifteen minutes."

I had another drink from the bottle before I called the hospital. "My name is John Lee," I said, forcing myself to speak slowly and clearly. "I've just been informed that my brother, Ashton Lee, and his wife Janet are in your intensive-care unit as a result of a fire. May I speak to the doctor in charge?"

"Would you please repeat that and spell the name."

I did so.

"Just a moment."

The moment drew out. The bottom of my foot began to throb. I sat down, noticing that most of the panes in the front windows were cracked or broken from the blast affect. I wondered why the news of the explosion had not also interrupted the very very late show. Ashton Lee was more important, or maybe they were saving the excitement here for the seven o'clock news. Come on, you bastard!

"Hello. This is Doctor Meldrin. To whom am I speaking, please?" The tone was slightly imperious.

"John Lee. I'm Ashton Lee's brother. I want to know—"

"Can you give me some sort of identification?"

That tore it. "For Christ's sake, Doctor, don't give me any crap! What's the situation! Are they all right!"

My authentic outburst, blood ties or no, was identification enough. "They're both suffering from severe smoke inhalation. It's possible he may have some lung damage. They're both responding to treatment and the prognosis is favorable."

"What about burns?"

"Second degree, not too serious. You might wish to come to the hospital, Mr. Lee."

When I had asked Bud Goss to stay in contact, it was with the half-formed thought that I might need him to drive me to the hospital. By the time he called again, I had other ideas.

The fire, of course, had been no more accident that the bomb in the car or the near-miss on the Parkway. Whoever these people were, they had not only traced me to Ashton's house, they had also been aware of who he was and what our connection meant. For all I knew, they had overheard our conversation through the use of some sophisticated electronic listening device in the van. Obviously, they had not caught up with me during my futile day or they would have moved against me sooner. Now it was only a matter of time until they moved again. If it had been one of them who had blown himself to bits, planting the bomb, that time could be very soon but not likely while the neighborhood was still swarming with police. If it had been some poor sot, trying to steal my car, he'd paid an awful price for an already battered heap. Naturally, I hoped the former was the case, but if it had been theft, then before the killers learned they had gotten the wrong man again, I had additional time to flee. I knew I couldn't count on it because it came to me that my phone might be bugged and any conversation would establish whether I was on the scene and where I was going. The only sure thing was that I was being hunted. I would have to run for my life right now. If I could reach the Quebec northland, I'd match my woodslore against any terrorist, but at the moment, Pete Scott-style, I made my plan of how to get there.

With the lights out and the coffee perking, I had dressed swiftly —corduroy slacks, hiking boots, shirt. I had removed the Bolex from its case and used the case for a few extras. I could carry the pack slung on one shoulder, my Hasselblad on the other, traveling light. The coffee was poured when Bud called: "Hey?" he said.

"They're going to be okay."

"Cheee! Thank God for that!"

"Yeah, and we'd better go to church. I'm going to the hospital about seven." That was for possible listeners as well as Bud.

"Let me know later."

"You better go to bed or you'll never get to the tennis court."

The yawn sounded prodigious. "Yeah. I turned that damned TV off. Hey, come see me Monday."

"I'll be in touch, and thanks."

Outside, the darkness was beginning to pale and the assembled crowd to drift away with it. The ambulances were gone and the fire trucks had noisily chug-chugged their way off toward the barn. Most of the police had also departed. An investigating team remained, sifting the wreckage, seeking information as to type of bomb used and ownership of vehicle. Of the four television vans and their crews that had converged on the scene, two were still standing by. I had one of them in mind as I left the house by the back door. The yard was a walled patio, relatively uncluttered with a scattering of crabapple and dogwood, too thin to conceal lurking savages. I made sure of this before issuing forth and going through the gate into the adjoining yard. Moving across lots, I came out on to the street at the top of the block and went down it camera in hand, a johnny-come-lately photographer headed toward the point of interest amidst the departing sightseers.

I spotted the TV newscaster named Max whom I had heard earlier reporting to Bob. He was talking to a cameraman who was loading his equipment into the rear of the mobile.

"Max," I said, approaching, camera now hanging around my neck, "I'm Pete Scott from the Post. That bastard Louie went off and left me. Can I hop a ride back to town with you guys?" We all laughed at the thought of my being left.

"Sure, but we'll have to drop you in Georgetown. We go up Wisconsin."

"No problem. I'll get a ride from there."

And so I began my run north. I would rather have been in the Arun Valley in Nepal between Everest and Kanchenjunga, or even in the jungles above Mu Gui Pass, but even so I felt a certain inner satisfaction in making the first step of my getaway in the back of a beige-colored van.

*

My return to Canada was indirect and by varied means. I used buses, trains and planes, and my course was roughly south by northwest by northeast by north and all the points between. A fox would have been proud of me, and a casual observer would have thought

I was out of my gourd. In the course of my travels, I made two calls. The first directly after reaching Washington, to the Fairfax County Police.

"The fire that burned down the home of Ashton Lee in McLean early this morning was set," I said without preamble. "His life is in danger and possibly his wife's. They should have round-the-clock protection until they have recovered." I hung up and went to board the milk train for Richmond. I felt that even though the police would consider the call that of a crank, Ashton Lee was well enough known that precautions would be taken, to stay on the safe side.

The next call I made was from Harry F. Byrd Field, outside of Richmond, before boarding a flight to Syracuse, New York. It was still early, but, I hoped, not too early. Mostly, I hoped she would answer the phone. Instead it was Edwin or Morcar, one of the Earls of York, who said he would fetch her. I realized I was keyed up waiting for the sound of her voice.

It was cool and crisp. "Yes?"

"Laurie, this is John Erikson. It seems I'm always calling you at inconsiderate times."

"Not at all." Her tone lifted and brightened. "I've been trying to reach you. I called last night."

"Not bad news, I hope!"

"No, good news for a change. Sam Catton is out of danger and he's recovering very nicely. Evidently nothing vital was damaged, and it was mostly a loss of blood."

"That is good news!" I felt a surge of relief, not only for his sake, but also because his improved condition might make it possible for us to talk, although to do so would change my original plan to skirt around Montreal. "Have you seen him, Laurie?"

"I expect to, sometime today."

"Look, Laurie," I had made up my mind, "I know about you and Mountjoy Aviation. Is there anybody in your operation who could fly down to Burlington, Vermont, and pick me up this afternoon?"

"Why, yes, of course. We have a Beach Baron, and we often fly to Burlington."

"I expect to be there about two. I'll be coming up from Albany." I didn't tell her by bus. "What will it cost me?"

She paused a moment, and I thought she was doing her sums. "John, does your coming here have anything to do with Dad?"

"Well . . . in a way, yes. I'd rather not explain from here."

"I'll pick you up myself."

I didn't want to involve her, but I already had, at least as far as Montreal. "Look, Laurie, I know this is a lousy time; wouldn't it be better if . . ."

"No, it'll do me good. There are plenty of people here to take care of things. I'll be waiting for you at Burlington."

And she was. I found her in the general aviation lounge, looking slim and elegant in pale-blue slacks and shirt, lemon scarf at the throat. With all my broken-field running added to an unrestful night, I should have been punchy. But I wasn't, not only because I had slept during most of the ride through the pastoral beauty of my favorite state, but also because the thought of her and then the sight of her, gave me the kind of lift I needed. I held on to her hand much too long for a greeting, and examined her eyes whose color I now determined to be a subtle teal blue.

"It's nice to see you again," I finally said, and we both laughed.

"We'll have to file a flight plan," she said. "Do you have a bag or anything?"

"Just what you see around me." We went out on to the cement apron and walked to the operations office, going past a line of parked aircraft. "Which one is yours?" I asked.

"The one on the end."

"Fiery-red and ready to fly. Are you a good pilot?"

She nodded and smiled. "Yes. The best." We laughed at that, too.

"I'll be your co-pilot. How long a flight?"

"Not long. About fifteen minutes unless we get held up in traffic."

"I'll want to pay for it."

"We'll talk about that later. Are you carrying contraband in your camera case?"

"My shaving-kit was smuggled out of Hong Kong." I held the door open for her and we went into the operations office.

I enjoyed the brief flight because it gave me a chance to sit beside her and observe her competence at the controls, the smooth motions of her hands, making mixture, prop and throttle adjustments on the flight pedestal. I had read the check list for her before take-off, and then with clearance from the tower, we were down the runway and climbing with Lake Champlain's long reach off the left wing and the hump of Mount Mansfield sliding behind on the right. She was a very different kind of pilot from René. He had a kind of devil-take-the-hindmost élan, while she demonstrated the soaring grace of flight, or so it seemed as I watched her at the controls.

There was no time to talk—a quick smile, a few words, a few gestures over the synchronized beat of the engines.

I wanted to reach out and fasten my hand over the top of hers as she set the throttles. Mostly, I watched her talking into the microphone of her head set, getting and acknowledging clearance from one control, contacting and being directed by the next. And finally, as we began our descent toward the river and the city veiled in the cocoon of pollution, receiving landing instructions and clearance from the Dorval control tower.

With all my efforts to shake off pursuit, I had known from the outset that to come into Montreal or Quebec or Sept Iles on a scheduled flight could have made all my running around pointless. My hunters might have any one terminal or all three terminals, under surveillance. I had no idea how extensive an operation this was, but from what had already happened, I had to assume they had manpower at their command and a broad capability to act. Still, I didn't think they could monitor all the private aircraft flying in and out of a major airport, particularly on a busy holiday weekend. But they could keep an eye on Customs for General Aviation.

I faced the problem after we had made our landing run and Laurie was pulling off on to the taxi-way. "Laurie, if I recall correctly, we go to Customs and stay in the plane until they ask us to get out and step inside."

"You recall correctly," she said lightly. "We're going there right now."

"I'd rather stay with the plane. I'm airsick. I've had a bad flight. Will that work?"

She gave me with a quick, questioning look. "I'm not sure. It will depend on who's on duty, but I'll see what I can do."

"Also," I said, pulling out my wallet, "my name is Peter Scott."

Now the look was longer and more serious. "Is that necessary? False identity is a criminal offense."

"It will be my offense, not yours." The thing was that long ago Pete had loaned me his official press-card so that I could get into an off-the-record hearing, and I had forgotten to return it. After his death I'd carried it because I never cleaned out my wallet, and also as a sort of memento.

She was no longer looking at me as I extracted it. "I'm doing this as a precaution," I said. "It's better that no one know I'm here. I don't mean I have anything to hide from your customs people, but there could be other interested parties."

"I hope you'll tell me who they are." She had become somewhat distant. "After all, I know you're here, and I assume you'll want to see Sam Catton."

"I hate to throw the old cliché—trust me—at you because you have no reason to trust me at all, but this is my doing, not yours. I'm listed on your flight plan as a passenger. It's not up to you to declare my identity to the inspector. If my name goes down on the form as John Erikson, it could be learned by others."

"And why shouldn't it be known?" She swung the plane around so that we were facing the *douane.* She leaned out the mixtures and the propellers wheezed to a stop.

"Because I've got to remain incognito for safety's sake." I said in the new-found silence, and my voice sounded unnaturally loud.

She opened the window beside her head and I wondered if she was worried that she had a psychotic on her hands. "And this has something to do with Dad?"

"Yes. Indirectly, at least. I'm sorry to lean on you like this," I said, knowing I had mouthed the same limp excuse when we had first met.

"We'll get out," she said, waving a return to the signal she'd gotten from the *douane.* "You can stay by the wing and act air-sick. I'll get André, I know him well."

"Thanks . . . for more than the ride." *Why don't you shut up?* I asked myself.

We got out of the plane, and I did as she suggested and leaned against the fuselage with my head lowered as though I might throw up. No one could see me from the Custom's office.

Laurie returned bringing André, a short, swarthy man in white shirt, black tie, and pants.

"You're not feeling so well, M'sieur, hey?" he said with genial understanding.

"I apologize." I shook my head. "This doesn't usually happen." I swallowed hard, "And with such a gracious pilot." I managed a weak smile.

"C'est la vie. Dommage, a pity. You have identification, M'sieur?"

I produced my Pete Scott card. The AP seal gave it an official look. André studied it and wrote down the particulars on the form attached to his clipboard. "A journalist, eh? Are you here on assignment, M'sieur Scott?"

"No. I'm here to see friends. I'll only be here for a few days."

"And what is in the sack? Have you anything to declare?"

"No." I opened up the Bolex case and he had a quick poke around in it. "Well, I hope you will be feeling better. You will sign here, and here; and when you leave Canada you will present this card at the point of your departure."

I damned-near botched the whole thing by signing my own name. As it was, my Peter Scott didn't look too dissimilar from the rightful signature. Laurie had remained silent throughout the exchange, although I could feel her tenseness. This sort of thing was not in the realm of fun and games, but when we got back into the plane, I noticed she was trying to cover a smile.

"Was I convincing?" I said, as I sat down beside her.

"Very! You actually looked ill. I thought you might be sick any minute."

"I nearly was!" And we were laughing again.

The Mountjoy Instrument Flight School offices were in a long, single-story, brick extension of a hangar on the opposite side of the field from the main terminal. I liked the location, out of the mainstream of activity. I also liked the fact that although the extension housed a number of aeronautical suppliers, because it was Saturday of the long holiday weekend, the place was largely closed down, and Laurie and I had Mountjoy to ourselves. But before we went inside, we sat in the plane, and I did most of the talking. "I know you're waiting for an explanation, and I'll give you one. But right now I have to think about getting to Sept Iles, and the only reason I asked you to bring me here instead of trying to get there directly, was your good news about Sam Catton. I want to see him and not just to tell him I'm glad he's feeling better. Can we call the hospital and find out when he can have a visitor?"

"Of course." I found her eyes disturbing, not just because they attracted me but because I saw wariness in them. But why shouldn't there be?

"I don't want to presume on you, Laurie. God knows, I already have. Do you know a pilot who can get me up there by tonight? I don't want to go on a scheduled flight, even if there is one."

She had turned her eyes away from me and was looking out across the field. "When do you expect to return?"

"If everything goes all right by tomorrow afternoon."

She turned back to me. "I can fly you there, John."

And, of course, that's what I wanted her to say because I believed at the moment I was safe and therefore she was, too. "I should say no," I said," but right now time is everything, and I'm in a race against it. It's two-thirty. Can we leave in an hour?"

"You can take my car and go see Sam."

"What about things at home?"

"They'll be all right, and I'd rather have my mind occupied. Do you think you can find your way to the hospital?"

"If you steer me in the right direction." We were back to examining eyes. "You know, I think you're something special," I was absently aware of the words I was speaking.

She didn't smile. "I'm also my father's daughter, John Erikson," she said, summing up her position and her willingness to assist me.

Sam Catton was propped up in bed, looking a bit on the pale side but hardly like a man only forty-eight hours away from having been shot. "The next time I borrow a room from you, it'll be a cold Tuesday in August," his greeting was peppy but the weakness of his voice gave an indication of what he'd been through.

"How are you feeling?" His grasp was firm and dry.

"It's not anything I want to make a habit. Sit down. What are you doing back here so soon?"

"Have they had any luck in finding who did it?" I sat down by the window.

"I don't think so, and I can't help them. I don't remember anything beyond taking a leak when I got in the room."

"I read your book," I said, "and forgot to bring the manuscript."

"No problem. I have other copies. What did you think of it?"

"Too bad you didn't get it published a couple of years ago. It might have made some difference."

He shook his head, "I doubt it, but maybe if you'd been around

—will you please tell me something, where did you disappear to? I certainly could have used your help." He looked and sounded reproachful.

"I went out to Vietnam for a Senatorial subcommittee on an ecology investigation into the use of herbicides and defoliants. That was right after I got back from being with you people." I stood up with my back to him, looking out the window down into a courtyard full of greenery where convalescent patients were taking the sun.

"And?"

"And I got shot down over the Ho Chi Minh trail, or one of them. I had a rough time of it there. . . . Back here, I lost my wife. She was killed in an accident. I was nearly six months in getting home due to injuries. When I arrived there wasn't much to keep me. I had an offer to go out to the Arun Valley in Eastern Nepal on a long term ecology survey, my job was birds. I took it. Call it therapy or whatever. I didn't come back to Washington until the beginning of last year. If you people ever answered any of the letters I sent, I never got it."

I turned around, and he was looking at me intently.

"I'm sorry to hear about your wife," he said quietly.

"Thanks. Sam, I came here to see you about something even more serious than the subject of your book, maybe an additional chapter. Do you have any idea whether MacMurry was involved in experimenting with the Weathermaker for any other purpose than making rain?"

"Well, I know he did a lot of experimenting, hail suppression and such. . . ."

"No, I'm not talking about weather modification."

"Well, what are you talking about?"

I took a breath and told him, but I made no mention of anything that had happened to me after I had gone back to Washington. Instead, I stuck to René Picard, Sept Iles and Angus MacMurry. "The photographs he received in the mail were taken over Lake Poitrine, the place where I took mine."

Catton's eyes never left me as I moved about the room restlessly, not liking the line I was pursuing but knowing it had to be developed; knowing, too, that the real reason for my reluctance was Laurie.

"This is a helluva thing," he finally said. "The photographs could have turned him to suicide."

"Exactly. His mental condition could have driven him into some kind of abnormal action. Didn't you say he'd come into some money. Do you know what it was for?"

"What you're saying is that Mac, in his bitterness and paranoia, may have converted the Weathermaker into a-a—"

"A weather killer. The possibility has crossed my mind. Maybe he sold it to somebody, God knows who, some way-out group of Quebec separatists, a terrorist operation—the woods are full of them. When he realized the enormity of what he'd done, he shot himself."

"I don't know, John," Catton rubbed his forehead. "He was never in the toxic poison field, and I should think he would have had to be."

"Not necessarily. He could have been working with someone else. Was there anyone else that you know about, someone from Iran? They're an awful lot of them, I understand, who don't love the Shah."

"If there was, I never met him. The only really smart people in that country are Armenians anyway, and I don't think they specialize in terror weapons. But what the hell," he sighed. "Maybe some of them do."

"One more question. What do you know about Ganin, the pilot you had?"

"That bastard! What about him?" He winced with the pain of recollection.

"I ran into him in Sept Iles. He flies survey for the power company."

He grunted. "Ganin would rob his mother's piggy-bank. He tried to steal the operation away from Mac by discrediting him with the Iranians. When I got wind of it, Mac fired him, had him tossed out on his ass."

"Well, if Ganin had succeeded, how could he have set up an operation? Could he have gotten the Weathermaker?"

"No, he'd have used snake oil or bat piss. He's a sharp con-artist."

"But do you see him connected with mass murder?"

"Not really. He's the kind who'd do most anything for a buck, so long as he could avoid unpleasant results."

"Well, how about this? Ganin got hold of the Weathermaker and sold it to parties unknown, who doctored it with a killing substance unknown."

He shook his head. "Not possible. He couldn't get hold of it. He wouldn't know how to manufacture it."

156

"Anything's possible, Sam. Even making rain. But whether Ganin's involved or not, that still brings us back to MacMurry."

"I didn't say he wasn't involved," a note of irritability had come into his voice. "I don't know. But I do know I'd sure as hell like to have the chance to question him, or beat some answers out of him. Of course, his being up there could be coincidence."

"I realize that but the photographs are not."

"Look, I told you I haven't seen or been in touch with Mac for a long time." A hardness was mixing with the weariness in his tone, and I saw he had grown paler and was looking more like a badly-wounded man. "Maybe Laurie can give you some answers." He put his head back, eyes closed again.

"I'm sorry to wear you down," I said. "I'll get out of here and let you rest."

"Where are you bound?" he said without opening his eyes.

"Back to the scene. I've got to pick up some fresh evidence, and as you said, I want to talk to Ganin."

He was looking at me again. "Who have you alerted on this thing? Are you going up with a team?"

"Half of Washington," I grinned. "Everyone from the White House to the DOD," which was true in a sense. "We've retained Laurie MacMurry's outfit."

He cocked one eye at me, "I'm too tired to question you on the wisdom of that." And then shaking his head he said, "It's a sad case . . . when I think of old Mac. I hope someone's going after the characters behind this thing."

"That's for sure."

"Yeah. What you should do is give the whole thing to the press right now. Blast it all over the boob tube. That's what I'd do. It'll protect you, too." He was falling asleep.

"Soon as we've got it licked, Sam. You rest easy."

"Good luck," he half whispered, "and let me know how you make out."

We were off the ground at three-thirty, climbing above the Isle of Orleans, paralleling the long ribbon of the river, glinting below in the bright sunlight. I could not help but think of the exact same flight I had taken such a short time ago. Then René had asked me to trust him. Now I was asking Laurie to trust me. If I hadn't trusted René, he might still be alive. I didn't know what that proved exactly, other than that the bomb planters had done better on their first try than their second. Or maybe it was that the wrong moon had come up to cast its influence on René's planet while it was passing through the house of Uranus—or something. Whatever it proved, there was going to be no chance for a repeat involving this lady at the controls. I thought I could see to that. She was going back to Montreal in the morning without me, and I didn't care what the bill would be.

She leveled off the plane, made the necessary power and stabilizer adjustments, and looked at me.

"Now, sir," she said. "We have plenty of time, and I don't expect we'll be interrupted. I'm a good listener, even if the engines sound brassy."

"You're also very patient."

"I'll agree to that, too, so please reward me."

"I'll have to start with a question."

"I've noted you usually do," she observed dryly. "Now tell me about Dad."

"You know a lot about your father's work, I realize that. But how much do you know about the Weathermaker? For example, how is it made?"

"Well, the rope-like part of it is blasting cord. The nucleator is impounded into the cord. There's a fail-safe firing mechanism that —"

"I understand all that, but what about the nucleator? Is it really silver iodide?"

She studied me, making up her mind before she answered, and then shook her head. "No, it's not. And I don't know what it is. Dad never said. He just said it would work in warm weather clouds as well as cold. He spent a long time experimenting."

"So it was a secret with him. Did he tell anyone, anyone outside the family, like Sam Catton?"

"He may have told Sam. From the way he acted later, I think he must have. But he wanted all the meteorological people to think it was silver iodide to hide what it really was. When they tested it at NCAR, that's what they thought it was."

"Well, who put whatever it was into the blasting cord—I mean when it was manufactured?"

"He did. He had a contract to buy the cord, I think with Imperial

Chemical. They supplied the cord, and he had his own little plant where he did the assembling."

"Can anyone buy blasting cord?"

"As I understand it, not unless you can prove what you're using it for. They're very careful about that."

"Okay, so he gets the cord and he does the assembling. How about the people who worked for him? Wouldn't they know what they were working with?"

"They were just that—workers. They simply carried out the process. Dad was very careful about security. He was always terribly suspicious."

"And people like Dufore—was that his name?—and that other fellow out in Iran, Stein. Did they know the process?"

"I don't know. I assume they thought it was silver iodide. I knew because Dad wanted me to know. He wanted me to be a part of what he was doing. I flew all the test flights over the Laurentians and then in Newfoundland."

"But you didn't go to Iran."

"No. The Iranians wouldn't agree to a woman doing the flying. Real male chauvinists. Actually, Dad didn't want me there. He wanted me minding the store. Now, John Erikson, I'm doing too much of the talking and it's past time you stopped playing Twenty Questions. What is this all about?"

I took a breath. "Laurie, it's about somebody making rain up around Sept Iles, only the rain is apparently killing everything it falls on." I tried to soften the last.

"Killing what it falls on!"

"There may be a connection with the Weathermaker. I don't know, but from what you've said—"

"But there couldn't be! There's nothing in it that would—that would—!"

"Not as your dad made it," I said, holding back the thought: we don't know what's in it, and then, "Maybe someone has modified it."

"But he's the only one who. . . ." And then it was as though we had suddenly run into turbulence. She had been keeping one eye on her flying as we talked. Now she turned, both hands gripping the wheel, staring straight ahead, seeing nothing, blinded by the sudden revelation. "Oh, God!" It came out of her in a choked whisper. She shook her head as though to free herself of the knowledge.

I wanted to put my arm around her, but I wasn't stupid enough to do so. I sat and waited until she got control of herself. Then, without looking at me, she said, "Tell me about it. How do they know it kills things? Who's doing it?"

"We don't know who's doing it, but it's been observed and so have the results. I'm collecting evidence—or trying to."

Now her eyes came back to mine, tear-filmed. "And someone is trying to stop you."

"It appears so. I thought it best to—"

"I know who it is, John." It was my turn to react. She returned her attention to flying the plane but went on talking: "When Dad's business failed, he still had a large supply of Weathermakers. He had them stored in a warehouse at the airport as engine parts. A month or so ago, not long after he'd come out of the hospital, he had a call from someone who said he represented a firm that wanted to buy the supply. Evidently he was willing to pay a lot of money. Dad said no. He told Mother, and although she understood his reluctance, she begged him to accept, if the offer was made again, because they were terribly in debt. The second offer was double the first amount, and Dad got his Scotch up and demanded, and got, twice *that*. The cash was mailed to his account. Then he sent the key and location of the Weathermaker to a postal box number. Two men in a truck took the supply away.

"That was two weeks ago. Mother was happier than she's been in years, and even Dad was a bit cheered up by. . . ."

"Laurie, who in the hell bought the Weathermaker!" I had to interrupt.

She looked at me. "I know everyone thought he was crazy, but dad said it was your CIA."

My breath whistled through my teeth. "He didn't know that. He just thought that." I couldn't keep the rejection out of my tone.

"He said he knew it!" She answered sharply. "He told mother he recognized the voice."

"Look, Laurie, the CIA could make its own Weathermaker if it wanted to. It did in Vietnam. Your father sued the U.S. Government over just that point."

"No, he did not. He sued them over patent infringements. He held the patents on explosive rain-making devices. They didn't know what he was using, but they must have found out through someone, maybe Sam Catton, that it wasn't silver iodide!"

I knew she was terribly upset, and I had done the upsetting. At the moment she needed to accept her father's belief that the CIA was behind his downfall and even behind his death. I had not mentioned the photographs, and for the moment I didn't plan to, for that would add nothing to what I already knew, and further convince her of who was to blame. If she brought up the CIA, I'd finesse the point. Instead, I tried another tack. "You mentioned Sam Catton. What about Liam Ganin? He's flying out of Sept Iles right now."

"I heard that. Certainly he could be paid enough to fly anything."

"And Dufore and Stein?"

"Maybe. Why not? Why not anybody?" Her voice spiraled angrily. And then, under control, "The last I knew Dufore was in Africa and Stein in Israel . . . Didn't you tell anyone about this in Washington?"

"Plenty of people know, but it's necessary to examine the effects of the rainfall in the laboratory."

"What about the government here. Does Ottawa know?"

"It will, it will, but it's a holiday weekend, remember." I tried to make the answer seem light and ironic.

She didn't reply, busying herself with a correction on the altimeter. "I know one thing," she said after a few moments of reflection. "There was nothing in the Weathermaker as Dad made it that was harmful, or it would have shown up in Iran and Cyprus. That means if it is being used for experiments—to make it into something awful, a weapon or something—whoever bought it is adding. . . . "

"I agree, but I think you're all wrong, Laurie—in fact, I know you're wrong—on who's behind it. I don't blame you for feeling the way you do, but. . . ."

"How do you know I'm wrong!" Her eyes were cold and hostile.

Her anger set off my own response. "Because if the CIA was out to kill me, they'd have done a lot better job of it, and they wouldn't have shot Sam Catton by mistake!"

That shook her into silence, and she went back to flying the plane.

I had a few thoughts of my own and a nagging doubt. How did I know she wasn't right? Hell, the CIA had a long public record of botched assassinations. If they couldn't get Castro, who said they could get Erikson? How did I know what experiments they might want to conduct on a weather weapon now that Biological and Chemical Warfare had been ruled out, and what better place to test than over somebody-else's wilderness? But good God! Would they go to such extremes to cover their tracks? I could almost hear the voice of Bud Goss issuing from the slipstream, *Now, friend, don't buy all that crap.*

We flew, for a long period, in silence. I studied the reaches of the horizon ahead and the ultramarine tint of the river below, with its scattering of power boats followed by the white tracings of their passage. One thing we did not want or need was a barrier between us, and I knew the sound of flight could create just that. Whatever else there was to say on the issue before us, it could be better said on the ground.

I spoke up brightly, "I've done a lot of flying, but I don't really know anything about it. Would you let me in on the secret? Would you show me how it's done? You can charge me extra."

Her smile was one of welcome and I sensed gratitude for having changed the subject and put us back on a safe track. The rest of the flight was pure delight, as Laurie explained and demonstrated how the plane flew and I tried to concentrate on learning, but distracted by her nearness, by her voice and laughter, by the curve of her cheek. Our hands touched now and again, as we winged through the mellowing afternoon. *Laurie, Laurie, Laurie,* was the voice in the beat of the engines. Thoughts of death far below, but here above, caught in the prison of flight with the lovely Lorelei, I had only thoughts of life and living.

Finally, she permitted me to make most of the let-down into Sept Iles. We came over the Saint Marguerite where it flows into the river, and passed the railway line to the left and the TV towers to the right, crossing Point Noir and the bay, turning to skirt the high-bluffed coast and the city, and turning again over the Indian Reservation at Maliotenan with the Moisie River beckoning to come cast a line. Then she took over, and we dropped down to land, the light softening and going into shadow as the bulk of terrain rose up.

After she had parked the aircraft and silenced the engines, I said, "That was great, Laurie. You'll have to give me more instruction."

"You learn very quickly. I'll make you a pilot in no time."

"Ahh, if only we could stay up there. I hate to bring us back to earth, but this is where we are. Because I've been here before, people in the terminal might recognize me, and I'm not anxious for that. I don't want to be bothered answering questions. Suppose we get a cab to town and stay at the Cartier House. And then I want to take you to dinner, that is if you don't have a previous date, of course." I put on my best grin.

She didn't reciprocate. "Where is the place you'll be picking up what you came for, and why didn't you pick it up before?"

"I did, but we need more, and let's not worry about that," I said quickly, determined to leave the thing alone for now.

And after a moment's hesitation I saw that she was, too. She smiled briefly, "Why don't we get out?"

My one worry at the field was being under surveillance, someone waiting for our arrival. The lack of anyone in sight was reassuring, but how did I know who was looking out the terminal window?

At the Cartier, Miss MacMurry and Mr. Scott could not get adjoining rooms, or even on the same floor—but while she was in hers, I had a chat with the male concierge about a good place to dine, since we were not dressed for anything fancy. He knew just the place —La Bon Auberge. He had it right: it was rustic with candle-light and excellent French-Canadian cuisine.

I found it difficult to sit across the table from Laurie, watching the candle's flame cast subtle shadows on the soft planes of her face while touching her eyes with glints of fire. I wanted to relax and sink into the mood, to give my interest in her free rein. But I couldn't relax. I had an eye for everyone who came in and everyone who left, and it was too dark to distinguish clearly most of our fellow-diners. Then, somewhere in the back of my mind, I began making comparisons, and I didn't like that either. No. There was no physical resemblance, but there were other similarities: the quality of quietness that didn't require conversation to feel comfortable or close. The manner of a woman who made you aware of the essential character and magic of her femininity. Nan with her painting, a delicate artistry. Laurie, her hand easing the throttles forward, a different kind of artistry, not less delicate, but a positive grace. And then a major difference. Nan was a follower, often uncertain and afraid, not wanting to dominate, loving but not daring. Laurie would give as good as she got, could stand alone, without compromise, carried by a strength of purpose. *I am my father's daughter, John Erikson.* Yes, and beyond that, you are yourself. Warmth and compassion lie beneath your careful look.

163

"You are very silent, John," she said to me, and her tone and her look momentarily banished my caution.

"It's because I'm warming myself in your glow, Laurie."

"Aren't you confusing me with the candle?"

I laughed. "Don't make fun of my being romantic."

"And whom are you romantic with in Washington?" She sipped her wine, teasing but still wanting to know.

"No one, really. What about you, how is it that some hero has not carried you off to his castle?"

"Because, as I'm sure you've heard, all the heroes are gone. Gone far away."

"Farewell, Clark Gable. Goodby, Gary Cooper."

"When I was a little girl, there were many heroes."

"Tell me about when you were a little girl." We were getting into the spirit of the thing, playing it in the right key.

"It was long, long ago and far away in Nova Scotia."

"It sounds like a song," and I sang the words back to her, and she laughed and said, "You missed your calling. You should have been a troubadour."

"I am a troubadour, Pierre Vidal by name, but I'm also the last of the heroes and all good heroes sing songs. Take Siegfried, for instance."

"This is the Saint Lawrence, not the Rhine."

And so it was, and although our point-counter-point was light and meaningless on the surface, it had its own underlying thread that began to draw us together. And when she suddenly broke off the game in mid-stride, asking quickly, "John, are you married?" I answered just as quickly, "No, my wife died five years ago."

And we sat and looked at each other, and when she spoke she didn't say the usual—*I'm sorry,* but instead, "Forgive me for asking."

"Why shouldn't you ask? I would have told you anyway." I sounded abrupt and annoyed. I stopped and tried again. "I'd like to take you dancing, but I'm wearing the wrong kind of pumps."

"It's getting late, isn't it? And we've got to think about tomorrow."

"Yes, we do." And the mood was broken, the spell gone, like coming down out of the sky with her earlier that day. "Laurie, do you know any of the flight operators here, the bush pilots?"

"Oh, yes, quite a few. The best is René Picard, if you can find him."

I had to swallow hard on that one. "The place I want to go is a lake about two hundred miles out in the brush. I'll need a plane with pontoons."

"That will be no problem. They all have them. I can make the arrangements in the morning. We'll charter one and I'll fly you to your lake."

"I appreciate that, and I'll need your help," I picked my way carefully. "But I don't want you to fly me there. I've been there, and it's very unpleasant. I want you to go back to Dorval in the morning. I'll be going out of here to Presque Isle and Washington."

She didn't answer right away, nor did she protest. She kept her eyes on her hands. "Well, let's see what we can do in the morning."

There was no way of taking a cab back to the Cartier, and I was skittery as a chipmunk until we got there. I saw her to her room which was on the floor below my own. We had not spoken since entering the lobby. "Thank you, John, for a very pleasant evening." She extended her hand, smiling, and I took it and held it.

"In this age of dead heroes and live dinosaurs," I said "I suppose I should expect to spend the night with you. I don't expect that because I'm not ready for paradise yet, but if anybody knocks on your door or attempts to storm it, for God sake, don't let them in. Call me, call the desk, call the police in any order that comes to mind, and yell bloody murder."

"You're serious, aren't you?" I liked the close intentness of her glance.

"I am. I don't know what kind of jeopardy I may have put you in by bringing you here. I pray we've been unnoticed, but that's one of the reasons I want you to leave tomorrow, without me."

And then while she was registering my latest, I kissed her. Before I became overwhelmed by the contact, I broke away and said over my shoulder, "I'll call you for breakfast at seven."

I went down the corridor and the stairs feeling her lips on mine, her body against mine, and the special scent of her like a touch of jasmine in the night.

Once in my room, I settled down, although her look and her presence were reflecting everywhere in the mirrors of my mind. "You've got eggs to lay and worms to scratch," I said, reaching for the phone book.

Captain Liam Ganin was listed, but he was not at home, I was sullenly informed by the Madame Defarge who answered.

"Can you tell me where I might find him?"

"Non," she snapped, and then added sarcastically, "I can't tell you whose bed you'll find him in. Who is this I am speaking with?"

"This is Mr. Richardson at Quebec Central. Is this Madame Ganin?"

There was a pause while she thought over the nature of the caller. "Oui." She sounded less truculent. "He went out earlier. He may be at Le Bijou. If you will leave your number, I will tell him you called."

"Is there any place else he might be beside Le Bijou?"

"Ask at Le Bijou!" she flared. "They will know where he is."

"Merci bien, Madame."

I found Le Bijou was a swinging, over-crowded waterfront night spot on the public pier. I could hear it long before I reached it, the mindless cacaphony of rocking and rolling coming up the street. The idea was that if you made a loud enough racket instead of music, eventually everyone would go deaf and it wouldn't matter anymore. Conversation, I realized, in such a spot was out of the question. But then, happily, the insensate caterwauling shuddered to a ragged climax just before I made my entrance.

The place was a box-like, low-ceilinged, dimly-lit fire trap that stank of pot and beer and sweat, noisy with trumpeting bulls just off the ships and out of the woods, their joyous, dirty, dungareed nymphets supplying a shrill soprano.

The performing quartet set the style with matted shoulder-length hair and headbands. Their glove-tight silver slacks outlined the their crotches as though the display would in some way make up for the musical talent they lacked. The bandstand was behind the bar, and a case of beer was passed up to them as they knelt and gyrated. The sight reminded me of newly-hatched birds in a nest, squeaking and sightless, their beaks perpetually open, searching, searching.

I had some searching to do of my own, and after I adjusted to the surroundings, I approached the bar by careful maneuvering and acquired my own bottle of Molson's ale. Then I began to drift with the multi-lingual tide and explore the wonderland. The thought of locating Ganin had ridden with me all day. Sam Catton had helped to solidify it, and kissing Laurie goodnight had set me off on the attempt. I fully recognized the incongruity of my action, for I had done my best to throw off the pack, to avoid recognition, and now here

I was, suddenly surfacing and openly announcing my presence to someone whom I believed might be joined with the opposition. Catton had wanted me to go public, not just to expose the whole thing but for my own self protection. I had that idea in mind but from a different point of view. What I was hoping to pull off was pure bluff. But in trying, I might learn something essential from Ganin, and he would get a message from me. On the other hand, if Ganin was no part of the thing, then nothing would be lost but some sleep and possibly my hearing—or so my reasoning went.

I had just about given up the quest when I spotted him in a corner booth with the blonde he'd had in tow at the airport. I had wondered why he would want to do his drinking in such a boiling cauldron of noise. From the way he ignored the blonde, who was talking to him, I suspected he chose the place so he wouldn't have to hear what she was saying. The number of glasses on the table and the cigarette butts in the ash tray indicated the session had been going on for sometime.

As I bore down on them through the smoke and general uproar, I caught a few of her strident words: ". . . you said you would . . . she's a bloodsucker! . . . go home. . . ."

"Well, Captain Ganin! Just the man I've been looking for!" I bellowed it forth, full of bonhomie and beer.

With heavily lipsticked mouth open, blood-shot eyes wide, and heavy blue eye-shadow, like a canopy, she looked up at me. Ganin simply glanced up.

"Do you mind if I sit down?" I said, as I sat down next to his annoyed lady. I gave her a smile that did nothing to improve our relationship. "Coincidence is the wine of life," I babbled, "although I'll settle for this now." I had a swig of my beer, toasting them. "I've been looking for you, and I wasn't going to come in here, but I flipped a coin and it came up heads. Do you ever flip coins?" I asked my unamused seat partner. "My name is John Erikson, and what's yours?" I extended my hand.

"Helen," she managed between her teeth.

"Helen! A noble name! Helen of Troy! Here's to Helen. Do you sink ships?" I had another slug of beer and noticed the empty glasses. "Hey, can I buy you a drink?"

"No! No thanks." Helen shook her wig.

"I'll have a VO-and-ginger," Ganin said, reaching for his cigarettes.

"Li, I thought we were going." Her voice rose.

"Oh, come on, Helen of Troy, the night's young," I nosed in. "How do you get a drink around here? Send up a rocket?" I had good laugh at that one.

Ganin reached over and pushed a button on the wall above the ersatz lamp. He was doing it to show her, not me.

"Li, you've got to fly tomorrow."

"So?" He raised his face and smirked at her.

"So I think we should leave."

"I'm not ready."

"Oh, you don't really want to go, Helen," I said. "Have one for the road."

She ignored me. "Li. I want to leave now!"

"Well . . . no one's stopping you." His words had a faint slur.

That tore it. She slammed her hand down on her purse, and I slid out of the booth before she could trample me. "You stupid bastard!" she swore at him as she swept out.

He sat motionless, showing no reaction. Then he set about lighting a cigarette. As I sat back down, I said, "Sorry about that. Hope my butting in didn't—ahh—interfere."

He exhaled a cloud of smoke, most of it in my face. "What the hell do you want, Erikson? Is that your name?" There was no inflection in the flatness of his voice.

I dropped the act. "Maybe I want you to do some cloud-seeding for me."

My sudden change caught him. He peered up at me. "What's that supposed to mean?"

"I would have used René Picard, but I can't find him."

That made him blink. "You won't find him. René bought the farm."

"Yeah." He was surprised that I didn't react, that I just sat staring at him. "I'd like to know who put the down payment on it," I said.

He studied his cigarette and the waiter emerged from out of the jellied consommé. "VO-and-ginger, and another Molson," I said. The waiter repeated the order in French and vanished.

I didn't say anything more and Ganin lifted his eyes up to brush mine. "What's with cloud-seeding?"

"All kinds of things. It's changed a lot since the old days in Iran.

You certainly must know that, particularly in these parts . . . up on the way to Temiscamie."

"There hasn't been any seeding around here. There isn't any need for it, and it's against the law."

I ignored his disclaimer. "And you know another way it's different since Old MacMurry's day is that it's changed color, and it's changed its purpose too."

He blinked again and knocked the ash off his cigarette. "I don't know what the hell you're talking about, Erikson."

"So I'll tell you, Ganin." Somewhere in me a fire was lit and I was beginning to burn, looking at his foxy, buttoned-up face, and thinking of René, of MacMurry, of the whole dirty thing. "I represent people who are willing to pay almost any price for some answers about the changed color and the changed purpose of some seeding that was done around here."

"You don't make sense to me." He was beginning to get ugly, as his eyes widened.

"Pale green rain, Ganin, and it doesn't matter where it starts falling. You can either talk to me, which will make you rich, or you can start talking to a flock of official investigators who are going to hit here tomorrow."

He reared up on that one. "Listen, Erikson, the one thing that bothers me more than stupid talk is stupid people trying to rig up half-assed bribes about things that don't make sense. I'm a pilot, a damn good pilot. People hire me to fly, and that's all I know, OK? Right now I fly survey for Quebec Central, and if anybody wants to talk to them about my work, they're welcome to do it. Now get off my back!"

"It won't be survey work they'll be talking to you about. If you've got any brains, you'll get out now while you're still able and before anyone else gets hurt like René and Sam Catton."

"Catton!" That hit him. "What about Catton?"

"He got shot in Montreal. He was on his way up here." I lied. "And in case, you haven't heard, MacMurry killed himself, and the RCMP knows why."

The lights went out in Ganin's eyes. He sat still for a moment, as though he was listening for something over the ragged wave of the conglomerate chorus. Then he shook his head and muttered, "I'm just a pilot."

"Yeah, and did you ever fly a Lear jet?"

I'd hit him. His head jerked up. "Erikson, get your ass out of here!" he snarled.

At the moment I was bigger than he was. I grabbed him by the front of his shirt and pulled him closer, my other hand fastening around the beer bottle.

"René Picard! Angus MacMurry, Sam Catton, Ashton Lee!" I hissed the litany of names at him through my teeth as he struggled to pull away. I let him go and his own reflexes slammed him back against the booth. Enraged, he was eager to get at me.

"Don't!" I snapped as I got up. I still had my bottle of beer in hand.

I got out of the place and back on the street with mixed feelings. I might have misjudged Ganin. Perhaps he wasn't involved, and I'd been so anxious to force something tangible out of him that I'd gone overboard. But there was no denying I'd shaken him up, and why should he be shaken if he didn't know what I was talking about? If he was in on it, he'd certainly be reporting what I'd told him. And in that way I had gone public—but to the opposition. Through Ganin, I had informed them the troops were on their way. I had hoped that by doing so, I was buying the same kind of protection going public would supposedly bring. It was a tricky move. I'd taken one helluva risk, and now I'd have to see what the reaction would be.

It was very fast in coming. There were two of them, and they must have been in Le Bijou, keeping an eye on Ganin—a possibility I had simply not considered—that, or they had managed to follow me, for all my care and cunning.

I had reached the place where the extended pier joined the wharf area proper, with the beach a long drop below. A street lay ahead, across the docks, which I could follow back to the center of town and the Cartier. On either side, the waterfront stretched away into the darkness, except for a flood-lit area which illuminated the bunkers for the ore ships. But where I was headed the lighting became sparse and there were few strollers about. In fact, I saw only the pair coming at me. They converged from opposite angles, making me the point of a V. They said nothing, nor did they need to, and I did not choose to remain a focal point.

The best that could be said for the situation was that I had not been taken by surprise, and that in spite of past injuries and recent jaw wrenchings, I was fleet of foot. Beyond that, all I had with which to defend myself was a nearly-empty bottle of beer and a mighty surge of adrenalin. I threw the bottle at the tiger moving in on my left. And although my aim was a bit high and on the outside, he knew something was coming out of the night at him, and took the time to duck and spin to the right, giving me a chance to skirt around him to the left and run for it.

His wing man saw what I had in mind and changed direction to head me off from the street. They wanted to hem in along the quay where they could run me down and finish me in private, knowing the bay would accept my remains. I recognized at once that, fast as I was, he was just as fast. I also saw the glint of a knife in his hand. And then, as I put on speed, the shuddering question was—would he throw it or wait to carve me up?

They had another advantage, if they needed one. They were on home territory, and I didn't know where the hell I was going or what lay ahead.

The thin finger of a pier jutted out on my left. Whereas the public pier had been wide as a city block and stubby, this one was long and narrow. I headed for it. I knew the tide was somewhat out, but I hoped not that far. If I could reach the water, I might have a chance of losing them in it. If not, drowning was less messy than butchery.

We pounded out on to the pier like three sprinters coming down the stretch. The finish line was two stanchion lights at the end. In the darkness beyond, I could see the lights of a ship riding at anchor —a peaceful oasis in outer space. The chase had not been all that long, but I felt as though I couldn't suck in air fast enough to put out the burning cotton in my lungs, and trying to do so only fanned the flames.

I didn't dare risk a look over my shoulder, but I could hear the man with the knife closing the distance between us, putting on that last spurt to win the race. I knew he was planning to either make a football tackle or try to see how far he could drive his knife into my back. The thought of being tackled triggered memory of the childhood trick of letting the tackler get one step from you and dropping sideways on all fours so that he would catapult over you. I didn't have to examine the idea. There weren't any others. I sensed his approach. I braked and dropped, trying to get my butt around and not to flip over on my side. His legs slammed into me, and it felt as though a battering ram had tried to break me in half. The impact knocked me sprawling crosswise, and only the pier stanchion kept me from falling off the edge. The knife man, unable to check his dash, had struck me and taken instant flight. Vaguely I heard his shout of anguish as he zoomed into the night. Perhaps he was afraid of getting wet, but at the moment I had two other interests. One was somehow to replace the air and stuffing he had knocked out of me, and the other, even more urgent, was to avoid his on-coming twin.

There was no way to get around him. As he slowed down and came at me in a crouch, I moved to roll off the pier, still anxious to seek the watery depths. My arm brushed something hard that moved also and made a clattering sound. My hand knew even before my head. The knife man had lost his weapon in our brief meeting, and I came up on to my knees with it extended before me. It felt like a claymore in my hand, and the sudden sight of its gleam and length gave my attacker pause.

I saw that he was bearded. Desperation is only a hop-step from blind rage. I took it, possibly taking in air through my skin since I didn't seem to be getting much by the normal method. I rose up and rushed him, not exactly a Bengal Lancer but eager for a pig-sticking.

He was quicker and far more experienced at mayhem than I. He side-stepped and belted me with a round-house that nearly unhinged my head and knocked me sprawling. I picked up splinters but held on to the knife, even though my skull was full of pieces of broken glass and my mouth was clogged with sulphur. Then he tried his own hop step. Only he added a leap. Why scrape your knuckles when you can stomp your man to a pulp with your logging boots? I managed to roll clear of his landing and come up on my knees again. He drop-kicked next, and I ducked and went under his leg, getting my arm around his boot, holding it on my shoulder as I put all my leverage and strength into the lift. He went down hard on his back, trying to pull his legs in either to roll free or to continue his kicking from a more horizontal position. I drove between them, coming down on him and thrusting wildly with the knife. I felt the blade go into him, and he reared convulsively with a shrill cry, throwing me off, trying to get clear. That wish was mutual. When I left him, he was in a sitting position, his hands holding his belly, the haft of the knife jutting obscenely.

I was staggering as I ran back down the pier, back down the way we'd come. I didn't give a damn what his condition was. I only knew that I was still in one piece and breathing, even if my heart was trying to pound its way out of my chest.

It wasn't until I was clear of the dock area and managing to walk in a fairly straight line that it hit me. Laurie! For Christ's sake, Laurie! If they'd known where I was, they'd know where she was! I began to run again.

The startled few who saw me go through the Cartier's lobby must have thought they'd seen a honest-to-god Wendigo. I took the three flights of stairs faster than any elevator, and then I was beating on her door, calling her name. When she opened it, I could only reach out and grab her shoulders and stare at her sleep-blurred face, shaking my head, trying to suck in enough air to say something and to stay upright.

Her reaction was different. "John! My God, what's happened to you! You're bleeding!"

I hadn't been aware of it, or if I had, there were more important things on my mind. I came into the room and shut and locked the door and looked for something heavy to put against it. "No high-boys?" I wheezed.

She turned on the overhead light and had a better look at me. "You're all torn up!" I sat down feeling weak, realizing I was shaking.

"You're all right," I gasped stupidly. "No one—no one came here?"

"No." She shook her head. "I've been asleep."

She was wearing blue pajamas, the same color as her slacks. "You must like blue."

"Are you all right?" She meant, was I nuts?

"I'm all right, if you are." I shook my head still fighting for air.

"You'd better come in the bathroom, and we'll see what we can do about your face."

"You can't do anything about it . . . it was your face I was worried about."

"Come on. I'll help you." She held out her hand.

I got up carefully, almost thinking I'd made a mistake and the knife had actually been left in *my* ribs. "God, I've been bent out of shape."

She sat me down in the bathroom and set about cleaning the cut on the side of my head. "He must have worn a ring." I winced.

My clothes were a mess. She helped me get my shirt off so we could see if I had any broken ribs, and while she was going about being efficient and nurse-like and lovely, she asked no questions, and for the moment I was grateful for that and proud of her and content to give myself up to her gentle ministrations, my breathing beginning to settle down.

I was sitting with my head lowered, feeling as though I'd had one too many, when she rested her hand on it and then ran her fingers down my neck.

"How did this all happen, John?"

She went to work kneading my neck and shoulders, loosening the tense muscles.

"Tell me, please."

"As I said, some people don't like me. A couple of them found me."

"Here! Did they come here to your room?"

"No . . . down by the waterfront. I think they were Ganin's friends. . . . if they'd known you were here, they'd have come after you. That's why you've got to leave first thing in the morning."

"I think we'd better go see the RCMP in the morning."

"Wouldn't do any good. I don't know who they were. Might recognize one by the knife in his belly. Couldn't prove anything anyway."

"Did you see Liam Ganin?"

"Humm." I didn't say anything more, absorbed in the strong suppleness of her fingers and their effect, acutely aware of her closeness. "Do you know that old song, 'The Touch of Your Hand'?"

"John, be serious. How do you know Ganin was responsible?"

"Male intuition. He had two subhumans try to kill me. I just did a better job of outrunning them." I reached up and fastened my hands around her wrists, holding her hands in place. "You're a fine nurse." I tried to look back at her, but the motion started things spinning.

She leaned over and brushed my forehead with her lips. "Let's go in the other room," she said softly.

I followed her into the bedroom, noticing there was a rip in the knee of my pants. I had brought an extra shirt but no extra pants. As I watched her move toward the door, I was aware that in pajamas and barefeet, she looked smaller, almost childlike.

174

She turned out the light and the only light was that from the bathroom. "Oh, Laurie, Laurie," I whispered, and then I had my arms around her, battered head and stoved-in ribs of no consequence. Nothing of consequence, but the close holding of her and the reciprocal feel of her arms, reaching up around my shoulders.

Sorrow is a short step from passion, and she was full of sorrow over the tragedy of her father. Loneliness is an even shorter step, and I had had five years of it laced with guilt and depression. My fear for her safety—her reaction to the sight of me—all these emotions coalesced and fused around and within whatever marvelous alchemy it was that had drawn us together.

*

In a darkened room when desire is spent, words flow easily and hidden meanings go by the boards. There is closeness and touching and the lovely gift of laughter.

"So I told him if he wouldn't let me solo I wouldn't come home. He was furious." Her laughter bubbled.

"You're a stubborn lassie. Do you know in the dark you have a Grecian nose."

"And I suppose in daylight I have a boney Highland nob?"

"No, a bonny one. I think I'll be so stiff in the morning they'll have to carry me out on a board."

"This sort of thing won't help you." And we both laughed.

"This sort of thing would cure rigor mortis." I ran my hand over the graceful curve of her breast.

"Oh, really," she said dryly.

"Laurie, I love you," I said, kissing her gently.

"Oh, John, all so fast. I think I'm bewitched. I never meant it to happen like this. I thought that things should happen more slowly."

"More genteelly, maybe." I took her face between my hands and began kissing her eyes, her nose, her lips. "I am very ungenteel, and time is ever too little and ever too fast."

"I know, I know. The formula is out of kilter." Her hands came up to my face, then dropped to my shoulders, pulling me toward her.

"I'll tell you a magic formula that can slow it down," I whispered. "One in one . . . is one."

"Oh, what a nice thought! Like celestial navigation."

Somewhere between the small hours and cock-crow, I told her

about Nan. "She never liked me leaving her, going off on trips—the Geophysical Year, that sort of thing—and I took her with me whenever I could. But when I got the assignment to go out to Vietnam on an ecology mission, it really hit her hard. She was pregnant.

"You don't have to tell me this."

"I want to tell you."

She began rubbing my back. "Confessional?"

"In a way. They say it's good for the soul. She didn't want me to go because she'd had a premonition I wouldn't come back, that I'd be killed. She was superstitious, believed in astrology, read Tarot cards. I'd always humored her about it, but I felt I couldn't let her fears stop me from doing a job which seemed important. Before I left I agreed to call her every three days. She'd go to my office, so I could also talk to Annie, my secretary, on any business matters.

"On the last flight of the assignment a SAM missile hit us and I had to bail out. I was trapped in the jungle, pretty badly hurt. I couldn't move from where I was. It was nearly a week before a helicoptor rescue team picked me up. The day I got hit was the day I was supposed to call Nan, and when I didn't, she tried to reach me. She got through to the headquarters I was operating out of and talked to a green second lieutenant. He knew I was missing, but he didn't know what to tell a guy's wife calling him from the States." It realized I was talking faster and faster.

"His boss was a Colonel Kilbourne. I guess the kid thought he'd put Nan on hold, but when he buzzed Kilbourne, by some fluke of transmission, she heard their conversation, at least enough of it. Annie was on the office extension, which is how I found out. The Lieutenant said something like, 'I've got Mrs. Erikson on the phone from the states. She wants to know about her husband. What shall I tell her?' The Colonel said, 'Well, don't tell her he's dead.'

"That was all Nan had to hear. She passed out, and when Annie got her on her feet again, she insisted on leaving, even though Annie wanted to drive her home. Naturally, she was in a state of shock. She didn't know what she was doing, even where she was, I guess. She walked out of the Press Building, right out on to 14th Street. There was a bus coming. He couldn't stop in time."

My mouth felt dry. Her hand on my back had stopped moving. Neither of us spoke for a while.

"When did you learn about it?" Her voice was so quiet I almost didn't get the words.

"In the hospital at Da Nang. I was there a long time."

"And I suppose you blamed yourself for it."

"I suppose I did. I was to blame."

"Not really, John. You must know better. No one is to blame for something like that. Things build up and happen. We can't see them coming. You can't control the workings of a cruel fate."

"I could have stayed home, and I didn't really need to take that last flight. The Colonel tried to talk me out of it."

"That's silly. It was your job."

"Not that important."

She was silent for a moment, and then she said coldly. "What do you want me to do, help you nurse your self-pity?"

That went in deep. "No . . . I just wanted you to know."

"All right, I know. I'm sorry for your tragedy, it's terribly sad, and your loss must have been shattering. But if we're going to have any future, John, that's not going to be a part of it." She was sitting up.

I rolled over and saw the upper half of her body in silhouette. I reached out. "Laurie, loving you is something new. Forgive me if I'm clumsy. I've been trying to get rid of the past for a long time."

She sighed and then leaned down and whispered into my lips, "I'll help you get rid of it."

At some point we fell asleep, and when we awoke it was not only to discover the pleasant shock of being in the same bed without the cover of darkness, but also that it was later than it should have been.

I sat up with care. "We've got to get going."

"I'm bashful," she said, pulling the sheet up to her chin.

"My head feels like a pumpkin and my body like the rusty Tin Woodsman. How do I look?"

"Shaggy and fierce."

"You look too good, so I'll close my eyes and you listen and take it all down."

"Yes, sir."

I remained sitting. "Even with last night, I think the odds are that no one knows we're here at this place even if they know I'm in Sept Iles. Can you contact one of your charter friends? Tell him I want to go fishing. He'll have to supply the equipment and the ice chest.

I have a special lake I know, where the walleye are bigger than in the Moisie. I'll want to charter him just for the day. If he can, he's to pick me up here in an hour. And my name is Mr. Scott. Got that?"

"I'll try Jacques Fortin. But I want to know something else." She was looking up at me, grinning.

"What's that?"

"How are you going to get out of bed without any clothes on?"

"Easily," I said and got out of bed.

She let out a shriek of laughter and hid her eyes.

As soon as I reached my room I called her. She answered sounding wary, on guard. "I love you," I said. "I'll order us some breakfast to be sent up to your room in twenty minutes. Okay?"

"Okay. But don't call me again and frighten me like that. And one other thing." She sounding very direct and like a woman liberated.

"What's that?"

"I love you, too, and I've already ordered breakfast."

While my cheek and the side of my head didn't look to grotesque, most of my body ached, and any sudden turn brought the knife man to mind with a vengeance. I hoped that he had gone out with the tide and that his partner was still trying to separate himself from his knife. Although during the night the world had become a different place for me, I knew the realities of yesterday had not changed one wit, and while delicious thoughts of Laurie ran through me like quicksilver and visions of her clouded my mirror as I attempted to shave, I had to keep my mind not on love but on madness, not on life but the threat to it. I must move swiftly, and Laurie and I must part almost at the moment of our joining. "Hard lines, John O' Gaunt," I said to my sunken-eyed visage, which appeared in the mirror longer in the tooth and lopsided of head.

Outside, I could hear the church bells summoning the faithful. Inside, my stomach was summoning me to breakfast.

She looked fresh and rested—something I could not say for myself. I kissed her again. "You look better with a shave. Don't ever grow a beard, please."

"I did in Nepal. The girls in Katmandu thought it was very attractive."

"I am not from Katmandu."

"Amen to that. Did you have any luck?"

"We'll have to take a cab. Jacques couldn't send a car, but he's perfectly happy to charter out a plane. A hundred dollars for the day, and that includes gas and fishing equipment."

"Good. What did you tell him about the location of my lake?"

"Just a lake you are anxious to fish. He'll be waiting for us at the yacht club. I said we'd be there by eight."

"Doesn't he operate out of the field?"

"Yes, but he also operates out of the yacht basin, and that's where he wants to meet us."

"Well, good. I won't have to show my face at the field."

"I thought it would be better. That's why I suggested it."

"I'm glad I found you, but where's breakfast?"

There was a knock on the door, and we both laughed. "Voilá!" she said.

Even though it was all light and sparkling, and I was blinded by her witchery, I opened the door with care. The waiter looked amused.

At breakfast we made no mention of our coming separation, but once in the cab, riding through the quiet early Sunday morning streets, where indeed the faithful were driving, pedaling and walking to church, I brought it up. "Laurie, when you leave me, please go directly to your plane. Check it over very carefully. Give it a very thorough pre-flight."

"You think someone might tamper with it?" She wasn't taking it very seriously.

"Believe me, I do. I know. It's already been done."

That surprised her. "Really? Where was it done?"

"There's no need to go into it. Just humor me, and do as I say." She gave me a salute, and I grabbed her hand and held it. "Soon as I'm back from my fishing, I'll call you in Dorval. Then we'll both know we're all right."

"There's a great deal you haven't told me about all this, isn't there?"

"There's a great deal I don't know about it myself."

"No, I mean that you do know." She turned to me. "Like, who you represent in Washington—"

"Myself. Just myself."

"Or why you are going there instead of Ottawa—or to the police right here."

"Two reasons—time and confusion. I'm afraid that whatever was done—may be done very soon again. I don't know that for sure. I only suspect it because the thing was done in the first place and what has happened since. My original evidence disappeared, I didn't tell you that, but that's the reason for going after more."

"And when you get your evidence, you're taking it back to Washington."

"Yes, and I'll call you from there, too."

"John, wouldn't it make better sense if I flew you to Washington?"

"Under the circumstances, no. It shouldn't be too long before I'll be knocking on your door again."

"I'd rather be your pilot."

The cab driver was watching us in his rearview mirror, grinning. A romantic, no doubt. Jacques Fortin was grinning as he kissed Laurie on both cheeks. He was round of face and round of belly, bald with a commanding dagger-point mustache and alert, shoe-button eyes. His grip was powerful. "Mademoiselle Laurie says you have come for *le pêche*, and the Moisie won't do." He had a resonant voice and his accent reminded me of René's.

"I know a place," I said.

"Ahh, oui, oui, everyone knows a place. Well, there is the plane. She is all yours. Come and have a look."

The yacht club had a private channel to the river and its own harbor, cluttered with various-size sail- and power-boats. Fortin had met us at the rear of the club proper, and now we looked down a ramp to a floating dock. Moored to one side of it was an aircraft with a high, red wing, and a sky-blue fuselage and tail. At the end of the dock was a dory with an outboard motor. There were three men in it, two passengers and a man on the motor. Anchored a short distance out in the harbor was a larger plane, an amphibian, and I wondered which aircraft Fortin was referring to.

We walked down the ramp in the bright sunlight, the breeze wrinkling the water and making the dock creak and the moored aircraft bob. A man dressed in cover-alls was on the dock, holding a wing strut, keeping the plane from banging against the siding. I thought he must be the pilot. Fortin chatted with Laurie in French as we descended, and I brought up the rear, thinking he had some nerve moving in on my girl.

"Is the plane an amphibian?" I called to him, seeing pontoons but no wheels.

"Oui! Oui! But of course," he called over his shoulder, and then he said something to Laurie in French and they both laughed.

We reached the dock, and I saw that the plane was a single-engine, four-place type, not anywhere the size of Laurie's Baron or even René's Beaver. I hoped it would get me there and back if this was the one we were taking, but the men in the outboard kept looking at us as though waiting for us. I still wondered which aircraft was Fortin's and what these other people had to do with it.

"You bring the camera to take pictures of what you catch, no?" Fortin joked.

"Always," I said. "Then there can be no fish-stories."

"Ahh, but what is better than a good fish-story, M'sieur?"

"Why, a good *fish*, M'sieur!" We all laughed, Fortin clapping his belly. "Bon! Bon! A good fish. I hope you will catch many of them. And now if you will pardon me, M'sieur Scott, I too must fly."

He extended his hand. "You may pay me through Mademoiselle Laurie when you return. A pleasure, M'sieur. Bon chance, bon pêche, à bientôt."

Stupidly I shook hands with him, watching him kiss Laurie and cross the dock to the waiting boat.

The crewman gave him a hand as he stepped aboard, then revved up the engine, accelerating fast, heading for the larger amphibian.

I turned around, knowing how well I'd been had. At the time her seeming acquiescence to return to Dorval empty-handed, so to speak, had struck me as being out of character. Now, I was too angry to speak.

She saw the look on my face. Her voice was very quiet. "It was the only way. He couldn't take you."

"Neither can you. Is this man a pilot?" I moved toward him. He smiled and nodded his head, gesturing for us both to climb on board. "Etes-vous un aviateur?"

"Ahh, non, M'sieur. Je suis le mécanicien. Mademoiselle, elle est une aviatrix, oui?"

"There's really no one else, John."

"Then I'll have to wait until there is, or go looking for someone." I refused to look at her.

"Darling, I know you're angry, but you're being silly, I—"

"What I'm being is sick!"

She came to me and linked her arm through mine, standing beside me. "Why the hell couldn't you have been willing to do it my way?" I said, fighting to keep my voice lowered.

"I suppose there are two reasons. I've fallen in love with you. I don't know how or why. It doesn't matter. But I do know that the things that are important we have to do together. The other reason is Dad. I have a stake in whatever you're doing or trying to do because of him. I don't want anything more to hurt his name. Try to understand that. I knew this would upset you, but if you want me, then you have to accept me and the things I can do. I'm good at flying anywhere." She laid her head on my shoulder.

Her soft words ate holes in me. "Laurie, Laurie," I sighed. "I understand, but you don't. You mentioned René Picard." I brought her around facing me, my hands on her shoulders, the breeze flagging wisps of her hair. "René's dead! Someone put a bomb in his plane." I felt her body jerk as though I'd hit her. "The attempt on me last night was the fifth or maybe the sixth since Thursday. That doesn't speak well for their killing average, but they'll go on trying. They could be planning to try next at the lake."

"I don't understand about René Picard."

"It was he who first asked me to come here. He saw the rain come down. It was green, it killed everything it touched. I think someone got hold of the Weathermaker and added a toxic substance—God knows what, but I'm trying to get specimens for laboratory testing so we'll know what! René saw a test. At least, that's what I think it was—a test. He took me to the site. It's the kind of hell I wouldn't want you to see, even if there weren't the other dangers. Now do you understand?"

"You have to go there again. And you said time was very important."

"Yes, but now it's been lost. I don't know how much."

"Doing things together means sharing whatever risk is involved."

"That's bird music!" My voice rose.

She lifted her head. "If this thing is so horrible, aren't you overlooking that it's your duty to use the time you have and the means at hand to do whatever you came here to do?" She stood away from me. "I'm going to get in the plane. I hope you'll get in, too."

I saw the outboard coming back from the amphibian, saw the big plane's engines starting. I watched the mechanic giving Laurie a hand into the cockpit. For all my words and protests, for all the emotions that were tearing at me, I knew I had no choice.

*

The yacht club lay a few kilometers northwest of Sept Iles, and when Laurie made her take-off, she turned out over the bay and then turned again, parallel with the city. I had not spoken to her since boarding the plane, and as she was climbing the aircraft, and I couldn't see just where we were headed. I said, "Fly over to the airport."

She turned her head. "John, there is no one there available. It's a holiday."

"Do as I say," I snapped, and then, "Are you required to file a flight plan?"

"I don't have to, but—"

"Then don't. Are there any maps in this plane?" The only thing I'd seen so far that had given me any kind of reassurance was a 30-30 in a rack on the bulkhead over the passenger seat behind us. I thanked God that a rifle was standard equipment in any bush pilot's plane. On the seat were a tackle box and several rod cases, on the floor an ice chest for the fish. But no maps.

"See if there's a pocket in the door behind you." She was making her own search as she flew.

There was a pocket, and there were maps.

She had leveled off, and I could see the field directly ahead. "Do we go up the Moisie?" she asked.

"No. We go over Lac des Rapides, then the Sainte Margurite, then the rail line. I remember the gyro heading René was on when we left Rapides was three hundred degrees. We went over a landing strip there." I got the proper chart folded on my knees and tried to recall the course René had marked on his.

"Didn't you say Temiscamie?"

"Yes, but it's not in a direct line." One thing I saw in our favor was the visibility. We were in the midst of a Canadian high, and we could see a long way toward forever. She circled the field, and I tried to get oriented. "All right, head for the lake. If you cross it, going over the island at the lower end you'll be on course. I think that's the way we went." Oh, how I wished I'd paid more attention to the way we went.

"Stay at about this altitude. How fast are we flying?"

"Our air-speed is one-four-five. Do you remember anything about the wind? It's our ground-speed that's important."

"No, I don't. What kind of a wind do we have now?" I was all business and not friendly.

"I'll contact the tower."

While she did so, I studied the map, hoping I could spot Poitrine, and if not it, something I could identify beyond the rail line. I did recall there had been a long thin snaking river off my wing. I found it, and showed it to her.

We had a twenty-knot wind about due west, and she made a course correction to compensate. I sat with my head lowered, trying to summon up René pointing out spots we had landed at in the winter. I could hear the sound of his voice, but I didn't get much of what he said: a large swamp area, and a cluster of lakes that formed a rough diamond. I marked the sites.

"How long a flight was it?"

"About an hour and a half I think, not much more than that." I checked my watch. "Every fifteen minutes I want you to do a complete circle, a three-hundred-and-sixty-degree turn. I want to know if we're being followed or watched."

"I have a mirror right here."

"Do as I say! " I flared angrily. I was more furious with myself than I was at her for having mouse-trapped me. The one thing above all that I had wanted to avoid was to endanger her, but beyond everything else, I knew that it was not so much her fault as mine that she, and not Fortin, was beside me now. While I seethed with worries, the fear grew that I might not be able to find René's lake. So much below had looked the same before. It looked even more so now. I made a note of the time on the map. "Is this where we are?"

She glanced at the chart and nodded. "All right, I'd like that turn now." I might be riding co-pilot but I was running this show, and it was best she should find out now what an ugly bastard I could be. I knew she was smoldering, her manner had become withdrawn and aloof.

She made the turn and we had a nice circular look at the empty blue sky. With the visibility, it was possible to spot the few check points I was able to remember long before we reached them.

But once we put the swamp land and the diamond cluster behind us, there was absolutely nothing for me to get a ground-fix on—ahead and off the wing lay the self-same scene of forested plateaus, ravines, groups of scattered lakes, many with thread-thin tributaries—like tadpoles in the spring. And all, suddenly, had the shape of Poitrine. *Oh, René, René, to have you here now!*

When it came time to make our fourth sky-sweep, we were an hour and ten minutes from our departure point over the airport, and I was trying to figure what that meant in relationship to the Beaver which I was sure had a faster air-speed. "Can you determine if there has been a wind-change?"

"Yes. No change."

"How much difference will it make in the respective air-speed of this plane and René's Beaver?"

"Very little." She offered no explanation why.

"Okay, if and when we find the lake, this is how we're going to operate," I said, deciding it wasn't too soon to have a clear understanding of the procedure I wanted to follow. "I don't want to anchor. There's rock ledge I can get off on from the pontoon. I don't expect to take any more than fifteen minutes to do my job. Once you drop me off, I want you to stay out in the middle of the lake, and if anything happens to me you'll take the hell off and go get *your* Mounties. The smell is so sickening that you'll want to tie a handkerchief over your face." I said it, wishing I'd thought to bring a jug of life-restoring McElroy's. "There is something in the after-effect of the poison that makes you sick and thirsty, so if there's anything to drink in this plane, have it ready. When I signal you, come in and pick me up."

She made no response, seeming to be occupied with peering straight ahead, her Polaroids giving her an added touch of remoteness. I was about to repeat my question when she said, "What about the surface of the lake—are there apt to be snags and logs?"

"René landed there twice. He didn't want to get in too close to the ledge for that reason. We anchored out and used a rubber dingy. As a matter of fact, we left it there. Maybe it's still usable. If it is, I'll try and use it, but I saw no logs sticking up in close, and this plane is much lighter than a Beaver, isn't it?"

"Yes." She was still intent on peering ahead.

I tensed. "What do you see, another plane?"

"No. Smoke."

Her eyes were better than mine and more accustomed to recognizing objects from the air. All I saw was a faint, whitish smudge on the horizon. "I'm afraid it's not a landmark I recognize. In fact, I'm not sure I see it."

"You will."

How right she was. In another ten minutes the smudge appeared to be a cigar-shaped cloud close to the ground. Then it changed very swiftly, extending upward in a ragged fan, dirtying the blue, and outward to cover a wide swath. Soon it transformed itself into a roiling black and white curtain with an irregular base of flame. Its advance was not directly in line with our course but off to the right, wind-driven and moving in an expanding arc. Behind its path lay a broad reach of devastation, blackened and smoking. By chance, the fire had led us to René's lake.

"How did it start way out here?" I said, searching the sky. "It's past our time to circle."

"Lightning," she said, beginning the turn. "It happens frequently this time of year. Usually it's the rain that puts it out."

"I remember your father saying he had put out fires like this."

"He did. I was doing the flying."

"No rain today anyway."

"Don't be too sure of that." We completed the turn and began passing a portion of the burned out area. The fire had husked the trees, leaving them blackened stalks, and had consumed the underbrush, leaving nothing but skeletal remains. Bodies of water stood out amidst the desolation. Some of them because smoke continued to rise around their boundaries, and one of them because it was shaped like a woman's breast.

"Oh, the bastards!"

"What's the matter?"

"The lake is over there." I shook my fist at it, "And this goddam fire wasn't set by lightning!"

Behind her glasses she was looking puzzled. "Can you think of any better way to destroy evidence than to burn it!" I shouted.

Laurie circled the lake while I sat numbly studying the woodland wreckage below. The fire had been started to the southwest of the lake and had moved in a line to burn everything on either side of it.

Outside the fire area, I sought for an indication that some of the originally-contaminated terrain had been missed by the blaze, but I saw none of the previous discoloration. From where I sat, it appeared that just as nothing had survived the fall of the killing rain, nothing had escaped the funeral fire, nothing but the lake and possibly its outflow and adjacent thin streams and rock formations.

"It looks like we may have trouble landing. The water is full of debris," she said. "I'm going down to have a look."

She brought the plane in over the blackened trees and flew the length of Poitrine, and we peared down to see how badly cluttered-up the surface was. We made three low passes, but I saw no sign of René's yellow dingy. "Most of the stuff seems to be in along the shore," I said.

"All we need is one log in the wrong place." She leveled the plane off.

"Let's think about this for a minute. If we were to hit that log, what kind of a spot would that put us in? No one knows where we are, and where we are is in the geographic center of nowhere."

"We have the radio. We could certainly be in contact."

"Providing we weren't too badly damaged and the radio was still working."

"Suppose you were alone, John, and you were doing the flying. Would you land?"

I thought that one over and knew what the answer was. "But I'm not alone."

"You'll have to make the decision." She gave me a wisp of a smile. "Don't you think it's been too long a flight not to try something?"

"It seems risking your neck has become a habit of mine. . . . What can I do to help?"

"Say a prayer, and if you see anything in our way, holler in that big strong voice of yours. I'm sure I'll understand." If she was worried about the prospect of our landing, her anxiety was well in hand, and I had the impression she was enjoying herself.

She brought the plane in at slow speed, trimmed nose-high, set-tling into the bowl of the lake, adjusting the flaps as she descended. I had my face pressed against the side window and just as I thought we had it made, I caught the sheen of a wet log dead-ahead. Before I could shout a warning, she had slammed the throttle to the stop, and for an exceedingly long instant it was a battle between lift and drag. I think one pontoon made brief contact before lift won the battle through her sensitive control of the plane.

Before we made a second try, she flew another low pass. "I'll try landing closer to the center this time," was her only comment. And this time we got down all right, splashing in, almost tail-first, slowing fast and no snags ahead.

My sigh was a good imitation of a ruptured balloon. "You get a big A-plus for that, Madam Captain. The ledge I spoke about is over that way. Would it help if I got out on a pontoon?"

"I think if you open your window and keep your head out on your side, and I do the same on mine, we'll be fine."

I had my head out the window, the propeller blast not aiding my search for obstacles, when it struck me that the stench I had anticipated was gone. The only smell was that of smoke, burned wood and pitch. Fire cleanses all. It was one thing to be thankful for, but it occurred to me that it might take a lot longer than fifteen minutes to get what I had come for, if I was able to get anything at all.

I felt her tapping my arm and I pulled my head in. "Down the lake a way from your ledge there seems to be a natural beach. The water's probably shallow there. It's full of branches, but maybe it would be an easier place to drop you, and you could wade in."

"We'll have a look. But there's been a change of plans. I can't leave you sitting out here for a couple of hours, dodging logs and wasting gas." I shoved back my seat. "I want to see what your pal Jacques has in this plane. There must be a mooring line."

There was, and under the lift-up seat, a twenty-pound anchor. Laurie was right, the gravel beach she had spotted did have a shallow shelf. While she maneuvered in close, I eased out the door on to the pontoon and made one end of the line fast to its forward strut. Then, at her signal, I dropped the anchor. She cut the switch and the plane drifted around tail to the shore, its nose into the breeze. I went off the pontoon into liquid ice up to my waist. It was nothing to stand around in getting used to. I lugged in the fish chest and the loaded rifle. It had a full magazine. Laurie was climbing down on to the pontoon when I returned. "Come on, I'll carry you." I was anxious for the opportunity.

"Sure you won't drown me?" She had taken off her glasses, and I liked that better.

"Not this trip." I held out my arms and she slid into them with care. When we reached the beach I set her down but held on to her, and we stood by the water's edge in the midst of desecrated woodland breathing the acrid smell of all that had been consumed, holding each other and not saying anything. There was something Dantesque in the setting—what it had been—what it had become. The aircraft was a brightly-colored incongruity in a land of the dead.

"Do you think the plane will be all right there?"

"As long as the wind doesn't pick up, or shift."

"I'll want you to stay close by." We were speaking very quietly.

"Is there something I can do to help?"

"Yes. This lake was full of dead fish. The rain killed them all. The fish net is in the chest. If you walk along the edge here, you might possibly find a couple, although they seemed to have disappeared, washed away through the outflow. I'll be checking that. If you find anything, don't touch it. Use the net and put your find in the chest."

"Where will you be?" She pulled her head back and looked up at me.

"Not far away. I saw some streams, and fire doesn't burn rock. There are plenty of ledges about. There may be something recoverable on them. If you hear, see or smell anything that doesn't look right, call at the top of your lungs."

"Nothing looks right here." She was gazing past me at the no-man's land.

"Believe me, bad as this is, the view is much better than it was. I'll be as quick as I can." I kissed her on the forehead, slung the rifle on my shoulder, and moved away into the carpeting of ashes.

It didn't take long to realize that the pickings were going to be slim. As to fauna, I knew they were probably non-existent. There had been normal rain here since René and I had made our visit, which would have had a cleansing effect. On top of that, the heat of the fire seemed to have consumed all vegetation. The rain-slaughtered animal life had been cremated, but my hope was to find a spot or two that the flames had missed. I carried a fish bucket to put my specimens in, and a hunting knife to keep my hands from making contact with my finds—animal or plant. Thus circumstances led me away, and on a longer hunt than I had intended.

It was a wretched hunt. While on the one hand my worries concerning Laurie's safety were less for the moment, it was a bitter anti-climax to return to the center point of the entire affair, only to find myself in check. I tried not to think about it as I moved through a limbo where the silence was almost as complete as it had been when everything in it lay newly dead. The ground was still warm underfoot. The breeze stirred up ash, twisting it now and again into whirlpools. I coughed and spit frequently, felt a growing thirst—normal enough under the circumstances, not like last time, I told myself. Intermittently, the silence was punctuated with the harsh snapping of limbs breaking free and thudding into the ground, sending up flurries of sparks. At one point I saw the hulk of what once had been a magnificent spruce come crashing down.

I traveled with care, following a stream bed. Then I moved up on to a ridge line so I could see on both sides of it and at the same time keep the lake in sight. I came on a large outcropping of granite, and I squatted down to rest and examine its surface for lichens. Off to my right I could glimpse a portion of the lake, but not the plane or Laurie. My thoughts were an unpleasant stew of present realities and the eerie feeling that what lay about me was a look into the future.

In spite of personal loss, until recently I had hewed to that not always defensible belief, that man, for all his failings and madness, was unique enough in his creativity and tough enough in his spirit and determination to survive. Angus MacMurry had been an example. I would always remember him in the airport terminal at Mehrabad, crying out: "What I have to say is—yes, to the world where there is too much bloody no!" The "no" had overtaken him. Perhaps it had overtaken us all. Something essential had become warped—lost in the technological wasteland of our age. I did not want us to go back to the cave or deny ourselves the benefits of mechanical genius. But in accomplishing the instantaneous compression of time and space, had we not broken some law of the universe? And at the cost of what? Was I perched here, examining a scene from our coming dissolution? The sense of pessimism that gripped me was stimulated by my surroundings and what had led me to them, but I knew that more and more I had begun to doubt the survivability of man. We had found too many ways to assure our own destruction, and we seemed eager to try them.

Something alien brushed my eyesight, obliterating my musings. By reflex, the rifle sling came off my shoulder. I am not a hunter of game, but I knew the workings of a gun. Below me I had caught a flash of movement in the screen of tree stalks. There was no repeat. I remained motionless trying to replay in my mind what I had seen, seeking identification. The best I could reconstruct was that there had been a brighter color amidst the grey and black of the scene. A shirt? I was startled and shaken by the possibility that those who had set the fire might still be in the area. If so, they would have heard us and seen us coming down to land in the lake.

I rose and headed off on an angle, rifle in one hand, fish bucket, with its pitiful collection, in the other. As soon as I was off the incline, I began to run. I tried to keep an eye on the area where I had seen movement and at the same time avoid tripping and going down in the mess of downed wood. The stiffness in my body was nothing, but the pain under my ribs was worse than the ache in my head, and I was forced to run half-bent-over. I was suddenly desperate to catch a glimpse of Laurie, and I knew that in my hunt I had traveled farther from the lake than I had planned.

I caught a glimpse of the plane first, its red wing, then the beach. But not Laurie. I forced myself not to call her name. I put on more speed, tripped over a log, and with the butt of the rifle managed to break my fall. The bad thing was that even with the fire's devastation, it was not easy to see any distance, and it wasn't until I was practically on the beach that I had a clear view of it. The fish chest was there, but Laurie wasn't.

And now it didn't matter who heard me. I shouted her name, an animal cry echoing in the awful silence. There was movement to my right and I swung with the rifle up, finger on the trigger. Laurie had risen from behind a rock, and as I stood frozen, a mixture of enormous relief mixed with the horror of having almost shot her, she raised her hand to her mouth and shook her head. I went to her, blood pounding in my temples, my breath coming in gasps.

She spoke softly. "John, I saw something on the other side of the lake." I spun around. "No, they're gone."

"They?"

"I think there were two of them, it's hard to tell. I'm not even sure I wasn't imagining. The light is funny over there. I thought I'd better stay out of sight until you came."

"How long ago?"

"It seemed terribly long—about fifteen minutes."

It had taken me about that time to make my return, so what I had seen had to have been something or someone else. I didn't believe four-legged animals would come into the area unless driven by the fire, and the fire would be driving game in the other direction. "I think it's time we got out of here. Find any fish?"

"Yes, they're in the chest."

"All right, I'll carry you out."

"No, I'll wade. The wind is starting to pick up, it could shift." She was in as much a hurry to leave as I was. For the first time I noticed that our pure-blue sky had been spoiled and was now over-run with a white brush of mare's-tails. Circus clouds meant winds high-up, and winds high-up meant changing weather.

We carried everything out and got it on board in one trip, a sense of urgency pushing at us. Empty of everything, the land bore an evil stamp. With unknown creatures creeping around in the ashes, the feel of danger was as tangible and pervasive as the smell of smoke.

I had hefted Laurie up into the cabin, when I saw movement down at the point of the lake's outlet. The distance was too far to make out details, but I was sure it must be a man, or possibly two. I mentally put myself back on the rock outcropping at the top of the ridge line and figured in what Laurie had seen and what I had first seen, and it added up to the possibility that three or more men had come over the low hills from the area where the fire had originally been set, and they were now moving in on us.

"Laurie," I said, "get that engine started. We'll owe Fortin a line and an anchor." As soon as she had the propeller turning, I untied the rope on the pontoon strut, and then I hauled myself into the cabin, muttering and cursing at the pain and effort.

"Nothing like flying in a goldfish bowl," I observed, slamming the door shut. The water sloshed off me as I maneuvered into my seat.

"We may drown before we fly," she said, busy with the aircraft. "You watch on your side. I'm afraid we'll only have one chance at this."

"Well, when you make it, don't take off from down at that end." I pointed. I brought the rifle around and rested it with the stock at my feet.

"To take off into the wind, I have to. It's too dangerous to try a down-wind."

"What about angling it cross-wind right from here?"

"I don't think we'd clear that ridge. I won't go all the way down to the outlet. I can start my run right about there," she indicated.

"You're the pilot." I had the window all the way open and I thrust the barrel of the rifle out, watching for obstruction in the water, watching for trouble on the land and hoping that if we were under observation, the sight of the gun might check intentions.

The surface of the lake had become curled, showing caps of white, and the sun scattered patches of gold dust on the surface. Laurie had to keep on a fair degree of power to maintain control. Twice we felt the pontoons come in brief contact with logs. Then she brought the plane around into the wind, her eyes checking the instrument panel. I pulled in the rifle and closed my window, "Good luck, chum," I intoned. She nodded, intent on her work. Her hand eased the throttle forward against the stop, sound and acceleration flowing out of the motion. Then it was up to her and the Lord God Almighty.

I didn't really know anything about flying skill, but I felt in my bones she must have done a superb job. She had the plane off the water and free of danger in a surprisingly short distance. But only *just*, and then we seemed to be hanging in that position as the propeller chewed at the air and she did a balancing act on the thin edge of flight. I saw that we were not gaining altitude, but the rim of the land and its graveyard of trees was. She brought down the nose, held it steady for an instant, and when she raised it again I had the feeling that we weren't so much going over what lay ahead of us as through it.

She didn't look at me until we had five hundred feet and were still climbing. There was a cagey glint in her eye. "I wouldn't want to try that every day . . . and with wet pants." She shifted from side to side.

"You made it seem like a joy-ride, Captain." I patted her arm. "Now I'd like to go back over the place and see what we can see from here."

We circled Poitrine at a thousand feet and saw nothing moving about under us that indicated either persons unknown or straying wildlife. It was possible that anyone down there could conceal himself, although why anyone would bother to do so was another question. After ten minutes of circling and getting dizzy, I said, "I think maybe we were spooked. We were seeing ghosts. But I'd like to add one other thing, Captain MacMurry. I'll fly with you anytime—anywhere."

"Changed your tune, hey? Can we go to Nepal and Katmandu?"

"I'll take you where the Himalayas and the Karakorums grow, but right now you take us back to Sept Iles." We were both feeling an enormous sense of relief in spite of the little my search had produced. I was amazed to see it was close to noon.

Ten minutes later, and we were nearly dead. Without any warning, I realized I was beginning to feel ill. It started with a numb ache in my chest, which spread downward. I couldn't breathe properly. My throat was becoming clogged and the same awful thirst which I had experienced with René took hold again.

Laurie turned to me, her eyes wide and glazed with bewilderment and pain. Her complexion was paper-white. Perspiration flecked the area above her lip. Her mouth was partly open and she was panting. "John, I feel awful . . . can't breathe!"

I needed no doctor's diagnosis. The smoked air we had been inhaling had been impregnated with whatever had come down in the killing rain. "Get your window open!" I gasped, hauling my own back. A storm of air rushed in, buffeting around us. It didn't appear to help. I couldn't seem to get any of it in my lungs. I could feel my heart trying to pound its way out of my chest. I was suffocating, while a knife was tearing my interior apart.

"John . . . got to land!" I was aware that we were in a dive, that Laurie had her head back, her mouth open, both her hands gripping the wheel. Through the windshield I saw rich, green forest and a narrow stretch of water rushing up at us. Her hand clawed back on the throttle, the nose rose sharply, cutting off the view of the trees. She slewed the plane into a shuddering side-slip, and we went skidding down the sky sideways. I saw we were going to crash into the trees or the water that had suddenly appeared again. Then she snapped the wings level, checked the rapid descent and we hit the water upright with a great jarring splash. Before it all faded out, I saw her face distorted in pain, her head swinging about wildly, as though she were trying to escape.

Out of the cradle endlessly rocking. The line came from nowhere and I kept repeating it. Endlessly rocking, and something cool and wet on the forehead to hold down the ache and the wonderful spice of pure northern air, going deep, deep into the lungs, putting out the fire, cleaning out the smoke. Inhale, inhale.

I opened my eyes, saw her crouched beside me, head bowed as though in prayer. My orientation was swift. I was half-lying on the back seat of the plane and Laurie was kneeling on the floor. The plane was rocking gently. "Hey," I said. It came out as a croak.

Her head shot up, "Oh, John, thank God!" She looked careworn, her face puffy, her eyes unguarded and distraught.

She laid her head on my chest and I put my arms around her, stroking her head, trying to put all the pieces back together. "Are you all right?"

She raised her head, brushing tears from her eyes. "What about you?"

"I'm not going to run up any mountains for a while. How did you ever get me out of that seat?"

"It's a long story, John Erikson," she said, and before she could say anything else, I took her face between my hands and kissed her. It was a while until she was able to tell me what had happened.

After landing, she had had the presence of mind to cut the switch. Then she, too, had lost consciousness. But her activity at Poitrine had been much less vigorous than my own, and the effect of what we had ingested was far less severe on her. At some point she had recovered to find that the plane had drifted down the pencil-thin lake, coming to rest in a mass of reeds. Bobbing about in them it had apparently suffered no damage. She hadn't felt strong enough or able enough to do anything but try to bring me back into the picture, and the effort had left her physically and emotionally exhausted. Both of us were extremely weak although the symptoms that had downed us were fading.

"What was it, John? What happened?"

I told her what I thought had happened. "Evidently, we have survived with no serious effects. Other than weakness and thirst, I think I'm all right." I sat up and grabbed my head as everything swung round to the left. "Spoke too soon," I groaned. I opened my eyes carefully and the result was bearable. "I can see you," I sighed, "so I must be okay, just take the pneumatic drill out of my head."

"You know another thing, we haven't had anything to eat since breakfast. I think maybe we're suffering from starvation," she took the wet cloth that had dropped from my head into my lap.

"Thoughtless of Fortin not to pack us a lunch, but I think I know something that might be in order in the place of food. Let's go skinny-dipping, and all the water I don't drink you can swim in."

The thought gave her pause, then brightened her. "Why not? But it will be terribly cold."

"Might shock some life back into us." It did, and she was right. The water had that white-cold burning quality that either kills or cures. As we thrashed about, I realized the cure would have to be brief. A great deal of time had gone by since she managed to flutter us down from the sky like a stricken bird. The sky, too, had changed its happy look. The circus had given way to a high covering of stratus, and under it, fat-bellied and dark with rain, a lower cloud-deck was starting to move in.

A chill rode on the gusting breeze, and the light was going by the time I managed to jockey the plane out of the reeds and swing the nose enough so that Laurie could get the propeller turning without chopping up a cord of pine boughs. She at least had been able to change to dry slacks, which she carried in her bag, while all I had was shorts from the Bolex case. I was sitting on the back seat, putting them on when she taxied out into the center of our lake and had us airborne even before I could haul on my damp corduroys. I felt weak, ravenous but alive. "How do you feel, Captain?" I said climbing into my seat.

"It's been a very long day, sir."

*

The change of weather in our return to Sept Iles reminded me of the earlier return I'd made with René; it was about the same time of day, too. As we came over the field in a greyish light, Laurie was a bit puzzled because the tower had instructed her to land heading westerly on runway 28, when the wind was right down 24. When she made the point, she was informed that 24 was temporarily closed to all traffic. I wasn't that interested on which runway we landed, just so long as we put a gentle end to the flight. I was now feeling like an Indian fakir who had been rubbed over his bed of nails the wrong way, and I suspected my pilot's condition wasn't much better. I had considered our next move, but I wanted to wait until there was solid ground under our feet and some food inside before I got to that. What I had in mind was the U.S. Air Force Base at Presque Isle, Maine, not just to safekeep possible specimens but also to do a thorough check on us.

"There's something wrong down there," Laurie informed me as she began a descending turn.

"That's been the theme for the day. What's the problem?"

196

"I don't know. I could tell from the tower operator's voice, it didn't sound right."

"It couldn't have anything to do with us?" I became alert.

She shook her head. "Maybe the police want to talk to you about last night."

I couldn't see what that had to do with landing on a different runway, unless they planned to rush out with tanks and surround us, and as Laurie lined up the plane on the final approach, I not only didn't see any tanks, I didn't see anything else that looked ominous —just the approaching runway and its ribbon of bordering lights. "I really can't believe my unexpected victim of last night was the type who would call in the Mounties even if he had known the name I was traveling under." Still, it was just one more thing to be uptight about.

After we landed, Laurie turned the plane off the runway and began taxi-ing along the apron. "I don't see any gombeen men looking for us," I said.

"Let's hope not. But he sounded so strange, sort of mixed up."

"Maybe he's new on the job. Look, I know we have to take care of Fortin, but first let's park next to your plane and we'll off-load the fish chest and our things. After that we'll find something to eat. Maybe the food has improved over the holiday."

"All right. You give me a check for Jacques, and I'll drop you off. I'll take care of the other details. He won't be here anyway, but he can bill Mountjoy for whatever else is owed, the anchor and the chest, and you can pay me. Here are the keys for the Baron."

She taxied in beside the Beachcraft, and I moved to get out of my seat. "Wait, John." She put her hand on my arm. "You see those two cars in front of the terminal? They're police cars."

So the gombeen men were here. I looked out through the windshield at the twin black marias—Canadian RCMP-style. No one was around them, but some distance away there was a mixed gathering of a dozen or so people. They were standing in a ragged line, and they seemed to have their attention focused on us or something beyond us, and since it was already half dark and drizzling, I couldn't imagine what the hell it could be. Suddenly I was fed up with the whole mess. "Ahh, the devil with it! If they want me, they can make an appointment." I had reached the point where I was perfectly willing to go public, even if it meant a beheading in the town square at high noon.

"If anyone lays a hand on you, spit in his eye and scream," I said. "I'll be lurking in your Baron." I kissed her on the cheek as I stood up.

After I watched her taxi away to leave Fortin's plane at its designated place in front of Alouette Airways, I turned my attention to the watching spectators. I decided they must be waiting for an incoming flight because they'd heard the Mounties were going to grab someone who was coming in on it. Nice piece of deduction.

I carried the fish chest and our belongings into the plane, and then I took a seat in the back and mulled over future plans.

The improved state of our health was an unexpected factor. Had we gotten over whatever had hit us or were we walking around with something ugly in the blood? René and I had suffered no lasting effects from the original contact, but then René had not really survived much longer in any case, and who could tell what I was carrying around? Would food and rest help, or did we have time to fool around to learn the answer? I didn't think Presque Isle was much more than 250 miles distant, and in this plane it wouldn't be a very long flight under normal circumstances. But the weather was turning stinko and there wasn't one damn thing normal about the circumstances, including us. We should probably be in a hospital under-going tests.

On the other hand, how dangerous would it be to spend another night here, get a good rest, and leave at daybreak? If I thought only about our present condition, it made very good sense. But if I thought about the dangers surrounding us, I knew we should get out of here as soon as possible. As soon as possible after eating, filing a flight plan, clearing customs. That brought up the reason for going anywhere—the contents of the chest. I knew there was an ice machine installed here at the airport for the convenience of home-going fishermen, but there was no fish market and anyone having a look at our catch would call for help. I figured with Laurie's charm and savvy we should be able to pass customs without having to open the chest. We'd have to bluff it, but I didn't think anyone was going to get that excited about fish around here, provided they didn't thiink we were a couple of heroin smugglers.

It was only ten minutes before I spotted Laurie walking down the flight line from the Alouette hanger. I moved out of the plane, locked it up and went to meet her, the question still hanging in the air, whether to go or not to go. She supplied the answer.

Even in the poor light I saw how drawn and shaken she looked. "You're feeling sick," I said.

She nodded. "I—I—took care of everything. Here's your receipt."

I put my arm around her shoulder. "You want to lie down somewhere?"

"No . . . I'd like to sit down. I want some black coffee."

"I don't think the police are looking for us, or for me, I mean."

"No." She shook her head.

"You sure you want something to eat?"

Again her answer was monosyllabic. She was walking a ragged edge. It meant either going to Maine in the morning or finding someone else here to fly me there tonight, a probable impossibility.

The airport restaurant was heavily populated this time, and there seemed to be a heightened tone to the table talk, as though everyone had something confidential to discuss. Perhaps the police were actually waiting to pick up someone and the rumors were flying. I found us an empty corner table and then I bought two large-size mugs of black coffee. We could take on the main course later.

She had nothing to say until she'd managed to drink half the coffee in her mug. She sat forward with her arms folded on the table, peering at the cup.

"Better?" Bad as the brew had tasted, I knew its effect on me was momentarily positive.

"John, I know why the police are here. There was a crash earlier. It was off the end of runway two four. That's why they didn't want to me land there. They're looking for evidence."

"That is sad news. How many on board?"

"One. Liam Ganin. He was killed." She said it as though she was counting, but she didn't raise her head.

I recalled the look on Ganin's face as I rose from the booth at Le Bijou. I saw myself running. "How did it happen?" I was holding the table-edge with both hands.

The details were grim and few. His wife said he had been called by the Company to fly to Chicoutimi, to pick up a party of engineers. The tower had reported a normal-appearing take-off. Just beyond the glide path, at about two hundred feet, the plane had nosed over and gone straight in. Cause unknown. What *was* known was that no one at Quebec Central had issued orders for Ganin to make the flight.

"I think I helped to kill him," I said. "I was with him. I was recognized. They weren't going to risk the possibility of his talking."

"This thing is so horrible." She shook her head. "My dad, Sam Catton, Liam Ganin." She lifted her eyes to mine, eyes filled with tears of anguish. "Who are these people who kill so easily? Who are *they!*"

"I could tell you generally that *they* are not really people, but that won't help. Laurie, do you feel up to flying to Presque Isle as soon as we can get out of here?"

"Why Presque Isle?" She was fingering her handkerchief.

I told her why. "In the morning at the Base, I'll get in touch with some VIPs I contacted when I was in Washington. I'm going to tell them they'd better put an official stamp on this whole thing and come running with their best toxologists or I'm going directly to the press and television. I'll let the Post and the Times fight over the exclusive. Fact is, I'm going to write it myself, whatever they do. But if we can reach the Air base, I think we'll be home free one way or the other. There's only one problem. I'm going to be so broke from having you fly me around that I'll have to go to work for you to pay the bill."

That brought a quick smile. "I've heard of worse ideas. Why don't you start by getting us something to eat?"

Clearing customs and the Fish and Game office was easier than I had anticipated. Jacques Fortin had already alerted officialdom, and Laurie, as a member of the Sept Iles Aero Club, made it all very routine. A member's word on the poundage of fish caught was his bond, and in Laurie's case, her smile and manner would have got us past far more difficult inspection.

Mostly, the conversation concerned the bad weather moving in, and the hope, by the inspector, that we would delay until morning to fly in it.

I was glad that he made no mention of Ganin's crash. He was garrulous and friendly, and although I was impatient to get going, I let him and Laurie ramble on about the kind of season it had been for the charter operators. When finally we bid him an effusive adieu, he insisted that when I came again I must fish Lac Cigogne with him.

Ordinarily, in mid-summer in northern latitudes, there's a very long twilight. But there is a type of weather that can creep in vampirelike and suck the blood from the day, leaving a pallid greyness, stifling visibility and although not producing complete darkness, creates almost the same effect. The tower beacon made only a limited penetration into the enveloping mist. The field lights and the lights in the terminal building were pale illuminations suggesting moisture content more than detail. I did note as we entered the terminal that the two police cars had gone.

Once inside, we took a moment to brush the wet off our clothing.

"Laurie, while you're filing a flight plan," I said, "Why don't I save some time by looking the plane over? Is there a flashlight on board?"

"On my side of the cockpit, just below the instrument panel. You can take off the aileron and elevator locks, too." She brushed her hair back with her hand and I was glad to see that she was looking better. Her color had returned, and her eyes were calm.

"Is it difficult to take off the engine cowlings?"

"My goodness, what do you expect to find there?"

"Nothing, I hope. But your plane has been sitting out there by itself for twenty-four hours."

That gave her pause. "Maybe you'd better wait for me. We'll do a thorough check together."

"I can save time by getting started. You go get us properly flight-planned."

I found that in walking out to the Beachcraft, I actually had to hunt for it. Like every plane on the flight line, it presented a shrouded silhouette and it looked very much the same to me as similar models. I began to worry that we would not have enough ceiling and visibility to take off. Then, from the position of the engines, I saw we were going to need a step ladder to unfasten the cowlings. More delay. *Better delay than an abrupt end,* I reflected to myself, seeing again the trees rushing up at us.

There was no one around. No planes warming up, no planes in the air. I had the feeling that the tower beacon was making a huffing sound in its circular path, but all I could hear were my feet on the pavement as I moved around the wing to take off the control locks. If someone put a bomb in a plane, it was undoubtedly fired by a timing device, not like starting a car and blowing yourself up. Where had they put the bomb in René's Beaver? In the cabin amidst his gear. René deserved better, but today it is not the victim's loss we mourn; it is his slayer's hatred with which we must come to grips.

I placed the three control-locks on the wing step and fished the cabin key out of my pocket, remembering it wasn't a bomb that got Ganin. I would have to ask Laurie what would cause a plane to dive straight into the ground. When I had unlocked the cabin before the key had stuck. Now it went around with ease, and I swung open the door.

I gathered up the locks and stepped up into the cabin, and I knew even before my rear foot made contact with the floor that I wasn't alone. Off balance, my arms full, I had no time to register anything but sickening awareness. Arms grabbed me and hurled me sideways. I went down hard, tripping over a seat leg, my head coming in painful contact with a solid object. Before I could move, a claw was fastened under my chin, cutting off life and breath. Something hard was pressed against my temple.

"You!" a voice rasped, "Say nothing! Do nothing!"

Under the circumstances the instructions were ridiculous. I was on about my last choke when the pressure around my throat was released. Dazed, I managed to gulp air and slowly pinch out the pinwheels and sparklers within my skull. I realized there were two of them—the one who had grabbed me and the one who had received me like a low pitched ball. The receiver did not remove the gun barrel from my head and remained crouched beside me. The grabber was outside my range, but I could hear him moving around. Then he went silent again, and I knew they were waiting for Laurie.

If I shouted I was either going to have my brains blown out or beaten in, but if she called my name or I could hear her approach, I was determined to cry, *Run!* If she heard me or the shot she would run. She'd have a chance, and that would give these bastards something else to think about. To make the try wasn't any great heroic decision on my part. I just knew it was the best I could do to save her, and I was going to do it.

Like hell I was. They were smarter than that. The grabber up front muttered a signal and my keeper clamped his hand under my chin again. I tried to wrench his wrist loose, but he bore down and I faded while he had all the best of it. And that was the way they neatly took us—no bomb, no noise, no unexpected crashes. But smartly, professionally, like using a forest fire to wipe out evidence, like two men in a plane, waiting.

While the grabber sat in the co-pilot's seat, instructing Laurie, I was permitted to sit on the floor, my captor sitting behind me, riding shot-gun. Before Laurie started the engines I heard her being instructed to call Air Traffic Control to change the flight plan from

Presque Isle to Goose Bay. Once we were off the ground and up to altitude, there was a change in the seating arrangements. The grabber, who spoke with a clipped British accent, moved into the left seat. Laurie was sent back to join me, and my watch-dog moved forward to become co-pilot.

I put my arm around my friend, and she rested her head on my shoulder. There wasn't much to say. Skyjacking and kidnapping were old hat. I could only wonder why we were being taken to Goose Bay . . . maybe to meet the Wizard of Oz. Shell-shocked as I felt about our capture, the immediate thing was that apparently no one was out to kill us. I clung to the thought for reassurance. As for the total failure of my long broken-field run to expose the effect of a small cloud of green rain, I refused to think about it. I had a single concern now, and her head rested on my shoulder. She whispered in my ear, "We're not going to Goose Bay."

"How do you know?"

"Wrong course. He's been turning."

How she could tell that, sitting as we were in a darkened cabin away from the instrument panel, I had no idea except that she was a pro.

We were in the air over two hours, and we came down out of it in blackness and rain and no sight of any place to land. The pilot made contact with someone and spoke very briefly into his mike, and then he continued to lose altitude but more gradually, props in low pitch, throttles retarded. Shortly, he began to circle, obviously looking for his destination. Apparently he spotted what he was looking for, and banked sharply. When he rolled out, he dropped the nose, and I had a feeling we were in a dive. Laurie's hand was wrapped in my own. The nose camp up, the aircraft slowed, the gear was lowered. Laurie pointed out her window, and below in the murk I saw a short bar of three flickering lights, and then as we turned I looked and saw a second pair of lights and realized that they marked the beginning and ending of a runway, though not a modern air-strip. I decided the pilot might be another Liam Ganin out of the cockpit, but he, too, was a pro at the controls, and he brought the Baron in with nothing but the primitive flares to guide him through a rain scoured windshield, landing on the wheels with barely a bounce.

For all we could see, it appeared that the pilot had brought us down in the woodland center of nowhere. The rain was thrumming on wings and fuselage as he reversed course, and, using his landing lights, taxied very quickly along the runway, which although somewhat bumpy felt relatively solid.

The co-pilot left his seat and gestured at us to come forward. I couldn't see him in detail, but I knew he had a gun in his hand. The resurging thought that he was going to shoot and dump our bodies, carved out whatever was left of my entrails. I moved in front of Laurie as the plane jerked to a stop.

"Open the door," the co-pilot ordered. "Get out." His accent was not British. It wasn't anything, just gutteral. Rushing him would only kill me. Getting out of the plane offered more hopeful possibilities. I opened the door against the churn of the idling prop and received a face full of wet. The smell of balsam was strong and refreshing.

There was a welcoming committee *a deux*. Bulky forms, they hurried us away from the plane toward a screen of trees where I saw dim lights gleaming. By the time we reached the trees we could hear the plane starting its take-off run. When it went by, already in the air, its engines sounded wet and flatulant in passage. I wondered how I was every going to be able to buy Laurie a new aircraft. The other thing I noticed was that the landing lights had been pinched out by the time we had left the plane, which meant that our hosts numbered more than two.

There were three canvas tents pitched in under the black spruce. We were taken to the larger central one where a pair of Coleman lanterns gave us a chance to look each other over. My immediate reaction was—they fit the bill! A couple of Che Guevaras—black-bereted, bearded, camouflaged coveralls, booted, holstered, submachine gunned—probably with the standard guerrilla weapon, the Soviet Kalishnakov. They looked like something out of a Made-for-TV Movie. The only trouble was, we were a part of the action. Was it my cue to speak?: *Why have you brought us here? You can't get away with this!*

The taller and heftier of the two was in command. His English was not good, and, of course, his accent was Latin. "Go there and re-main," he pointed.

"I decided not to mention the fact that I spoke a little Spanish.

Where we were to go and remain was at the rear of the tent. There was a camp cot for us to sit on, which we did. The scene I decided was on a par with the players. The right side of the tent was dominated by a short-wave radio with receiver and transmitter. It was perched on a makeshift table with accompanying chair. To the left, there were stacked an assortment of food cartons, camping equipment, including axes, jerricans, shovels and similar gear. Undoubtedly, the other two tents were for housing the troops, and when presently two more of the same came in out of the wet, we had the full complement. The two late-arrivals had been the runway lighters and the runway light-putter-outers. Suited and bearded like their bridge partners, they eyed us with the same degree of welcome. Their conversation was in Spanish, which seemed to disqualify them as members of some extreme Quebec separatist group, although I knew such organizations had an international following. Their conversation was swift and brief. I caught only a few phrases, but enough to know that Pepé had the first watch. Pepé was the one who had given me the shove. After the others had left him to see to our cares, he lit up and settled down in the chair facing us.

Laurie had been sitting hunched forward taking it all in as had I, searching for answers. "Why do you suppose they brought us here?" she said suddenly.

"Señorita! Not to talk," Pepé waved his finger commandingly. "You keep the silence."

"I'm damned if I can figure it, certainly not for ransom."

Pepé was on his feet, coming toward us, unslinging his weapon. "You! I say, stay shut! You open I kick your teeth in, si!" He stood before me, waving the muzzle of his gun under my nose.

I thought it better to stay shut. After he got tired of standing in front of me, blocking the light, he went back and sat down. It certainly wasn't going to be a night for sitting around the campfire telling old wives' tales. I looked at Laurie and gestured that she might like to lie down. She gestured that we might like to lie down together. It was a cot built for one, but by lying on our sides and putting my arms around her it was possible, and since there was no blanket, and it was bound to get cold, I decided to try.

My arm fell asleep before I did, but until then I lay listening to the wind pecking at the tent, water showering down when the heavily-soaked boughs shook, and thinking about the whys and wherefores of what had happened. Obviously, the four had been camped here making the runway serviceable; perhaps they'd even built it, although I doubted that. Probably it had once been an emergency air strip.

Judging from the pile of food cartons and other equipment—and even the beards—they must have been camped here for sometime, which indicated long-range planning. Everything had indicated that. Their action also suggested that, for the time being at least, they did not mean to harm us. What could we expect after the time being was ended? Maybe a helicopter descending out of the dawn—a Buff or a Jolly Green—emblazoned with a U.S. Government seal and from it would step the deputy assistant undertaker for covert actions in northern Quebec, to inform us that if we would be willing to sign form A in triplicate, attesting to our good faith and silence, we could be taken on as alternate members of Team C in the pursuit of special weaponry to assure the peace and tranquility of mankind. Such wind-blown meanderings were a measure of my state of mind. Our hosts looked and sounded like escapees from a revolutionary finishing school. I didn't really want to entertain the thought that it might have been a CIA-directed Cuban refugee finishing-school, but—. Out of a sudden shower of rain drops splattering the canvas, I heard old Bud Goss snorting, *"For Pete's sake, Erikson, don't you have any more faith in our guys than that?"* And because Pepé didn't want any more talking I told Goss to be quiet and fell asleep.

When I awoke, I lay trying to orient myself and place the sound of the rain, because there was something familiar in it and in my waking. And then I knew what it was.

When I had bailed out over Mu Gia Pass, my chute had not fully opened before I went plummeting down through the jungle. The canopy had caught in the trees and checked my descent, but not altogether, and when I had recovered consciousness it was dark and rain was falling, pecking at the leaves. That was the familiar sound.

Laurie had shifted in her sleep, and my arm partially pinned by her shoulders, was numb. My legs felt numb and stiff, too, and that was the way it had been when I was hanging by the chute shrouds, for by some fluke I had hit near the edge of a limestone cliff, and the lower part of my body was trapped in a fissure. When I had tried to pull my legs free, the pain was so agonizing I had to stop. I was sure my back was broken. I knew when daylight came the Viet Cong would find me.

Instead it had been the helicopters that came, three Buffs from the Aerospace Rescue and Recovery Service—ARRS. They fanned about, the PJs in them searching for me, trying to spot my chute, and drawing heavy ground fire in their effort. Vietnam had been such an agonizing mess, but those PJ helicopter birds were something special, so utterly self-sacrificing in their job of trying to bring home the downed—the best of our best. I managed to extract my arm from under Laurie's weight. She turned in her sleep and snuggled her back into me and we lay spoon-fashion.

Laurie and I here, and the rain coming down, and five years ago caught on a jungle mountain-side, thinking of Nan.

For some reason they couldn't spot my chute; it had become too entangled and hidden in the jungle growth. I had two methods to signal, a beeper radio in my vest and colored smoke. The beeper wasn't working and I didn't dare use the smoke. Off to my right, on the same ridge and down below me, they were shooting at the Buffs. I knew if I signaled, I'd give my position away, and if they sent down a penetrator with a PJ crewman on it, he wouldn't be able to get me out in time, even if he could reach me.

I was trapped four days, and every day the Buffs and Jolly Green Giants came back looking for me. The V.C. were looking for me, too. I could hear them all around. If they found me, they could shoot me as a spy—Kilbourne had warned me of that. At night curious monkeys found me, but finally I didn't think anyone else was going to unless I started signaling. I was weak from injuries and lack of food. Rain water and a jungle water-vine kept me alive, but I was beginning to spend more time out of the world than in it. On the fourth night I had awakened somewhat delorious, not really knowing what night it was. I decided I was going to get out of my volcanic rock garden or die in the attempt. I talked to God about it, and told Him I could really use His help if He had any to spare.

Laurie's body jerked and she woke up. "It's all right," I whispered. She took my hand and pulled it under her chin, a pretty lousy blanket. She gave a long sigh and pressed against me for warmth. I lifted my head and saw that Pepé had been relieved by one of his bigger brothers. He was keeping company with the standard cigarette, looking off at a brighter tomorrow when he and his pals would be king. I settled down and went back to my own yesteryear, when all the world had changed for me. I had been a man of few doubts then, of much zest and great assuredness—which proved I didn't know much. One thing I didn't know afterward was how I managed to get unstuck from the rock vise I was in, or how with a broken leg—some of the flesh of which I left behind—cracked pelvis, damaged vertabrae, and other assorted injuries I navigated down the cliff-side through the jungle by night. When the rain awoke me it was daylight. I was lying in an open area, a valley, and a figure was descending on a line from a Buff, probably the Angel Gabriel. Over the sound of the rotor blades I could hear the nasty staccato of a machine gun.

Now the only remaining sound was the rain on the tent roof. The hell with it. I'd let my thoughts fly me back to Nepal and a different kind of valley—the magical Arun. I'd take Laurie there, and we'd awake in the soaring presence of the great white peaks—*Everest, Kanchengjunga, Makalu, Dhaulargiri, Annapurna.* I fell asleep reciting their names like a litany.

When I awoke once again, it was to the sound of voices in the damp dawnlight. I rose up stiff and cold and saw the guerrilla quartet quietly harmonizing over the old Mexican breakfast of spit and a cigarette—although I did smell coffee.

"Good morning, gentlemen." I gave it my best and had the satisfaction of seeing startled reaction as they swung toward me in concert. "Don't shoot!" I raised my hands, and stood up stretching, and when I glanced down at Laurie she was looking up at me laughing.

"I won't ask you how you slept."

"You!" commanded Numero Uno, "Stay shut!"

I considered what would happen if I told him to go screw himself. Probably something more vigorous than nasty words—like starting the new day with half a head. The hell with valor. I sat down beside Laurie, leaned over and kissed her good morning. She yawned mightily, also stretching out the kinks and I helped her to sit up, and we sat together on the cot hunched over against the damp chill, our eyes on our guards, wondering what came next.

Two things came next—hot coffee in paper cups. Pepé brought it, and when I thanked him I was glared at but not told to stay shut. And while we were drinking it, they began cleaning everything out of the tent.

Obviously camp was being broken. We and the cot were the last items to be removed, and I was glad to get out of the tent and have a look at where we were. The campsite was well concealed under the trees. Because they were not tall trees, I guessed we were farther north than Poitrine. I could see no higher land around us, which seemed to indicate that we were on a plateau. From what little I could observe of the runway I gathered that its existence was also well concealed—a narrow slash in the wilderness, camouflaged, except when ready for use, by neatly placed clumps of forest growth. Again, the whole set up indicated fairly elaborate pre-arrangement.

The weather was solid overcast with low-hanging patches of fog. The rain had slacked off to an uncomfortable drizzle, no doubt preparatory to a three-day downpour.

As I stood beside Laurie, watching the troops bring down the big tent, having struck one of the other two, a very ugly feeling took root in my very empty stomach. Obviously, they were planning to depart, but were they planning to take us with them?

The shortwave radio had been lugged into the remaining smaller tent, and, I heard a brief untranslatable exchange between Pepé and someone he was hearing through his earphones. No doubt orders were being sent concerning us. I noted also that in breaking camp they had made a small, neat pile of equipment which included personal gear and a couple of square cartons; all the rest lay scattered about, dropped anywhere.

I felt Laurie tugging my sleeve, and as I cocked my head to hear what she had to say, another sound intruded—an approaching aircraft, a jet. I could tell it was a jet by the way its sound shredded the air, like the tearing of a rag. Pepé came out of the tent, a different man. He was dressed in civilian clothes; only the submachine gun kept him in form. The other three went into the tent and left him to watch us. I figured they, too, were making a quick change.

Laurie said, "Those two boxes . . . our company name, Weather Operations, is on them."

"They've used this as a base for their testing." My lips felt numb as though I'd had a shot of novicaine. It didn't matter a damn what they had done, it was what they were going to do now. Pepé had unslung his weapon and was checking it. I moved Laurie around to face me as I turned my back on him. "Laurie, when I turn around again, you run for it. Get into those trees!"

Her eyes were enormous, her fingers pressing into my arms. "No!" I didn't know whether she meant no, she wouldn't run, or no, she couldn't accept what was about to happen.

"Run!" The jet over head blanketed my command. I spun around to do my own running, and Pepé was right there to block me. I didn't have anything left but a prayer. He studied me with eyes of stone.

They were impressive in their quality of alertness, their cold glitter revealing their emptiness. It suddenly struck me that he was anxious for us to run, which would give him an excuse to shoot us. Whereas if we didn't move, he was under orders only to watch us. We had no choice.

The jet had come down through the overcast, and as it whistled by, I was not surprised to recognize its white needle-like lines. My legs were shaking not only in reaction to having just survived what I had believed was to be our own end, but also in the new-found belief that we were going for another ride.

The pilot landed with the same skill exhibited the night before, and if he was a different man at the controls, it was clear that however large this operation was, flying skill ranked high. I could see the employment ad: *experienced cloud-seeding pilots wanted.* By the time the plane had been brought to the edge of the campsite and the turbines silenced, all present were dressed in civilian clothes and the third tent taken down. No one got out of the jet. Someone inside activated the cabin-door mechanism, and its steps extended automatically. Pepé no longer paid any attention to us. He joined the other three in quickly loading the shortwave radio and the other selected equipment, including the tents, on board.

"There's an ejection tube on the bottom of the fuselage," Laurie said.

"I don't think it matters right now. I think maybe this would be the right time for us both to run like hell. I'm going to grab that ax in passing."

"No, wait!" As we spoke, the quartet, their loading completed, had boarded the plane without so much as a backward glance. Now a new figure appeared, stepping down from the plane. His coloring reminded me of nut-brown Zahedi. He had a neatly-trimmed Sam Catton mustache, a somewhat round face with rather limpid dark eyes, and to keep him from the wet he wore a Burberry trenchcoat and a wide-brimmed fedora. He was of middle height and middle age with grey at the temples, and when he spoke I could not place his accent. For an incredible moment I thought my night-time fantasy of a strange Greek bearing an official U.S. Government seal was about to unfold.

"Well, Mr. Erikson—Miss MacMurry," he tipped his hat to Laurie, "I regret that it has come to this, but you will understand I have my duty. You—"

"We don't understand a damn thing!"

He ignored my response, continuing to speak, almost as though he had been programmed. "You learned of our earlier test of Newrain through the pilot, Picard. The test's purpose was to examine the effect of Newrain on wildlife. Now because of your continued interference, we have selected you to test the effects of Newrain on the human anatomy." He had a quick look overhead as though to assure himself that the overcast was still in place.

"And what is this all supposed to be in the interest of, you bastard!" I moved toward the axe.

Of course, he had a forty-five. "I can shoot you in the leg, Mr. Erikson.

"Why are you doing this?" Laurie got back to basics.

"For the total liberation, Mademoiselle. We in the World Liberation Front are determined to bring justice to the impoverished and oppressed everywhere. We are a global crusade, well organized, and our scientific brains are the best—as you have perceived, Mr. Erikson."

"Justice for all, as you kill millions with rainfall."

"We need kill only a few to have our demands met."

"What demands, you stupid bastard!" I hoped I could get him angry enough and close enough for me to try for the impossible.

He was untroubled by my insults. "The resignation of your President and his Cabinet are of priority. WLF has plans for negotiations with the capitalist imperialists of North America. Newrain on Kansas City or Denver will have a positive effect in Washington, London and Paris."

It was strictly from Graustark. He was cliché—his words were cliché—his troops were cliché. But behind all the clichés sat the Lear jet with its ejection tube. He moved toward it, having concluded his early morning spiel. He stepped on board as the turbines began to whine. Now I did run for the ax, planning to chop a few holes in the plane's wing, but the pilot saw me coming and pulled away fast, swinging the tail so I got driven back by the blast. The best I could do was throw a can of food at them as they went by. I prayed something would go wrong and they'd hit the trees.

Laurie let out a long weary sigh, watching the plane disappear.

"Laurie," I said, taking her hand, feeling suddenly as though I had run a very long way, "we've got to find some way to get in out of the wet, fast!"

"A cave!" Her voice was a fleeting cry of hope—a bird call in the awful emptiness of our plight. She was looking upward, my own words having stimulated recognition of the terror lurking not by night but in the sky above.

"No caves here, not in this kind of terrain."

"We can run!" She was tugging at my hand, set to flee.

"Not far enough or fast enough." I was a hope-killer as I fought to hold down a growing sense of helplessness, my mind and eyes casting about desperately for some way out. *You're the great woodsman, Erikson, so put your vaunted knowledge to work! Grow feathers and fly! Why the hell didn't you realize they brought you here for this!*

"Laurie, grab that shovel!" I hefted the axe and began running toward the end of the runway.

She caught up with me, shovel in hand. "What are we going to do?"

"They had to clear this runway of a lot of brush and undergrowth. There could be a pile of it off the end. If there is, we'll try to make a shelter."

For the first time in a long time, I was correct in my reasoning. There was a hefty pile of wood and brush piled at the runway's threshold which was on a slight incline. "Here, we'll swap," I said. "You chop bows for extra covering. I'll do the digging."

From the expression on her face I could see she didn't think much of my choice of a shelter. "I'll dig down under the pile and make our own cave. It will protect us." I tried to sound confident. I even managed a sick smile.

"What will protect us from the effects we felt at Lake Poitrine?" There was anger in her tone and look.

I didn't have to answer because her question was topped by two muted detonations from above. We could hear the jet circling high up. They had launched not one, but two, Weathermakers.

I went at the leavings furiously, modern man stripped of his armor, back to basics, frantically trying to find shelter.

I had one small bit of luck. Within the pile I found the rusted skeleton of an old tent. I straightened some of its kinks and used it as a frame to support a roof and floor. While Laurie laid logs and spruce bows on the top, I concentrated on footings and drainage ditches and, withal, attempted to tunnel us a warren that not only would protect us from the coming downpour, but just as important, would shield us from rain dripping through the entrance.

Even as I worked, I knew the chances of our staying free of the rain once it began to come down in earnest were poor. This was going to be such a pitiful abode. There was no time! No time to do a proper job.

As I flung earth and piled brush, I had to fight down the wild urge to throw down the shovel, grab Laurie's hand and run!

"John, listen!" I straightened up. She was standing above me. She had her head raised and posed in profile with dirty face, wet clothes and no make-up, she looked like a woodsprite. What she heard was nothing. "They've gone," she said.

There was only the new morning sound of the breeze fingering through the pine tops. It was whispering a funeral dirge. "So have eighteen minutes," I said. "Come here. We've got to move in now." I gave her my hand and she jumped down beside me and looked at the mess I'd made. "It's not home," I said.

She shook her head and I saw that she was fighting back tears. I put my arm around her and held her against me. "That silly fool man in his big hat," she choked. "He wasn't real! None of them were. They're something made out of a nightmare. They're not people! Not people!"

I pressed her down on her knees, feeling the need to hurry. "Go in feet first," I said.

"I never thought I'd crawl into my own grave." She tried to make a joke of it but couldn't.

It was a tight, miserable, mucky fit, a lousy place to get in out of the wet, but if it was a saving one, that was all that mattered. I'd gone as deeply into the incline as time permitted, and I'd burrowed a drainage ditch to carry the run-off away from the entrance. Now, if only the roof of brush and bows remained—if it was thick enough and tight enough—but we both knew that escaping the rain was only half the battle. Escaping its after-effects was the other half, possibly lost before we started.

As I burrowed myself in beside Laurie, the utter hopelessness of our position overwhelmed me. I wished now we had taken the twenty minutes to run. We might have found something better than this gopher hole.

It was dark in our tomb. By careful maneuvering I managed to wrap her in my arms. "I was hoping we were going to have a long life together, John," she said into my chest.

"We will, we will." I stroked her hair. "It's just having a rough start."

She raised her head and I kissed her, and we held on tightly and waited for the gentle green rain to fall.

At some point she took her lips from mine and lay with her head on my shoulder so that she could have a view of what was going on outside. I closed my eyes and thought of all the things I'd done to bring us to this. How neatly had these insensate murderers trapped us . . . with my help. *When all else is gone, the man of little or no faith is apt to pray in the face of death. It is fitting and meet that he do so. The Lord is my shepherd . . . Our Father who art in Heaven. What prayers do you know, John Erikson?*

I felt Laurie's body start to shake and then she began to laugh wildly, and I held her tighter, saying "It's all right, it's all right! We'll be all right, Laurie!"

"Yes, I know!" she choked through the paroxysms that tore her. "I see sunlight!"

And she did! Cautiously I stuck my head out of our warren and glimpsed the early-morning rays burning holes in the cloud deck. I could hear the wind starting to shush through the pines. "Rain before seven, clear before eleven," was the best I could summon at the moment.

Clear a lot sooner than that. No more than fifteen minutes later, we crawled forth to face the new day. We saw the new sun's rays making rising smoke of fog patches, saw new blue overhead, saw torn reaches of broken cloud moving off, saw the high deck turning paper-thin. And no green rain. I began to tremble.

"They'll be coming back," I said. "We've got to move out of here." Then I had a better idea. "No, by God, we'll block the runway!"

Laurie sank down on her knees. "I don't care what we're going to do. First, I'm going to say a prayer of thanks."

I was all in favor, but not until I had the runway fixed so they'd bust their asses if they tried to land. Then I heard the sound and began to run, shouting, "They're coming back Laurie!" I grabbed a pile of brush from the top of our hiding-hole and when I turned around Laurie was on her feet, listening. "That's no jet," she said, rubbing mud off her face. "That's a helicopter!"

And by God, it was! Not a buff or a Jolly Green from Da Nang, not the deputy assistant undertaker for covert actions, not even the 7th Cavalry and John Wayne, but welcome nonetheless. Royal blue with RCAF in white on its side complete with emblem. "Over here!" I yelled, waving my arms. "Over here!" I began to run down the runway as the big chopper thumped its way overhead.

*

I never did learn where the base was that they took us to. Laurie said it was near Chicoutimi. It didn't really matter. What mattered was the knowledge that action had been taken, the ordeal ended. There were two paramedics on board to check our condition, to sympathize gallantly with Laurie's appearance and to supply us with quantities of coffee.

When we landed at the base things went zippity-zip—shower, shave, complete physical (everything appeared normal) and some borrowed clean clothes. I only needed pants because my Bolex case was handed to me right after we landed by an obliging flight officer.

"Where did you find that?"

"Oh," a long pause and a dry smile, "We picked it up with Miss MacMurry's plane."

He had no other answers to my questions, leaving me to the mudcoated wreckage of myself.

When I joined Laurie again, we had a magnificent breakfast in the officer's mess, and then it was off to the de-briefing room, or so I hoped.

It was in fact a board room with a long table and comfortable chairs. There were three of them waiting for us, two RCAF officers, Colonel Bowers and Major Hancock, and a Mr. Sutterby. The officers were smart looking in their uniforms, deferential in manner and anxious to question us-me, in particular. Mr. Sutterby had a leonine head of blond hair and exuded a quiet aloofness typical of the high-ranking civil servant. Colonel Bowers announced that everything we said was being recorded, and I held nothing back.

It was Sutterby who asked the obvious question. "Why didn't you report Picard's findings to the RCMP at Sept Iles?" He had pale-blue eyes and a Grecian nose which he appeared intent on looking down.

I explained, as I thought I already had done in my response to Colonel Bowers' questions. He was not satisfied. He wanted to work me over the coals on it, and euphoric as I was feeling, I had a question of my own, which I directed to Colonel Bowers, cutting Sutterby off in mid-stream. "How did you know where we were, Colonel?"

The Colonel had a thin face, lean and all sharp angles. He eyed Sutterby for a green light to reply and Sutterby answered, "We had information from your people in Washington."

"General Kilbourne, no doubt," I said, wanting him to know I knew some of our people in Washington, too.

"We were aware you were in Sept Iles with Miss MacMurry." I had the feeling Bowers was not willing to let the impression be gained that he was in anyway subordinate to a civilian, particularly in his own board room. "When you took off last night, Major Hancock's people were having you tracked on radar." He nodded in deference to the Major's good work. "Later, when your Beechcraft landed in Quebec to refuel, we picked it and its crew up. We have it here for you, Miss MacMurry." He turned his attention to Laurie, but his explanation had driven my attention right out of the room.

Whatever blasphemy I uttered was unclear to them because I managed to cough half way through the requiem.

"I beg your pardon?" The Colonel's steady grey eyes had opened a bit wider. Major Hancock was patting his black, pencil-thin mustache, and Sutterby had discovered something on the table that held his attention.

"I—ahh—you say you had us on radar," I spoke to Hancock, clearing the debris from my throat, trying to hold things in place. "Did you track us to Lac Poitrine, the place where we landed?"

The Major shook his head, checking with a glance to the boss to see if he wanted to interrupt. "No. Only from the time your Beechcraft took off."

"But I thought you said you knew we were in Sept Iles."

"It was known you were there, but not about your flight the next morning," Sutterby said waspishly. "If you had done as any sensible person might have, then we would have known where you were all the time." He wasn't going to let me off the hook of his official displeasure. I wanted to ask him where he had been on the holiday, but instead I threw one from another angle.

"You mean, in fact, that you knew what the World Liberation Front was up to."

"Oh, we've known about these people for some time," Bowers said, "at least from the point of view of aircraft."

"Well, if you knew what they were doing, why didn't you stop them?"

"I'm afraid that's the part we didn't know until—" he looked down the table at Sutterby.

"It's enough to say, Mr. Erikson, that my Government and yours have long been aware of the WLF."

Sitting up he was a big man and, in his white suit and maroon tie, he had an ambassadorial look.

"Then undoubtedly you know they've managed to develop the deadliest toxin on earth."

"You need no longer be concerned, and you never would have been if—"

"Did you know they were experimenting with my father's Weathermaker?" Laurie interrupted and there was no friendliness in her tone or her look.

We all had a moment of silence while Sutterby fed embarrassment into his computer. "That's really outside my area," was the best he could manage.

The glint in Laurie's eye was all MacMurry. "I think you knew, all right. You could have told my father. You could have saved him."

That brought another momentary silence, and Colonel Bowers stepped into the breach. "Had we known what you and Mr. Erikson have told us, Miss MacMurry, then the experiment would never have taken place. What Mr. Sutterby has pointed out is that there was knowledge and information known on both sides of the border but hardly enough. It's a pity Mr. Erikson didn't come to us when he first learned of the matter."

"It wouldn't have mattered whether he'd come to you or not. If you people had gone to my father, it never would have happened." Laurie was not backing off.

"We do the flying, Ma'am. Major Hancock felt the RCAF had done its duty, and on that score so did I."

There was a long pause then, and I could sense Laurie taking stock and making decisions. Then I said, "If we haven't thanked you for saving our lives, gentlemen, we certainly do now. Excuse us for being in somewhat of a state of shock."

"Perfectly understandable. Our pleasure," the Colonel offered us a wisp of a smile. "I have no doubt, Miss MacMurry, that you'll be queried further when you return home." He didn't look at Sutterby. "And you may wish to bring up the matter you spoke of then. But as you feel we have done you a good turn, perhaps you would be willing to do one for us."

"I'm sure we'd be glad to, if it's possible." I wasn't sure I knew what was coming next. My mind was still spinning like a propeller.

"Let's put it this way," he said as he built a steeple with his fingers and spoke slowly, picking his words. "If there once was a threat of this rain weapon being used—it has been taken out of the air—so to speak. It no longer exists." Now he did look down the table at Sutterby to see if he had it right. "Let's say it never did."

It hung there before us for a moment, a question, and then I said, "Do you think you can sell that to the World Liberation Front?"

"We have its principal members in custody," Sutterby's tone was peremptory. "Those we don't have are no longer in possession of the means to tamper with the elements. What we're suggesting to you, Mr. Erikson, and to you, Miss MacMurry, is that this thing never happened. Further, there is absolutely no proof to show that it did."

"In other words, we will refrain from going public."

"Exactly." The Colonel was pleased that the message was so clearly understood.

"There's nothing to be gained by going public, as you put it," Sutterby wanted to get in the last word, "and it might cause you lots of trouble."

"Don't threaten me, Mr. Sutterby," Laurie said quietly. "I've had enough of threats."

We flew back to Dorval that afternoon. It was a flight spent mostly in reflection. We discussed Colonel Bowers' request and Sutterby's implied threat. I had already made up my mind, but Laurie was in doubt, wanting to restore her father's reputation but not wanting to bring further grief to her mother. We discussed our future together briefly, but too much had happened too fast and life was too complicated to plan in competition with two untiring aircraft engines. All we decided was that when we landed she would go home to see how things were there, and I would report to Sam Catton.

I found the patient's progress remarkable. He was sitting in a chair by the window, reading a paperback edition of book one of Goethe's 'Faust'.

"Good Lord, you are improving your mind."

"I find Mephistopheles a far more interesting fellow than Faust."

"Well, why not? He's the Devil."

"I guess you've got something there. Well, how did you make out? Did you get what you went after?"

"I've got quite a story. Some different than when I left you."

"I was worried when you left. How's Laurie?" The words were correct but there was no excitement in them.

As I talked, his eyes followed me while I paced about the small, antiseptic room.

I came to the end: "Now the RCAF people have asked us to forget the whole thing. But I've decided to go ahead and give the story to the press, as you suggested. It will at least bring attention to what the Weathermaker can do when used as MacMurry intended. It should also do something for his name."

He didn't answer right away, and when he did he was looking out the window. "You two were very lucky. I'm glad somebody got off the dime in Washington before things became too wet. But John, to go ahead now and publicize this thing—and without proof—will only scare the hell out of people and do nothing for cloud-seeding." He brought his eyes to mine. "After all, did the news that it was successful in Vietnam do anything to stimulate its positive uses?"

"It's all a matter of how it's told. The Weathermaker does have a successful track-record. Your book proves that, regardless of what the Met people have to say. But who could prove how well the technology worked over enemy territory? And, of course, there was the antagonism to the way it was used there."

Catton shook his head. "Look John, I can sympathize with how you feel, particularly after what you've been through, but my book hasn't been published, and it won't be for a long time. Nothing is going to be helped by going to the press now."

"That's not what you were selling the other day."

"I didn't know what you just told me the other day. The thing has been buttoned up. Let it lie." He made a small, cutting gesture with his hand.

I looked at him a moment without answering, and then I said

quietly, "I had an idea you'd say that, Sam. You remember I told you I was shot down in Vietnam?"

"You mean you almost got shot down again?"

"In a manner of speaking. But that's not my point. When I was finally rescued, I was picked up in an open area. There were no leaves on the trees. Later, when I was in the hospital, a Colonel who was in charge of the operation I was investigating came to see me. You know what he said to me? 'Erikson, I hope that when you write your report on how bad our defoliation program has been on the ecology up north, you'll include in it that it saved your life—that if you hadn't managed to get into an area that we'd already defoliated, you'd never have been retrieved. You'd be dead.' That's real irony, isn't it, Sam?"

He gave me a quizzical look. "Well, I hope you included it. What's that got to do with Sept Iles?"

"Same kind of irony." I moved from the bed and sat down in the chair facing him. "Laurie and I were dead a couple of times over—even rescued by a helicoptor—a lot of similarity." I took a breath. "Sam, only one person knew where I was going. Only one person knew I was with Laurie and her Beechcraft, even if I did give the impression others would be there, too. Not anybody in D.C., Sam. Just you."

He had become very still, his eyes holding mine, the wheels of his mind clicking smoothly. "We owe you our lives, Sam."

"You've got it mixed up, pal. I'm here in a hospital room."

"With a telephone. Sutterby told us they had been tipped off by Washington. By Washington through you, Sam."

"Well, thanks for all the credit, but really I—"

"Oh, you get the credit, all right. But old Angus MacMurry wasn't so paranoid after all. That's the parallel with Vietnam, Sam."

We suffered ourselves a long pause, then he shook his head and said, "You're a tired man, John."

"Beat to the nines, Sam, but I'm still working up top."

"Obviously too hard. Are you saying I was some kind of CIA plant in Mac's camp?"

"That's the way I see it, Sam."

"Well, I resent the implication." The familiar hard note was in his voice and in his face. "With Mac I could understand it. With you —look, for one thing why would I write my book if—"

"As you said, it won't be published for a long time. Now, maybe never. Maybe your orders were to write it as a cover—to keep yourself free from any possible suspicion, or maybe as a sop to your conscience, if you have one."

"And why would the CIA want a plant in Mac's operation?" He seemed faintly amused.

"That's easy, Sam. To keep an eye on it, to see how well it worked because you were giving it a try in Vietnam. You said it in your book. Once it was a proven success in Iran the decision was to kill it off. That's why you didn't want me to write that article. It had nothing to do with the Iranians. You people had to cover all bases. You had to protect your operation at all costs. You had to reason that if the process became publicly known, someone out there might suspect that what worked in Iran could be working in Vietnam."

"Oh come now, John, that's awfully convoluted thinking. I don't recall our Vietnam protesters being quite so esoteric."

"I'm not talking about college students. I'm talking about the World Meteorological Organization, the Russian Met people for starters. They were watching Iran, just as you were."

"Well, what's that got to do with Southeast Asia?"

"I would think from where you people sat, a very great deal. Meteorological people knew the monsoon season in the area, particularly over North Vietnam and Cambodia, had gone out of whack, that the season began early, lasted late, and that the rains had become abnormal over four or five seasons running. You couldn't risk a connection being made."

"No, of course, not. You should have written Mac's story. You're better at fiction than I."

"Yes, but Mac's story is not fiction, is it? Convoluted? Sure it is. The whole thing is. It's the name of the age we live in, when nothing is quite what it seems to be . . . like you."

He held me with a steady look, then shook his head and sighed. "I suppose I should humor you."

"Not really much humor in it, Sam. I can even understand the fears you people must have had. With the public attitude on Vietnam, news of climatological warfare would have pulled the bung from the barrel. The Administration, the White House, LBJ would have been blown sky-high. I'm sure it was a very touchy business. Suspicion today is like instantaneous news. Whatever is happening in one place is bound to be happening in another. No doubt it's on that kind of wave-length you people had to operate."

"Well, it's nice to know," he said sardonically, "but what I don't understand is how anyone could link up a Canadian rainmaker's operation with a U.S. war."

"Easily. With you. You're the American connection, a Canadian-American enterprise. Even the code name for the operation in Vietnam seems to fit . . . Intermediary Compatriot, isn't that what you called it?"

"John, I'm just a guy that got shot by mistake. Don't try to turn me into some kind of James Bond."

There was an edge of annoyance in his reply, and I knew my own tone matched it. "I don't have to. I got it all put together this morning at that meeting. I think the person who shot you meant to do that. It wasn't mistaken identity. You were up here looking into the sale of MacMurry's Weathermaker."

"On and on you go!"

"Sure. What do you think the WLF proves?"

"Proves! Hell, obviously that terrorists can be technical people, too. Aren't we worrying about them building nuclear bombs?"

"It proves that somebody did know what you were doing in Iran really worked, and they converted it, with God knows what kind of toxin, to their own uses."

He nodded. "That may be the one assumption you're right on. We did train some Iranian students. Ganin palled around with a couple of them, although I suspect he didn't know what he was getting in to."

"Yeah, but you did!" I stood up, my temper rising with me. "Goddamit, if you'd only gone to MacMurry and told him what you were doing, you could have saved him! He'd be alive right now!"

That did hit him. He came up straight, and it made him wince. "John, I don't have to take that! I don't have to take any of this. You've had a rough time. So have I. Go spin your wheels someplace else!"

"No, you don't have to take any of this, and what's more, I have to stand here and apologize because I wouldn't be standing here insulting you if you hadn't saved our lives. So there's the irony of it. I went all the way to Vietnam to expose the wickedness of herbicides and defoliants, and you guys were right there all the time, making rain. As Mac would have said, what a bloody laugh." I went toward the door.

"Wait a minute, John." He stopped me with my hand on the knob, and when I turned he was looking out the window.

His question, when it came, took me by surprise. "Do you think trying to flood the infiltration trails was a bad idea?" He swung around and met my gaze.

"I don't know . . . I suppose anything that can shorten the killing is a good idea at the time you do it. Why?"

"There's nothing new in the observation that sometimes what you're compelled to do to protect your own can have an adverse effect on a particular individual. We fight to survive on a number of levels."

"Yes, I'm sure we do, and I'm not so fixed in purity that I can't recognize how expediency works in a time of need. Flood the infiltration trails, block the supplies coming down, and so forth. But my God, look at the cost! Mac and René dead! Whether you people meant it or not, you've done a lot to suppress a badly-needed technology, and the end result is the near-miss we've just had with the WLF! You figure it out!" I had spewed out the final words in anger.

"Obviously, you think you have, he said." And evidently anything I might say about anything right now won't change your mind."

"Nothing you've said so far has."

"No . . . well, whatever you believe, I'm sure Mac's work hasn't been lost. It's going to be recognized. It's going to be used." He suddenly looked worn out, all used up.

"Does that make you feel better? Does that make it all right with the world? Don't sling me any hash, Sam. We owe you our lives, but don't expect me to accept justification for what's happened. It's all going down on paper. Maybe you'd like to write the dedication."

I left him sitting there with his book in his lap, the harshness of my words to fill his thoughts, his eyes once more turned toward the window.

*

I was wrong—not about Sam Catton. He's off somewhere in the Middle East using an oil rig or a Sumerian zigurrat as cover. No, I was wrong about the story. It didn't go down on paper in 1975, not because of very determined governmental pressure on both sides of the border, but because of Laurie. We went ring-hunting that next day. The sun was bright. There were no clouds in the sky to seed, and she made me realize, as only she could, that the one thing in the world that mattered for the moment and offered any real hope for the future was a man and a woman in love. Let the past rest, she said.

Unfortunately, it wouldn't. And now, today, I'm releasing this account. The reason for doing so is not that the technology of cloud-seeding remains a pitiful pygmy in our drought-stricken land—down-played and stunted by the No-men—but because of a brief news dispatch from northern Brazil. Annie brought it to me off the ticker, and I have a call in to Ashton Lee.

Indians in a remote village near Boa Vista reported that rain, pale green in color, had fallen nearby, and their investigation revealed the rain had killed everything it touched.